Praise for
Evan Help Us:

"Bowen's quiet humor and her appreciation for rural village life make this a jewel of a story."

—*Publishers Weekly*

"Satisfying as a Guinness pint."

—*Booklist*

"Entertaining."

—*Detroit Free Press*

"Fans of the delightful Welsh policeman Evan Evans will rejoice in his latest adventure . . . There's plenty to enjoy in this well-written tale."

—*Contra Costa Times*

"Rhys Bowen is a craftsman when it comes to creating believable characters. *Evan Help Us* is a most literate, enjoyable addition to the genre of detective fiction."

—*Benton Courier*

"Cheers, Rhys Bowen, Iachyd da! May your delightful series continue for many more years!"

—*Booked for Murder Casefile*

"Should delight fans of M. C. Beaton."

—*Poisoned Pen*

continued . . .

EVANLY CHOIRS

Rhys Bowen

BERKLEY PRIME CRIME, NEW YORK

This is a work of fiction. Names, characters, places, and incidents are either the product of the author's imagination or are used fictitiously, and any resemblance to actual persons, living or dead, business establishments, events, or locales is entirely coincidental.

EVANLY CHOIRS

A Berkley Prime Crime Book / published by arrangement with St. Martin's Press, Inc.

PRINTING HISTORY
St. Martin's Press hardcover edition / 1999
Berkley Prime Crime mass-market edition / August 2000

All rights reserved.
Copyright © 1999 by Rhys Bowen.
This book may not be reproduced in whole or in part, by mimeograph or any other means, without permission. For information address: The Berkley Publishing Group, a division of Penguin Putnam Inc., 375 Hudson Street, New York, New York 10014.

The Penguin Putnam Inc. World Wide Web site address is http://www.penguinputnam.com

ISBN: 0-425-17613-4

Berkley Prime Crime Books are published by The Berkley Publishing Group, a division of Penguin Putnam Inc., 375 Hudson Street, New York, New York 10014. The name BERKLEY PRIME CRIME and the BERKLEY PRIME CRIME design are trademarks belonging to Penguin Putnam Inc.

PRINTED IN THE UNITED STATES OF AMERICA

10 9 8 7 6 5 4 3 2 1

For my Thursday hiking friends, who are also my fashion advisors, culinary experts, travel companions, and, above all, therapists. What would I do without you?

And again with heartfelt thanks to John, Clare, Jane, and Tom for their critiques and great suggestions.

The Eisteddfod

THE *EISTEDDFOD* IS A WELSH tradition, going back to the Middle Ages, when every court had its bard. The competition for the honor of being chaired or crowned bard is still the focal point of all *eisteddfodau*. The contest begins with a dramatic procession of bardic contenders in flowing white and green robes, preceded by flower girls and heralded by trumpets. The bards then present their poems, written to a strict traditional form.

The *eisteddfod* is also a music festival with harp, dance, and vocal competitions, including the famous Côr Meibion, the Welsh male voice choirs that are still part of life in many villages.

Peripheral to the main competitions are displays of Welsh crafts and enjoyment of Welsh food and drink. *Eisteddfodau* range from the huge National Eisteddfod, held alternately in North and South Wales, to small regional and local festivals, keeping culture and tradition alive in every corner of Wales.

—Glossary of Welsh Words—

annwyl gyfeillion Dear friends (pronounced *annoo-eel ge-fy-chleon*)

bach Small. Used as term of endearment (*ch* pronounced as in the Scottish *loch*)

bore da Good day or Hello (pronounced *booray dah*)

Côr Meibion Literally choir of sons. Male voice choir (pronounced *cor meye-beeon*)

diolch am hynny! Thank goodness for that! (pronounced *deeolh am hinny*)

diolch yn fawr Thank you very much (pronounced *dee-olh n vower*)

eisteddfod Welsh cultural gathering (pronounced *eye-steth-vod*) (plural: **eisteddfodau**, pronounced *eye-steth-fod-ee*)

iachyd da Cheers (pronounced *yachy dah*)

Llanfair Fictitious village in North Wales (pronounced *Chlan-veyer*)

noswaith dda   Good evening (pronounced *nos-weye-th thah*)

plisman   Policeman (pronounced *pleesman*)

y Parch   The minister (*y* is pronounced here like the unaccented ending to *butter, parch* pronounced *parh* like Scottish *loch*)

ydych chi'n siarad Cymraeg?   Do you speak Welsh? (pronounced *idich-een sharad cumr-eye-g?*)

EVANLY CHOIRS

ONE

THE GIRL CHEWED ON HER lip as she drove up the pass. She wasn't a very experienced driver—only a complete idiot or a masochist would own a car in the middle of London or Milan—and the rental car felt enormous on the narrow Welsh mountain roads. All the way up from the coast she was conscious of the rock wall on one side of her, the sheer drop to the valley floor on the other. Once she had met a bus, taking up the whole road as it negotiated a hairpin bend and once a sheep had jumped out in front of her, causing her heart to do its own leap against her chest wall.

She was tense enough without the hazards of an unfamiliar road. *What am I doing here?* It had seemed so simple when she landed at London airport and rented the car. He would be happy to see her and everything would be just fine. Now she wasn't so sure.

Clouds covered the peaks above, parting every now and then to give tantalizing glimpses of rocky cliffs, down which bright ribbons of water were cascading, and high green pastures dotted with white sheep. Through the open car window she could hear the sound of running

water and the distant bleating of sheep. The air smelled
green and fresh. It was a completely unfamiliar landscape
to someone raised in a genteel London suburb and she
looked about her with awe. What could possibly have
made him want to come here?

Just when the road looked as if it were about to be
swallowed into the clouds, a village came into sight. She
slowed the car to a crawl and drove up the only street.
It was a simple little place, two rows of whitewashed
stone cottages, a couple of shops, a petrol pump, and a
friendly looking white pub with a RED DRAGON sign
swinging in the wind. She stopped the car and opened
her map. Surely this couldn't be the right place. She read
the signs on a row of shops. R. EVANS, DAIRY PRODUCTS,
G. EVANS, CIGYDD, with the word *Butcher* in parentheses
in tiny letters, and T. HARRIS, GENERAL STORE, and in
small letters after that, SUBPOSTOFFICE, LLANFAIR.

So this was the place. She knew that Llanfair was a
common enough name, the same as St. Mary's was always cropping up in English villages. She had picked out
a dozen or more Llanfair-somethings when she had
checked the map of Wales. But only one Llanfair nestled
close to the top of the pass beside Mount Snowdon. This
had to be it.

The girl shook her head in disbelief. This wasn't his
sort of place at all. She couldn't imagine him in one of
these little cottages. He was definitely a five-star kind of
person—Nice, Portofino, Beverly Hills—those were the
kind of places she'd expect to find him. Maybe the news-
paper had got it wrong. They often did, didn't they?

She drove on up the street, past the village school, now
deserted for the summer holidays, and came to two chapels, facing each other squarely across the narrow road.
They were almost mirror images of each other—squat
gray stone buildings with the minimum of adornment and
high, thin windows. The one on her left had a billboard
outside its front door, announcing it to be CHAPEL

BETHEL, REV. PARRY DAVIES. Its neighbor was CHAPEL BEULAH, REV. POWELL-JONES.

They must do a lot of praying here, the girl thought with amusement. The village searcely looked big enough to fill one chapel. There were biblical texts pasted on the billboards. Chapel Bethel's text read: "To him that has, more will be given," while Chapel Beulah's proclaimed: "It is easier for a camel to pass through the eye of a needle than for a rich man to enter the Kingdom of Heaven." This made her smile. She realized that smiling was something she hadn't done a lot of recently. Her face felt stiff and strange as it stretched into this unfamiliar shape.

The chapels were almost the last buildings in the village and she stopped the car again. There was only a plain stone cottage beside Chapel Bethel, but she now saw that a much larger house was set back in spacious grounds behind Chapel Beulah. It was black and white with gables and lots of Victorian gingerbread trim. The girl looked at it doubtfully then her gaze swept on, up the pass to where the road met the clouds. A large ornate building was perched on the hillside, a kind of overgrown Swiss chalet, complete with carved balconies and geraniums in window boxes. It was so completely unexpected, materializing from the clouds on an austere Welsh hillside, that she wondered for a moment if she was seeing things. A Walt Disney fantasyland came to mind. The tastefully lettered wooden sign beside the road said WELCOME. EVEREST INN. THE MOUNTAINEERS RETREAT. RESTAURANT, HEALTH CLUB. SPA ON PREMISES.

Its parking lot was full of luxury cars. Now this was more his kind of place, although he wouldn't have liked the phony chalet touch. But she had definitely understood that he was renting a house, not staying in a hotel. So it had to be the black-and-white Victorian behind the chapel.

She switched off the engine and got out, conscious of

the silence. At least it wasn't exactly silent up there. She
could hear the sigh of wind through grasses and the subtle murmur of a brook over stones. Sheep were still calling to each other somewhere up in the clouds, but there
were no familiar noises: no rumble of traffic, tooting of
horns, or blaring of sirens that punctuated life in the big
city. She felt very far away from home.

Taking a deep breath and smoothing down her crum-
pled black skirt, she opened the gate and walked down
the gravel driveway to the front door. It was opened by
a tall, gaunt woman in an unbecoming pea green cardigan
and tweed skirt. The woman ran her eyes over the European cut of her clothes and the alarming jet black bob
that overpowered the pale elfin face and wide blue eyes.
Dyed hair. The woman made a mental note and sniffed
to show her disapproval.

"Yes? Can I help you?" The voice was polished with
barely a trace of a Welsh lilt.

The girl stared at her in disbelief. "I'm—uh—not
sure," she stammered. "I'm not sure if I've come to the
right place." Her London-suburban flat vowels hadn't
completely been eradicated by an expensive education.

The woman folded her arms across the pea green cardigan. "If you're looking for bed and breakfast, we do
not take in trippers," she said, "and if you want to see
my husband . . ." she paused as she noticed a reaction in
the girl's face, "I'm afraid he's very busy at the moment.
He's working on next Sunday's sermon."

"Sermon?" The girl realized she was beginning to
sound like a parrot.

"He takes his preaching very seriously," the woman
went on. "He gives his sermons in Welsh and English,
you know. Quite a feat of oratory, even though that Parry
Davies person across the street thinks that he somehow
owns the title of bard around here."

The girl continued to stare, mouth open and uncomprehending. It could have been Martian or Chinese coming out of the woman's mouth.

"I'm sorry," she said, starting to back away. "I must have made a mistake. I was looking for a friend, but he's obviously not here. Sorry to have disturbed you."

"I could go and see if my husband can spare you a minute," the woman said, relenting. "He wouldn't like me to send anyone away who came seeking his help. He takes his Christian duties very seriously."

"Your husband is the minister?" the girl asked.

"Of course he's the minister. Who did you think he was? The Reverend Powell-Jones. I am Mrs. Powell-Jones. Maybe I could help you? I am known around here for my tact and counseling skills . . ."

Without warning the girl started to laugh. "The Reverend Powell-Jones? This is your house? I'm sorry. I really have made a mistake. I have to be going."

She fled down the laurel-lined front path, anxious to get back to the sanctuary of the car. As the girl put her hand on the gate a young man stepped out from between the bushes and barred her way.

"What are you doing here?" he demanded.

She tossed her head defiantly. "It's a free country. I can go where I want."

He grabbed her arm. "Don't be such a bloody fool, Christine. Can't you get it into your head—it's over. Finished. You are history, my sweet."

"Let go of me!" She tried to shake herself loose.

"Go back to London, Chrissy, please, before you make a complete idiot of yourself and someone winds up getting hurt."

"I said let go of me." Her voice had risen dangerously. "Leave me alone. I'm a big girl, Justin. I can take care of myself."

She pulled herself free from his grasp. "Bugger off, Justin!" She was yelling now. "I'm not just going to go

home like a good little girl and forget it ever happened.
You can't get rid of me that easily!"

She pushed past him, slammed her car door, gunned
the engine, and drove off with tires screeching. The
young man watched her go, then punched angrily at the
Powell-Joneses' gatepost before cutting across their garden and disappearing through the hedge.

Mrs. Powell-Jones had been watching the whole thing
from her sitting room window.

"Edward!" she called, her voice echoing through the
house. "Edward! Something very strange is going on."

The Reverend Powell-Jones's head appeared around
his study door. "What is it, my dear? I'm really very
busy. I was just getting to the good part about eternal
fires and sins of the flesh."

"Edward, this is important, or I should not have
dreamed of interrupting your sermon writing. A young
man has just gone through our hedge, and we've just had
an extraordinary visit from a young woman. I got the
impression that she wanted to see you, but then she
changed her mind." She glared at him as only Mrs.
Powell-Jones could glare. Boy Scouts and Sunday school
students had been known to confess to any number of
sins under the searing intensity of Mrs. Powell-Jones's
stare. "Edward," she said with icy softness. "You don't
have anything you want to tell me about, do you?"

"To tell you about, my dear? Of what nature?"

"The nature of your sermon, Edward. Sins of the flesh,
I think you called it."

Edward Powell-Jones looked puzzled. "I don't think I
follow you, my love."

"Then let me make myself clear. I was merely wondering why a young girl should be anxious to see you
and ask me pointedly if I were your wife. I wondered
exactly what might have gone on at that Christian youth
conference you attended in Bangor last month."

"You are not suggesting . . ." Edward Powell-Jones broke into horrified laughter . . . "that I, of all people . . ."

"It happens, Edward, even to the best of men. The beast lurks, even in the bosom of saints, and you are still an attractive man."

Edward, who was fiftyish, grayish, frailish, and had never been what young girls would describe as sexy, flushed with embarrassment. "I do assure you, my dear, that there has only been one woman in my life—will only be one woman in my life."

"Then what did she want?" Mrs. Powell-Jones demanded in exasperation.

"I have no idea."

"And a very angry young man, walking across our lawn, as if he owned the place."

Edward Powell-Jones's expression changed as if a new and troubling thought had just entered his head. His wife, who never missed a thing, didn't miss this either. "What is it?" she demanded. "You do know something."

"It just occurred to me that this might have something to do with that estate agent from Caernarfon."

"What estate agent?"

"The one who's been pestering me to let the house for the summer."

"Who's been what?"

"I'm sure I must have told you. He called several times this week, while you were at your mother's house."

"No, Edward, you did not tell me." Mrs. Powell-Jones's voice was icily calm.

"Didn't I? I meant to . . ." Edward Powell-Jones was distinctly flustered now. Icy calmness from his wife was worse than raging storms. "My memory, it's really letting me down these days, but I suppose I dismissed the matter as being of no consequence . . ."

"Exactly what did this estate agent person want from you, Edward?"

"He said he had a client who was very anxious to rent this house for the summer."

"This house?"

Edward Powell-Jones shrugged. "The client apparently wanted a large house with privacy in the vicinity of Llanfair and this was the only one that came to mind. I gather he was willing to pay a substantial sum for it."

"The nerve of the fellow," Mrs. Powell-Jones exclaimed.

"Exactly my thoughts, my dear. Showing up uninvited and fully expecting that we were going to comply just because he was waving money in our faces. I soon set him straight. I am the minister of the most important chapel in Llanfair, my good man, I told him. My flock needs me and I have no intention of going anywhere. Furthermore I told him that money was of no importance to us."

"On the other hand, Edward . . ." Mrs. Powell-Jones said thoughtfully, "maybe we should not dismiss the matter out of hand. You could have been overhasty."

"How so, my dear?"

"This might just be the answer to my prayers."

"Your prayers? You were praying to let the house?"

Mrs. Powell-Jones sighed at his stupidity. "About Mummy, Edward. I've been praying about Mummy." She perched herself on the arm of the faded print sofa. "You remember that the doctor told Mummy that she needs her hip replaced. She's been putting it off and putting it off and now the poor old dear can barely hobble around. I didn't offer to go and nurse her because my place is with you and the flock. How could I leave you to cope alone in this big house? Now, don't you see, a solution has presented itself. Mummy could get her hip replaced and I could take care of her."

"And what about me? There's no room for me at your mother's and anyway, I'm not closing up my chapel for the summer and letting Parry Davies get his hands on my congregation."

"Of course not, dear. We'll find somewhere in the village for you to board. Several villagers take in visitors don't they? I'll find somewhere suitable for you, don't worry." She looked around the room with satisfaction. "This couldn't have come at a better time. It is definitely a gift from heaven. And think of what we could do with the money . . ."

Edward's face lit up. "The organ has needed working on for some time. It's very distressing when the pedals stick during 'Cwm Rhondda.' "

"Organ be blowed. We need a new three-piece suite for this room." Mrs. Powell-Jones's voice rose alarmingly. She rose and pointed at the threadbare arm on which she had been perched. "Look at it, Edward. I've been ashamed for some time when we have had to hold chapel meetings here with the coils almost sticking through the cushions. And I am all too aware that the Parry Davies have that Naugahyde monstrosity, which, while only imitation leather and quite unsuitable for a pastor's home, is almost new."

"We could look into a new three-piece suite, I suppose," Edward Powell-Jones said with a resigned sigh. "If you really think that is the best use of the money."

"I do, Edward. I really do. Now get on the phone and call that estate agent. Tell him we've changed our minds and we can be out of here by the end of the week."

The young girl slowed the car to a crawl as she came to a crossroad at the top of the pass. One way led down to Beddgelert and the coast, the other to Betws-y-Coed. She stopped, undecided which way to turn. Tears were welling up, blurring her vision. She had no idea what to do now.

TWO

CONSTABLE EVAN EVANS CAME OUT of the Llanfair subpolice station and stood breathing in the good fresh air. He could smell the salt tang from the ocean today. He glanced up at the racing clouds. He hoped this didn't mean a storm coming in just in time for the weekend. He was really looking forward to his day with Bronwen.

His friendship with the young schoolteacher had been deepening and the village was already speculating, although they had only been on a handful of dates together. Evan was keeping any thoughts of wedding bells firmly out of his own mind.

They had a long mountain hike planned for the next day—if the weather held. It wasn't the sort of terrain you'd want to tackle in the rain, boggy in places and high enough to be mostly in cloud. If the wind kept blowing briskly like this it might clear out all these threatening clouds by then.

He glanced at his watch. Mrs. Williams, his landlady, would have his lunch waiting for him and would be upset if he let it get cold. It was Friday, so that probably meant fish. Mrs. Williams was very predictable in her choice of menus. He hoped it might be grilled herring today. There were wonderful fresh herrings at this time of year and Mrs. Williams cooked them to perfection, nicely crisp on the outside and moist in the middle, with maybe the added bonus of a soft row inside. Mrs. Williams was a wonderful cook and seemed to think that Evan would starve to death if he wasn't fed three large cooked meals a day, and tea as well if he happened to be home.

He locked the station door and set off for Mrs. Williams's cottage, his salivary glands working in anticipation.

"*Bore da,* Evans-the-Law," Roberts-the-Pump called from his garage next door.

"*Bore da.* How's business?" Evan asked.

"Can't complain. Plenty of tourists around at this time of year, isn't it? Of course we all know the one person who is complaining, don't we now?" He laughed and indicated the butcher's shop across the street. "Evans-the-Meat would build a bloody brick wall around the village if he had his way . . . and only let people through who spoke Welsh. You should have heard him ranting and raving this morning because some young fellow comes in and starts asking him questions about who lives where."

Evan smiled. He was all too aware of Evans-the-Meat's firm belief that foreigners had no business in Wales.

At that moment he heard raised voices, higher up the village street. He listened with interest. Speaking English, not Welsh. Probably tourists then. A woman's voice had risen to a scream. Evan hesitated then started up the street. A young girl was struggling to break free from a young man's grasp.

"Hey," Evan yelled but at that moment the girl broke loose, ran to a waiting maroon Vauxhall Vectra, and drove away, tires screeching. The young man yelled something after her, then turned back into the front garden and was lost among the bushes. *Lovers' tiff or something more serious?* Evan wondered. It took him a moment to register in surprise that the front garden belonged to the Powell-Joneses' house.

"What was that all about?" Roberts-the-Pump asked him as he returned down the street.

Evan shrugged. "We'll never know. They'd both gone by the time I got there. And I don't suppose it was any of my business, apart from the speeding, and I can hardly chase her on foot, can I?"

"They should provide you with a squad car," Roberts-the-Pump said. "I can get my hands on a lovely second-hand Ford Granada if you can get them interested."

Evan chuckled. "It's hard enough to get a new supply of paper clips out of them," he said. "And anyway, the whole purpose of having me here is that I can do all my patrolling on foot."

"And keep an eye on all the wicked goings on in Llanfair," Roberts-the-Pump laughed. "Got it made, haven't you, Evan *bach*?" he asked, although "little Evan" was hardly an accurate description for a six footer who climbed mountains and played rugby.

Evan smiled and walked on. He knew that this sentiment was echoed by most of the villagers—that he had a cushy job with little work. He also knew that they were glad enough to have him around.

"Is that you, Mr. Evans?" Mrs. Williams's high voice echoed from the kitchen. Always the same greeting, even though she knew he was the only one with a key. As usual he was tempted to answer that it was a homicidal maniac.

"Yes, it's me, Mrs. Williams."

"*Diolch am hynny!* Thank goodness for that." She came bustling down the dark hallway, smoothing down her apron as she spoke.

"Is something wrong then?" Evan asked.

"Only that I was worried you wouldn't come home before your dinner dried out." Mrs. Williams belonged to the old working-class tradition of calling lunch dinner and dinner supper. "I've made you a lovely fish pie, just," she added.

Fish pie—that was one he hadn't thought of. Not one of Mrs. Williams's usual specialties either. In fact he couldn't remember eating fish pie at her house before.

"I had to make it a fish pie today," she said, by way of explanation. "Jones-the-Fish didn't have a single decent herring in his van this morning. No mackerel either on account of the rough seas we've been getting." She turned and headed back to the kitchen with Evan following her. "I blame it all on that El Niño," she commented over her shoulder as she opened the oven door. "It's all the Americans' fault."

"El Niño? Isn't it a natural phenomenon?"

Mrs. Williams sniffed. "They started it with their atom bombs, didn't they? We never heard of El Niños in the Pacific before the Americans started testing their atom bombs there."

Evan kept wisely silent. He was steeling himself to face a fish pie, or wondering how to politely refuse it. Fish pie had never been one of his favorite foods. He associated it with school dinners. At school, fish pie had been a concoction of watery mashed potato with slight overtones of fish. He had never actually found fish in the pie, but there must have been some somewhere as he always got one or two bones.

While he was thinking these gloomy thoughts Mrs. Williams bent into the oven and produced a pie dish topped with a crispy, cheesy potato crust. The smell was definitely appetizing. Mrs. Williams scooped a big helping onto his plate. "Get that inside you and you won't do too badly then," she said proudly.

Evan prodded it with his fork. The bottom half of the slice was composed of chunks of firm white fish in a creamy sauce, then a layer of hardboiled egg and then the potato topping, fluffy underneath and crisp on top. The whole thing was crowned with bubbling cheese. One bite confirmed that it tasted as delicious as it looked.

"It's very good," he said in surprise.

Mrs. Williams nodded with satisfaction. "Now that's what I call a meal for a man," she said. "Good wholesome food that sticks to the ribs." Immediately she started ladling runner beans and marrow slices onto his plate.

Evan lamented silently that more food sticking to his ribs was the last thing he needed. Mrs. Williams's generous helpings were already beginning to show around his waistline.

He had only taken a couple of bites when there was a knock at the front door.

"Now who can that be?" Mrs. Williams demanded in annoyance. Evan often wondered if she expected him to be psychic or if this was merely a rhetorical question.

"I'll go and see, shall I?" He got up from the table only to be pushed back into his seat.

"You'll finish your dinner. I'll go," she said firmly.

"He's in the kitchen," Evan heard her say, "but he's only started in on his food just."

Then the kitchen door opened and Charlie Hopkins came in. He was one of the older men in the village, scrawny and undersize with thinning hair. He always wore boots that seemed too big for the rest of him—a throwback to the days when he worked in the slate quarry. He might have looked frail but Evan had seen him walk up mountains as if he was on an afternoon stroll through the park.

"Sorry to interrupt you when you're eating, Evan *bach*," he said.

"No problem, Charlie. Sit down and join me. You can see that Mrs. Williams has cooked enough for an army as usual."

"Oh, no thanks. I can't stay. I've got a delivery to

make in Llandudno," Charlie said. He operated a local hauling service. "I'm here on official business."

Evan looked up, his fork poised in his hand. "Official business?" Charlie was the usher at Chapel Bethel, but other than that held no office.

Charlie cleared his throat. "I've been asked to come and speak to you in my official capacity as secretary of the Llanfair and District Men's Choir," he said importantly.

"Oh really? You've got a problem with the choir, have you, Charlie?"

Charlie nodded. "A pretty big problem if you ask me. With the baritones."

"And you need my advice or you want police help?"

"We need help right enough. We need another baritone," Charlie said bluntly. "We've got the *eisteddfod* coming up in another month and we sound terrible, so Austin Mostyn asked me if I'd talk to you."

The choir director was Mostyn Phillips, who was also the music master at the comprehensive school in Caernarfon. He drove a very ancient Austin Mini, hence the nickname.

"I don't see why you've come to me, Charlie . . ."

"We've heard that you've got a good voice."

"Me? A good voice? Who told you that?" Evan laughed.

"Mrs. Williams," Charlie said, looking up to catch her eye as she lurked by the door. "She's heard you singing in the bathroom."

"I wasn't listening, you understand, Mr. Evans," Mrs. Williams said apologetically. "I just couldn't help hearing like. And you do sing lovely."

"I might sound okay in a tiled room or after a rugby match." Evan gave an embarrassed laugh. "But I've never sung properly in my life—well, not since the mixed infants choir."

"You couldn't be worse than what we've got," Charlie

said. "Pathetic, that's what it is, Evan *bach*, and the regional *eisteddfod* in Harlech is less than a month away.
Won't you come and help us out?"

"I really don't see that I'd be much help, Charlie. I
can't even read music."

"You wouldn't need to. Austin Mostyn will have you
going over the music so many times that it will be drilled
into your head. A right stickler he is—takes his duties
very seriously. He expects us to be the bloody Welsh
National Opera or something." He gave Evan a grin that
revealed a couple of missing teeth. "At least say you'll
come to the rehearsal this evening. I promised you'd be
there. I'll treat you to a pint in the Dragon afterward."

Evan sighed. "Well, I had no other plans for the evening . . ."

Charlie chuckled. "No hot dates with the schoolteacher?"

"Give over, Charlie. Bronwen and I are—"

"I know, just good friends, like the politicians say in
the *Daily Mirror* when they're caught in the Caribbean
with a French bit of crumpet." He gave Evan's shoulder
a nudge. "You want to take out young Betsy-the-Bar.
You'd do more than bird watching with her!"

"I don't doubt it," Evan said dryly. He was getting a
little tired of the constant matchmaking efforts that went
on in the village.

"Betsy-the-Bar?" Mrs. Williams demanded. "She's not
right for him. Mr. Evans is a serious, refined young man.
You can't see him taking out a girl who wears skirts
halfway up her thighs and necklines almost to meet
them? What he needs is a nice refined girl who can cook.
Now our Sharon, for example—"

"Gracious, is that the time?" Charlie interrupted, mer-
cifully sparing Evan from having to hear more about Mrs.
Williams's oversize granddaughter.

"I'd better get a move on, too," Evan said, turning to
look at the kitchen clock above the Welsh dresser.

"So you'll come tonight?" Charlie paused in the doorway.

"I'll be there," Evan said, "but I'm not making any promises."

THREE

"I'M MOST APPRECIATIVE, CONSTABLE EVANS."
Mostyn Phillips shook Evan's hand as they came out of
the village hall. It was almost dark and as they took the
shortcut to the Red Dragon, the peak of Mount Snowdon
glowed black against a silver sky.

"I do hope you decide to join our little endeavor,"
Mostyn continued. "As you can see, or should I say hear,
we could really use the extra voice."

Evan thought privately that the modest addition of his
somewhat-in-tune voice was hardly going to turn the
Llanfair Côr Meibion into an award-winning choir, but
he kept quiet. He felt sorry for Mostyn Phillips, who took
his duties so seriously and was faced with a choir of
aging voices. Most of the singers were more of Charlie
Hopkins's vintage—former slate miners to whom singing
in the choir was almost a requirement of living in Llanfair. There were only a few young men in the village
now and those teenage grandsons and nephews who were
dragged along thought the whole thing was a bit of a
joke.

"This used to be a fine choir in its heyday," Mostyn

went on, voicing Evan's thoughts out loud. "When the slate mine was working, every man in this neighborhood was proud to sing with the choir. Has Charlie shown you the cups we won in those days? My, but they were fine— the National Eisteddfod, too, not just local ones."

Evan glanced at Mostyn Phillips. He was a dapper little man with a neat Hitler-style moustache. He always dressed formally in a blazer and striped tie, or tweed jacket and cravat, but he gave the impression of being frozen in a time warp in both his dress and his behavior. He could never forget that he was a schoolmaster either. It must have been a constant annoyance for him to face an undisciplined group of men who couldn't be threatened with detention.

"Sometimes I wonder," Mostyn went on. "I wonder if I'm doing the right thing, entering us for the *eisteddfod* again. My whole reputation is riding on it. I'm well known for the quality of my choirs, Mr. Evans."

"Then maybe you should think twice about this *eisteddfod*," Evan said. "I doubt very much that you can whip us into shape in a month."

"But it's good for the men to compete. It gives them something to aim for—and we're only entered in the small choir division—under one hundred voices." He leaned confidentially close to Evan. "I hope to stun the judges with my choice of music."

Evan kept quiet about this, too. After all, what did he know about music? But none of the songs they had sung tonight were familiar to Evan. None of the old favorites that you could belt out with confidence, like "Men of Harlech" or "Sauspan Fach." It seemed to be all modern stuff and rather strange.

They had reached the Red Dragon at the same time as a couple of village women and Mostyn sprang ahead to open the door for them.

"After you, ladies," he said with a little bow, reducing both of the round village matrons to giggles.

"*Diolch yn fawr,* thank you very much," they mumbled.

"Nice to know that old world chivalry isn't dead yet, eh Sioned?" one of them exclaimed with a glance back at Mostyn.

"Holding the door open for us then, Austin Mostyn?" Roberts-the-Pump gave Charlie Hopkins a nudge as they walked through the open door. "Nice to know that old world chivalry isn't dead yet, eh Charlie?"

Mostyn flushed and gave a half laugh to show that he appreciated the joke.

"No, Constable Evans. I'm going to keep plowing ahead regardless," he said as they followed the men inside. "I'm an optimist. I keep hoping for a miracle."

"I don't think miracles come around too often, Mr. Phillips," Evan said.

"Well, look you, here he is now!" Betsy's high clear voice cut through the murmur of voices in the crowded bar. Her face lit up as Evan ducked under the big oak beam at the doorway and made his way through the crowd. "Charlie's just told me to pour you a pint of Brains courtesy of him, to celebrate your joining the choir." She beamed at Evan and smoothed down the Lycra tank top she was wearing, pulling the already-low neckline even lower. As Evan approached the bar, he was interested to see that the neon green top finished a good four inches above her waist, leaving a delicious exposure of flesh above her frilly white apron.

"I didn't say I was joining," Evan commented as he pushed his way to the bar between Charlie and Evans-the-Meat. "I only promised to come along and see. And I did come along and I did see. And now that I've got my free pint . . ."

The other men knew he was joking, but Mostyn Phillips turned a horrified face to Evan. "Oh, but Constable Evans, you can't leave us now. We need you, man. We can't do without you."

"See, Evan, you're going to be the star," Betsy said, her eyes smiling into his as she handed him the over-flowing glass of dark liquor. "I always knew you must have hidden talents if the right person knew how to draw them out of you." She put such meaning into this and stared so frankly that he had to take a large gulp of beer.

Why couldn't he just tell Betsy that he wasn't inter-ested and then maybe she'd stop all this embarrassing nonsense. He wondered if, deep down, he really did want her to stop.

"So Evan, did you hear that there's a Musicfest down on the quay in Caernarfon tomorrow?" Betsy went on as if the two of them were alone, not surrounded by the rest of Llanfair. "Live bands and dancing and all."

"Half my students are playing in those bands," Austin Mostyn commented. "I keep trying to educate them to like real music and what do they want—heavy metal, whatever that is."

Betsy laughed. "Heavy metal? That went out years ago, Mr. Phillips. Get with it! You should go to the Mu-sicfest and see what the young people like today. I thought I might go. My cousin Eddie's in one of the bands. The Groovin' Druids, they call themselves. They're ever so good." Her gaze moved toward Evan. "How about you come with me, Evan? Remember I promised to teach you the latest dance steps? You haven't even learned the macarena yet."

"You're wasting your time, Betsy love," Charlie Hop-kins said while Evan was still forming an answer in his head. "He's off with Bronwen-the-Book again tomor-row."

"Her again? Bloody bird watching, no doubt," Betsy muttered as she set down a glass, none too gently, in front of another customer. "Sounds like a barrel of laughs to me." She ignored Evan and leaned closer to Charlie. "Now if he came on a date with me, Mr. Hopkins, I'd show him that there was more fun in life than watching birds. He wouldn't have the time or energy to notice bloody birds if he was with me."

This was greeted with noisy laughter. Evan was glad that the public bar was dark. He was always embarrassed at blushing so easily—one of the problems of fair Celtic skin, he supposed. He took a long drink and emptied his glass.

"I'm not giving up, you know," Betsy said, taking the glass from him and refilling it without being asked. "I'm going to get you dancing with me one of these days, Evan Evans, and when you're out there with me, you'll wonder what hit you."

"The floor, probably, when I trip over my own feet," Evan said, grinning at Charlie.

A blast of cold air made everyone turn to the door.

"It's y Parch, the minister," Charlie muttered, digging Evan in the ribs. "Better watch our language from now on. Evening, Reverend," he called as the crowd parted to let the Reverend Parry Davies, the more worldly of the two ministers, approach the bar.

"Good evening, one and all." The Reverend Parry Davies nodded genially to those around him. "A pint of your best Brains, please, my dear. I've a thirst that could drain Llŷn Llydaw tonight."

"Been practicing your sermon for Sunday, have you, Reverend?" Evans-the-Meat asked. It was well known in Llanfair that he was a regular at the other chapel and thought that its preacher, Mr. Powell-Jones, was far superior. "When are you going to try sermonizing in Welsh, then? Isn't our mother tongue good enough for you?"

"I have to cater to everybody, Gareth," Reverend Parry Davies said, still smiling genially. "And not everybody speaks our mother tongue as well as you and I do." He looked around with pride. "As a matter of fact, I've just been reciting some of the finest Welsh words ever written. It's for the bardic competition at the eisteddfod, you know. This year I'm doing a poem based on the story of the Lady Rhiannon in the *Mabinogion*."

"The what?" young Barry-the-Bucket the local bulldozer driver, asked in a stage whisper.

"The *Mabinogion*," Evans-the-Meat hissed back. "One of the oldest books in the world, and full of stories of Welsh heroes, too. What do they teach you in the schools these days?"

The minister nodded. "Magnificent it is! The drama of it—the pathos when her little son is taken from her and she searches in vain. There won't be a dry eye in the pavilion, I can tell you."

"Why? Are you going to bring onions with you, Reverend?" Barry-the-Bucket quipped to his friends.

"You be quiet, Barry-the-Bucket," Betsy said fiercely. "You wouldn't know culture if it jumped up and bit you. I think the reverend is going to do just fine. He'll be a credit to us all."

"Your faith in me is very touching, my dear," Reverend Parry Davies said. "I have to confess that I have high hopes of being chaired bard this year."

"Good for you, Reverend," Charlie Hopkins said. "But what about Mr. Powell-Jones? Isn't he entering the *eisteddfod,* too?"

"My fellow minister doesn't believe in getting involved in secular declamations."

"What?" Barry-the-Bucket asked.

"He thinks it's sinful to enter competitions," Evans-the-Meat clarified.

"Only because he's not good enough," Evans-the-Milk muttered, loud enough for Evans-the-Meat to hear.

"What's that you're saying?" Evans-the-Meat demanded. "You're talking bloody rubbish as usual. The Reverend Powell-Jones has the finest voice this side of the mountain. That's my opinion and I don't care who knows it."

"I don't dispute it," the Reverend Parry Davies said

easily. "He does have a fine voice. Almost as good as mine."

This got general laughter.

"But I don't even know if he'll be here for the *eisteddfod*," he went on.

A hush fell on the room.

"Not be here? Where's he going then?" Evans-the-Meat asked.

"Haven't you heard?" The Reverend Parry Davies looked from face to face. "He's letting his house for the summer. His wife's going down to Barmouth to look after her mother."

There was a muffled cheer and someone at the back of the room muttered, "Good riddance."

"He's letting his house?" Harry-the-Pub appeared at Betsy's side, wiping his hands on his apron. "The Powell-Joneses are moving out for the summer? Where did you hear that?"

"Our daily woman, Elen, is friendly with their daily woman, Gladys. Elen heard it straight from the horse's mouth, so to speak. She said he was on the phone this afternoon arranging things and then he asked Gladys if she could come in over the weekend to help get their things packed away and give the place a good cleaning. Gladys said he offered an extra fifty pounds."

"Fifty pounds? That's not like him," Betsy exclaimed. "He's usually an old skinflint." She saw Harry-the-Pub's frown. "Well, he is," she repeated. "It's common knowledge in the village. He only had one go when I was in charge of the coconut shy at the last fete."

"You should have been in charge of the kissing booth, Betsy," Barry-the-Bucket said. "Then you'd have made a fortune."

"And I wouldn't have let you, even for a hundred pounds," Betsy responded quickly.

"Hold on a minute," Evans-the-Meat interrupted. "Did Gladys say who was renting the house for the summer?

I can't imagine Mrs. Powell-Jones letting strangers into her house. That's not like her at all."

"I've no idea," Reverend Parry Davies said, "but I got the feeling it was someone important."

"I know who it is," a voice spoke from the back of the crowd. Heads turned to see young Trefor Dawson, a newcomer who did maintenance at the Everest Inn. "At least I think I do," he added, conscious of being the center of attention.

"Well, spill the beans then, man," Charlie Hopkins said.

"My cousin works for Jenkins and Jenkins—you know, the posh estate agents in Caernarfon?" Several people nodded. "Well, you'll never guess who asked them to find a house in Llanfair?" He looked around with satisfaction. "Ifor Llewellyn."

"Ifor Llewellyn?" Mostyn Phillips demanded.

"THE Ifor Llewellyn?" Betsy shrieked. "The famous opera singer?"

For once the residents of Llanfair were momentarily speechless. Then Evans-the-Milk voiced what everyone was thinking. "Why on earth would he want to spend the summer in Llanfair, of all places?"

"And what's wrong with Llanfair?" Evans-the-Meat demanded. "Isn't it beautiful enough for you then? And peaceful and quiet and free of all those bloody tourists?"

"Yes, but . . ." Evans-the-Milk began. "It's nothing special, is it? I mean, if I were famous, I'd be spending my summers in Nice or Monte Carlo or California, not Llanfair."

"Especially someone like Ifor Llewellyn," Barry-the-Bucket added. "If what we read in the papers is true, you'd expect him to be on some woman film star's yacht."

"Perhaps he's bringing a lady friend to a little love nest in Llanfair," Charlie Hopkins chuckled. "Maybe that Italian Carla what's-her-name."

"I don't know how he does it," Barry-the-Bucket said.

"Does what?" Betsy demanded.

"How he gets all those beautiful women. I mean, it's not like he's young and he's heavy enough, isn't he?"

"I think he's ever so sexy," Betsy commented. "But then there's something about big men that I find very sexy." Her gaze moved unabashedly to Evan again. Evan hoped he wasn't beginning to look as heavy as Ifor Llewellyn.

"Love nest in Llanfair!" Barry-the-Bucket shook his head. "I don't think so, somehow."

"No, he's bringing his family, that's what Gladys said," the reverend interrupted. "Bringing his family here for the summer."

"He's probably had enough of Nice and Monte Carlo," Evans-the-Meat said. "After all, he is a local Gwynedd man, isn't he? He's coming home to his roots."

"Is that so?" Evan asked. "Ifor Llewellyn comes from around here?"

Several heads nodded. "He lived for a while in Llanfair, didn't he? When he was a little boy?"

"That would be when his mother was a maid at the big house," Charlie Hopkins informed them.

"The big house?" Evan asked. "You mean the Powell-Jones's?"

"It used to belong to Mrs. Powell-Joneses' family in those days. The Lloyds, they were. Owned the slate mine. She used to be Patsy Lloyd—" he laughed. "I remember her right enough. She was a toffy-nosed little thing, even in those days, wasn't she? They sent her away to boarding school in England and she came back even more toffy nosed. Then the slate mine closed and eventually she inherited the house."

"Very handy for Mr. Powell-Jones, right next door to his chapel," Evans-the-Milk exclaimed.

"Why do you think he got that chapel, you dummy?"

Evans-the-Meat exclaimed. "He got it because it was on land owned by her family."

"And Ifor Llewellyn's mother was the maid there?" Betsy asked, leaning forward across the bar until her neckline was stretched into a dangerous view of cleavage, causing every man in the room to stop drinking momentarily. "No wonder he wants to come back and rent it. What's the betting Mrs. Powell-Jones put him in his place when they were young. He probably had to bow to her."

Evans-the-Meat laughed. "Nothing like coming back in victory, is there. I wonder how he got them to leave?"

"He offered a huge sum of money, that's what I heard," the Reverend Parry Davies said.

"It must have been a huge sum to make her hand over the place to her former maid's child," Charlie Hopkins commented. "Well, isn't this a turn up for the books."

"I think it's a great honor for Llanfair," Evans-the-Meat said grandly, "as long as no bloody tourists come wanting to catch a glimpse of him."

"Now if we could only get him to join our choir for the *eisteddfod*," Charlie quipped.

"Oh 'deed to goodness, yes. He'd want to do that, wouldn't he? Make a change from La Scala. Do you think he'd be good enough for us?" The low-ceilinged barroom echoed with jeers and noisy laughter.

"Why don't you go ask him, Charlie," Harry-the-Pub suggested with a grin. "After all, you persuaded the constable here to join us."

Mostyn Phillips cleared his throat. "I happen to know Ifor Llewellyn," he said. "He and I got scholarships to the Royal School of Music in London at the same time."

"Is that a fact?" Suddenly Mostyn was the center of attention.

"You really know Ifor Llewellyn?" Betsy asked, wide-eyed and impressed.

"He and I shared digs together, our first year in London," Mostyn said. "I—uh—also knew the lady who is now his wife. I introduced them, in fact."

"Almost like one of the family, isn't he, boys?" Barry-the-Bucket clapped Mostyn on the back, sending him off balance and into the bar. "Good for you, Austin Mostyn."

"Well then," Evans-the-Meat said grandly. "You'll be the one to ask him to join us, won't you?"

Mostyn cringed with embarrassment. "Be reasonable, man. I can hardly ask one of the greatest tenors in the world to sing with the Llanfair Côr Meibion."

"I don't see why not," Evans-the-Meat insisted. "If it was a favor for a very old friend, like."

"Maybe you could ask him to sing a few solos—sort of drown out the rest of us," Evans-the-Milk suggested. "It would certainly make the judges sit up and take notice, wouldn't it?"

"If you really do know him as well as you say," Barry-the-Bucket commented.

Evan put his hand on Mostyn's shoulder. "You were asking for a miracle a few minutes ago, Mr. Phillips. I'd say you just got it."

FOUR

"I DON'T KNOW IF WE were wise to choose this route on a day like this," Evan said to Bronwen as he helped her over a stile. "It looks like we'll be walking in the clouds most of the time."

Bronwen took his hand and stepped nimbly up onto the stile. She was wearing khaki hiking pants today instead of her usual long skirts, and a blue-green jacket that gave her normally blue eyes a greenish glow. Her fair hair was back in a long braid but a few stray wisps swirled in the wind around her face as she smiled down at Evan.

"I like walking in the clouds," Bronwen said. "I like that feeling of unreality—being somewhere magical, quite apart from the real world down below."

They had been climbing steadily into the mist until they reached a high moorland of springy turf and heather. A pair of red grouse rose flapping from the grasses in front of them and from high in the mist came a plaintive wailing cry, like the call of a frightened child waking from a nightmare. It was so eerie, echoing from unseen cliffs, that they paused, alarmed for a second, then both said, "Raven," at the same moment.

They laughed and walked on but the unearthly quality of the cry haunted them. Evan felt his skin prickling.

"How about eating our lunch down by Llŷn Crafnant?" he asked. "The sun might be out there."

"Sounds fine to me," Bronwen said.

They reached a high pass where the wind swirled up from unseen waters below them, then picked their way down cautiously over rocks slippery with moisture and moss. Suddenly there was the lake, its surface steaming as the sun melted away the mist.

"Perfect," Evan said. "We should have blue skies by the time we've dropped down to the water. And we'll get a grand view of Snowdon on the way back."

He reached out and took Bronwen's hand as they made their way down over lichen-covered rocks. Suddenly Bronwen stopped. "Oh," she said in disappointment. "We're not going to be alone. Look, there's a car parked on the other side."

"A car?" Evan looked toward where she was pointing. Far below them, on the steep far shore of the lake, a maroon sedan was parked. A figure was standing behind the car, blending into the dappled shade of the trees. It seemed to be a young man in jeans and a leather jacket. "How on earth did someone get a car up here?" Evan asked.

"There's the forestry track up from Trefriw, isn't there?"

"But I wouldn't have thought it was suitable for cars, especially after the wet spring we've had. It must have been awfully bumpy. I didn't think cars were allowed."

"What some people will do to get out of walking," Bronwen said scornfully. "They want the views and the solitude, but they want the convenience of driving there."

"That's funny," Evan said, staring hard at the car. "That looks like the car I saw yesterday. Unusual color, isn't it?" He frowned, then shrugged. "No matter. Let them enjoy their day and we'll enjoy ours, eh Bronwen? Room enough for both of us."

The path passed through a stand of woodland, ancient hawthorns and oaks, still draped in mist. It was completely silent. Their feet made no noise on the rich carpet of decaying leaves. Overhead the raven cawed again, its plaintive cry echoing unnaturally loud. Then the path emerged from the woods and began a zigzag descent to the lakeshore.

"We don't need to worry about the car anymore," Bronwen said, her eyes scanning the lake below. "It's gone."

"That was quick," Evan said.

"Probably one of those tourists who come, take a snapshot of the kiddies in front of the lake, then go again."

Evan was about to move on when he saw bubbles rising from the surface of the lake. Once he spotted them, the outline of the car was clearly visible.

"It's in the water, Bron," Evan shouted. "The car's gone into the lake! Oh my God. We'll never get there in time."

He took off like a madman down the narrow path, leaping from rock to rock, his arms flailing to keep his balance around the precarious bends. He heard Bronwen shrieking, "Evan be careful. You'll fall!" but he couldn't slow down. The image of the submerged car blotted out everything else. He started peeling off his jacket as he ran. Where was the closest cottage? They had passed nothing since a farm above Capel Curig. Which would be the best direction to go for help—back the way they had come or down the forestry track to Trefriw? But that had to be a good two miles or more.

I'm going to be too late! The words echoed through his mind as the blood pounded in his temples. He was not conscious of the ground beneath his feet or of the drop to the lakeshore below. The descent seemed to take forever. He was running in slow motion, like the running he sometimes did in dreams, away from pursuers or wild beasts.

At last he reached the lakeshore. The level was down and he slithered over loose shale to skirt the end of the lake. Bubbles were still rising, marking the spot where the car had gone in, but nobody had managed to get out. How many people would he have to deal with? Why hadn't they jumped out when the car started to move?

He struggled out of his boots before he went in. The icy water took his breath away. He took a big gulp of air and dived into green darkness. The water was clear and he could see the outline of the car below him, moving steadily downward. The lakeshore fell away quickly into the depths. If he couldn't get to the door soon, it would be too deep for him to reach. He came to the surface again, took in more air, then went straight down. The door handle was in his hands. Please don't let it be locked, he prayed. He pressed on it and tried to pull it open. The force of the water held it shut. Inside he could make out a figure slumped in the driver's seat. He braced his feet against the doorpost and pulled again with all his might. Water rushed in through the crack he had opened. His lungs were bursting and the water was singing in his ears, but he struggled to let the water equalize the pressure.

At last he felt the door yield to his tug as the water engulfed the interior of the car. He grabbed at a jacket sleeve and pulled, kicking with all his force to get away from the car. He felt the body floating behind him as he kicked for the surface.

Bronwen was standing there, clutching his jacket, her face white and anxious.

"Help me . . . get to . . ." Evan started to say but Bronwen was already wading into the shallow water and grabbed the person's other arm.

"Is she dead?" she asked.

"I don't know." He was still gasping for air. "She couldn't have drowned. There was no water in the car."

They laid the limp body on the grassy shore. Against her jet black hair the face looked a ghastly white.

"We should start CPR," Bronwen said. Evan searched for a pulse and found one. "She's alive," he said.

The girl stirred and moaned. Then she opened her eyes and looked at them with surprise. "Where am I?" she asked. "What's happening?" She moved cautiously. "I'm all wet."

"You've been for a swim," Evan said. "Your car went into the lake."

"The lake?" She tried to sit up and looked around her, puzzled. "Oh yes, I remember now. I parked on the shore. I must have fallen asleep."

Evan was looking at her closely. "Fallen asleep?" he asked. "So how did the car get into the water?"

"I don't know." Her voice sounded young and scared. "Maybe the brake didn't hold properly. Maybe I knocked it with my leg while I was sleeping."

"And what about the man who was with you?" Bronwen asked, squatting down beside them.

"Man? With me? It was only me. I was all alone," the girl said steadily.

"But I saw a man there, didn't you Bronwen?"

"I think so. There was a man behind the car, at the edge of the woods."

The girl looked at them blankly. "I've no idea," she said. "I didn't see anyone."

"So what do we do now?" Bronwen asked.

"Get her down to a hospital to be checked out."

The girl struggled to get up. "Hospital? I don't want to go to any hospital. I'm fine—just a little shaken up, that's all."

"You were unconscious in a car at the bottom of the lake. That's not fine," Evan said.

"I told you, I must have fallen asleep, but I'm fine

now. Honestly I am. And I don't want to go to any hospital—please."

Evan shrugged and helped her to her feet. "I suppose we can't force you," he said, "but how are we going to get you back down? The easiest way would be to send for an ambulance."

"I told you, I'm perfectly okay." Her voice had a sharp edge to it now. "I can walk back the way I came. I can pick up a bus from there."

"You're not walking back alone," Evan said. "I don't think you'd make it back to my car, though. It's quite a climb." He looked at her black patent slingbacks and then at Bronwen.

Bronwen got up. "I'll go and get your car, Evan," she said. "It won't take me long."

"I don't know if I want to be left with a strange bloke," the girl said.

"He's a police officer," Bronwen said. "Very reliable. Never been known to take advantage of a girl yet." She gave Evan a little sideways glance, then picked up his jacket. "Here, put your jacket on. She can have my rain gear. I'll try not to be too long." She set off up the steep zigzag path.

"Thanks," the girl said as Evan helped her into the parka.

"What's your name?" he asked.

"Christine." She looked away, uncomfortable under his gaze.

"I've seen you before," Evan said. "You were in Llanfair yesterday. You were shouting at someone. You drove away fast."

"So?" She looked at him defiantly. "I wasn't breaking the law, was I?"

"You were probably speeding," Evan said, "but I've no way of proving that. I'm just interested. You have a fight with your boyfriend and then your car just happens to go into a very remote lake."

"He's not my boyfriend," she said emphatically. "So what are you getting at?"

"I'm wondering if the brakes really were faulty," Evan said. "If not, there are two scenarios that come to mind. Either you took the brake off, or he did. Suicide or attempted murder. Neither of them sound very nice, do they?"

The girl shuddered. "I was on my own, I tell you, and I don't know what happened. I woke up and found you looking down at me. That's all I can remember."

She hugged her knees tighter to her. She was shivering now.

"At the risk of sounding like an old fuddy-duddy," Evan said, "nothing is worth killing yourself for. You might have a broken heart right now, but trust me, you'll get over it."

She looked up with scorn in her eyes. "What do you know about anything? What can you possibly know?"

"Only that life's too good to waste and you're only given one chance at it," Evan said. He held out his hand to her. "Come on, let's start walking down the fire road to meet Bronwen. There's no sense in sitting here and freezing."

"What will happen when we get back?" the girl asked as she walked cautiously in squelching shoes. "About the car, I mean?"

"I'll drive you back to Llanfair and you can file a police report."

She leaped as if burned. "Police report? Wait a second. I haven't done anything wrong."

"There's a car worth a few thousand quid lying at the bottom of that lake. Someone will want that explained, I'd imagine."

"They won't expect me to pay if it was an accident, will they?" She sounded ridiculously young. "Do you think they can get it out?"

"I imagine that's what they have insurance for," Evan

said. "They might want to know why you drove it up a forest track?"

"I lost my way," the girl said. "I made a wrong turn and then I couldn't find a place to turn around before I got to the lake." She sounded as if she was working out the statement as she went along.

They walked for a while in silence. "Do we have to go back to Llanfair? I'd rather not," she said.

"I suppose you could make your report at any police station. Where did you rent the car?"

"Heathrow."

"And where are you staying?"

"Nowhere in particular. I slept in the car last night."

"So where do you live?"

"I don't have a place yet."

"What about your parents?"

"They live in Surrey. Don't worry. I'll handle it. London's fine. I know people in London."

"I'll take you down to Bangor," Evan said. "We'll get you some dry clothes, then you can file your report and we'll put you on a train back to London."

"I don't have any money," the girl said. "My purse is back in the car."

"I'll lend you the fare. You can send it back to me."

"I don't know why you're being so nice," she said suddenly.

"It's my job," Evan said, "And you better be thankful that I was the one who found you. You could easily have wound up in a psychiatric hospital for a full medical evaluation. They do that for attempted suicides, you know. But I'm giving you the benefit of the doubt. We'll call it an accident, but only if you promise never to try anything so bloody stupid again."

FIVE

"DO YOU THINK YOU DID the right thing?" Bronwen asked as they drove back into Llanfair after putting the girl on the London train.

"Letting her go, you mean?" Evan shrugged.

"You don't really think it was an accident, do you?"

"Not for a moment, but I don't see how sending her to hospital would help her. Most likely she's an emotional young girl who has been dumped by her boyfriend and overreacted. She'll feel differently tomorrow."

"It's strange that she should be covering up for him, though," Bronwen said. "I'm almost sure I saw a man behind the car."

"Me, too," Evan said. "Which makes me wonder if it was attempted suicide. Would he have had a chance to tamper with the brakes, do you think? And why was she unconscious when we got to her? You don't sleep so deeply that you don't notice your car going into a lake, do you?"

"You think he might have wanted her conveniently out of his way?" Bronwen asked, pushing her hair back worriedly from her face.

"Then why would she deny he was there? She must have suspected the same thing."

"Because she loved him, you dolt," Bronwen said. "Women do ridiculous things when they're in love."

Evan looked at her for a long moment. Then he said, "We never did have our picnic, did we?"

"It doesn't matter. We did our good deed for the month."

"I think we should go out to eat somewhere, to make up for it," Evan said.

Bronwen's face lit up. "That would be lovely. We'd have to go home and change first. You're still damp and steaming and I'm in my hiking gear."

"The fish-and-chip shop down by the docks doesn't care how you dress," Evan said casually, watching her face fall again. Then he put his arm around her shoulder and squeezed her to him. "Of course we're going home to change. Then I thought that Italian place wasn't too bad, was it?"

Bronwen beamed as they drove up the pass toward Llanfair.

Evan came to an abrupt halt in the middle of his room. A strange white nightshirt was laid out on his bed.

"What the . . . ?" he began.

Instantly Mrs. Williams appeared behind him. "Oh, there you are, Mr. Evans. I'm so sorry. I was hoping you'd be back earlier. He insisted, you see, or rather she did."

"Who insisted, Mrs. Williams?"

She glanced over her shoulder, then hissed, "The Powell-Joneses. He's moving in here while his wife goes to take care of her old mam. And Mrs. Powell-Jones said that her husband had to have this room because the one at the back is damp and he's allergic to damp and mold and fungus." She spread her hands helplessly. "I didn't like to touch your stuff. She wanted to clear it out, but I drew the line at that. I hope you'll understand. It's only for a little while, look you."

"It's alright, Mrs. Williams," Evan said, although he wasn't feeling too happy about the thought of moving to a room at the back that was apparently covered in mold and fungus. He knew the effect that Mrs. Powell-Jones could have on people. She'd had the same effect on him. It was hard to say no to her.

"Oh dear me, *diolch am hynny*, that takes a load off my mind," Mrs. Williams said, putting her hand to her ample breast. "I've been getting myself into a tizzy worrying about how you'd take it. I told her you had prior rights, but she just wouldn't listen."

"Where are they now?" Evan glanced at the door.

"Putting the final touches to the house before the new people move in tomorrow. Then the reverend's coming back here in time for supper tonight."

"I'll be out," Evan said. "I'm taking Bronwen out for a meal."

"Now isn't that nice." Mrs. Williams's face lit up. "I am pleased to hear that. She's a lovely young girl—a little serious for my mind. Too much bird watching and not enough dancing, but you can't have everything, can you. Our Sharon, of course, she's a lovely little dancer . . . light on her feet . . . you've never seen her dance, have you, Mr. Evans?"

"I'll start moving out my things, Mrs. Williams," he said quickly.

On Sunday morning Evan woke to the unfamiliar darkness of the back room and sniffed the air. Sunday morning meant Sunday breakfast, his favorite meal of the week. He glanced at his watch. Usually the delicious smells of sausage and bacon cooking would be rising up from the kitchen at this hour. Maybe Mrs. Williams had overslept for once, or maybe the Reverend Powell-Jones wanted his breakfast later—which wasn't likely as he had a sermon to preach at ten.

The bathroom door was locked. Evan sighed, put on cords and a sweater, and went downstairs.

"Ready for your breakfast, are you, Mr. Evans?" Mrs. Williams asked.

"Is it ready? I didn't smell any good frying smells." Evan sat down with an anticipatory smile on his face. The smile faded as Mrs. Williams put a bowl of what looked like brown twigs topped with mushy brown pulp in front of him.

"What's this, Mrs. Williams?" Evan asked.

Mrs. Williams glanced at the door. "It's what she ordered for him. It's bran with pureed prunes on top."

"That's all very nice for him, maybe, Mrs. W., but what about me?" Evan demanded, his good nature pushed to its limits. "I like my usual Sunday breakfast."

Mrs. Williams twisted her apron nervously. "Ah, well, that's it, you see. That's the problem. The reverend can't abide fried foods. His wife said the smell of them turns his stomach, especially before he has to preach. And we wouldn't want to get in the way of his doing the Lord's business, would we, Mr. Evans?"

"And how long is he planning to stay?" Evan asked gloomily.

Mrs. Williams shrugged. "They didn't say. As long as the house is let, I suppose. I was the only one who had space, seeing as it's the height of the tourist season."

Evan thought that it wasn't the number of tourists in Llanfair that had made other landladies turn away the Powell-Joneses. They must have known what they were getting into. He sighed. "I'll just have some toast, Mrs. W."

He was on his way upstairs again when an awful cry erupted from the front bedroom. "Help me, or I perish!" echoed through the hallway. Evan sprinted the last few stairs and burst into the bedroom. The Reverend Powell-

Jones was standing at the foot of his bed in long johns and a white undershirt. He looked up in horror as Evan burst in.

"Just what do you think you are doing, young man?" he demanded.

"I heard you yelling for help." Evan looked confused.

"I was merely vocalizing in preparation for my sermon," the reverend said dryly. "One must warm up the voice, you know. I was reciting a portion of the Lay of Olwen that I mean to perform at the *eisteddfod* bardic competition."

"I didn't know you were entering, too, Reverend," Evan said. "I know that the other reverend fancies himself as a bard . . ."

"Precisely. He fancies himself. Gives himself airs," Reverend Powell-Jones said. "I decided it was about time I showed him what a real orator sounds like. My wife persuaded me to enter the competition myself, since I'll have ample time for practicing during the next few weeks."

"Great," Evan muttered to himself as he clomped back down the stairs. A summer of damp, prune eating, and bardic oratory stretched unenticingly before him.

Later that day Evan took his usual walk around the village. He liked to check on things, even on his days off, and he found Bronwen working in the schoolhouse garden. To his annoyance she laughed when he recited his woes to her.

"Maybe a few weeks of pureed prunes is what you need," she chuckled. "Lick you into shape!"

"It's not funny, Bron. You should try living there," Evan said.

"You could always move out." Bronwen was yanking weeds between rows of gooseberries.

Evan looked at her in surprise. "Where would I go?

Everyone knows Mrs. Williams is the best landlady in the village."

"You could try living on your own." She looked up with a large dandelion in her hand. "Everyone does it at some stage, you know. It's called leaving the nest."

"Yes, but what about all the conveniences—all my meals cooked for me and my shirts washed and ironed? I'd have to give up all that if I lived on my own."

Bronwen snorted. "And what sort of husband do you think you're going to make someday if you don't know how to wash your own shirts?"

"Isn't that what wives are supposed to do?" Evan asked.

"If that's what you think, I can tell you're going to have a hard time finding a wife." Bronwen picked up the basin of gooseberries and started to walk back to the house.

"Bron, wait, I was only joking," he called. Then he sighed and walked on. Women were very hard to understand.

Sometime late on Sunday evening a big black car turned into the Powell-Joneses' driveway. The inhabitants of Llanfair were usually indoors with their curtains drawn by nine o'clock, especially on Sundays when the pub wasn't officially open, so nobody saw or heard the newcomers arrive. But by early Monday morning the word was all around the village. The great man had arrived!

When Evan reached his office at nine o'clock, the first thing he saw was a police car, parked outside.

A head poked out of the car window as Evan approached. "I'm glad you finally showed up. I'm dying for a cup of tea," the car's occupant said. Evan recognized Jim Abbott from headquarters—not his favorite member of the force. For some reason Abbott always had to make jokes about living among the sheep.

"What are you doing here?" Evan asked, attempting to sound civil.

"You'll be seeing a lot of me," Jim Abbott said. "I'm here on a hush-hush mission. You probably don't know about it, but there's a celebrity staying in your village at the moment."

"Don't know about it?" Evan gave a derisive snort. "The whole village has known about it since Friday. He moved in last night."

"Is that a fact?" Jim Abbott looked impressed. "I was told that he didn't want anyone to know that he was going to be here."

"You can't keep anything secret in a village," Evan said.

"Anyway, they're sending up extra patrols to keep an eye on him and handle the press," Jim Abbott said. "He was worried there would be trouble with the paparazzi. He wants peace and quiet."

"Why didn't they talk to me about it?" Evan said, trying to control his annoyance.

"Ah well." Jim Abbott paused noticeably. "I think they wanted someone with experience in this kind of thing. I mean, I'm sure you're a thoroughly good chap, but handling lost cats isn't exactly the same somehow, is it?" He grinned at Evan. He had an annoying grin with even white teeth. Evan had never trusted anyone with perfect teeth.

"So you've done a lot of this down in Caernarfon, have you?" he asked pleasantly. "I'd imagine there'd be world-class celebrities passing through almost every day down there."

The sarcasm wasn't lost on Jim Abbott. "I've done my share of crowd control at the rugby games," he said. "And we had a rock concert last year."

Evan said nothing. He felt that he had scored a point. Jim Abbott obviously thought so, too. "The boss just wanted an extra man on the spot, ready to call in reinforcements in case any crowd control was needed, that's all."

"I don't think there's much of a crowd to control at the moment," Evan said, surveying the street that was empty apart from Evans-the-Post, sitting on the bridge, reading the morning mail.

"What does he think he's doing?" Abbott asked. "He's not reading the mail, is he?"

Evans glanced back at the lanky mailman, who went on with his reading, completely oblivious of their presence. "He does it all the time," he said with a grin. "He's harmless and nobody seems to mind."

"A lot of dafties you've got up here," he said. "Now be a good chap and make me that cup of tea."

Ifor Llewellyn didn't show his face outside the house all day, although a big voice, doing vocal exercises, confirmed that he was indeed in residence. No other voice sounded like that. No hoards of paparazzi appeared either. Much to Evan's delight Jim Abbott had to spend the day doing the crossword and drinking cups of tea. When he left he muttered that he didn't see why they needed him up there, when Evan had a perfectly good telephone and could get reinforcements in fifteen minutes.

That evening Evan went to the Red Dragon soon after opening time.

"You're here early tonight, Mr. Evans," Harry-the-Pub commented. "Got a thirst on you, have you then?"

"I wouldn't say no to a pint, but what I'd really like is food."

Harry shrugged apologetically. "I've only got the usual things, Constable—you know, meat pies, sausages, fish fingers, that kind of thing."

"Lovely," Evan said. "A meat pie, a couple of sausages, and some chips would go down a treat."

"Is Mrs. Williams not feeling well then?" Harry asked.

"I'm the one not feeling well, Harry," Evan said. "We've got old Powell-Jones lodging with us and he's dictating the menus. It's muesli and prunes in the morning and it was steamed fish and spinach tonight. He's allergic to anything fried and he won't eat pastry or starch in the evenings—bad for his digestion. So I'm getting it, too—he's convinced Mrs. Williams it will be healthy for us all."

Harry rolled his eyes. "Don't you worry, Mr. Evans. We'll make sure you don't starve," he said. "Betsy love," he called. "I've got your favorite young man in here and he's dying of starvation. Get some sausages going for him and put a meat pie in the microwave, will you?"

Half an hour later, as the pub began to fill up, Evan was a happier man.

"Imagine her trying to starve you," Betsy said, turning her searchlight blue eyes on him. "You can come in here any time, Evan *bach,* and I'll take care of you. I know exactly what you want—"

She broke off suddenly and looked at the door. Her face took on the appearance of a saint, having a vision.

"It's him," she whispered to Evan.

Every head in the public bar turned in the direction she was looking. Ifor Llewellyn was filling the doorway with his commanding presence. He was a giant figure of a man, not fat, just big, and made even more impressive by the curling black beard and shoulder-length curling black hair. The impression was that of a biblical giant— Goliath or Samson.

"*Noswaith dda, gyfeillion,*" he said. "Good evening, my friends." His smile lit up his whole face. The crowd parted as he walked up to the bar. "*Ydych chi 'n siarad Cymraeg yma?* Does everyone still speak Welsh?"

"Oh we do," Betsy answered, still gazing at him in awe. "Most everyone does around here."

"I'm a little rusty, but I'll give it a try," Ifor Llewellyn said. "You'll just have to be patient if I've forgotten too much."

"Oh no, you sound lovely just," Betsy said.

He did sound lovely just, Evan thought. His speaking voice had that rich, rumbling quality that made his singing so unique.

"And who might you be, young lady?" Ifor asked Betsy.

"I'm Betsy Edwards . . . sir. I . . . work here." For once Betsy was almost lost for words.

"Don't call me sir, I haven't been knighted yet." Ifor Llewellyn chuckled. "They'll wait for that until I retire and I've still got a few good years in me yet, Miss Betsy." He reached out across the counter and took her hand. "Betsy. A beautiful name, to match a beautiful person, but tell me, why do you dye your hair that color?"

"My hair, sir . . . I mean, Mr. Llewellyn," Betsy stammered. "I don't really dye it, just touch it up, you know, bring out the blond highlights . . ."

"You women," Ifor said, shaking his head. "If you only realized that brunettes are far more alluring than blonds. The Italian girls with their black hair . . . they exude sexuality, not like the pale dreary English and Welsh girls. You'd be stunning as a brunette, Betsy."

"Would I, sir?" Betsy was lost for words for the first time since Evan had known her. She put her hand up to touch her flyaway blond curls.

"Absolutely stunning," Ifor said. He was still holding her hand. "I hope you'll take good care of me this summer, Betsy. I'm going to rely on you. You could show me around the old place sometime, and maybe I'll need some Welsh lessons, too?"

"I'd be happy to. Anything. Anytime," Betsy said, her face bright pink with pleasure and confusion.

He certainly was a smooth operator, Evan thought. No wonder he had broken hearts all over Europe.

Ifor turned to the men in the bar. "You don't know

how good it is to be back here among friends," he said. "When my doctor told me I had to take it easy and rest, this was the first place that sprang into my mind. I said to Margaret, my wife, let's go home, shall we? And I've come home and it feels wonderful."

He stopped and looked around, almost as if he was expecting applause. Instead he saw nodding, smiling faces.

"We're honored to have you here, Ifor," Evans-the-Meat said. "It's a great honor for Llanfair."

"Oh, don't make a big thing of it, man," Ifor said. "I just want to lie low and fit right in. Think of me as a neighbor, just like anyone else. Invite me to play darts or whatever you do these days. I'd like that." He turned his soulful dark eyes back to Betsy. "The first request I have of you, my love, is to get me a double whiskey—Jameson Irish Whiskey, if you have it: No ice. Then you can get these gentlemen anything they want to drink. The first round's on me."

There was loud approval from the crowd. Betsy and Harry began drawing pints. Ifor picked up his glass. "*Iachyd da.* Cheers," he said and drained it in one gulp.

"So you're here to take it easy, are you, Mr. Llewellyn?" Roberts-the-Pump asked.

"Call me Ifor. I don't go for ceremony. And yes, I'm here on doctor's orders. I'm not hiding out from the Mafia or some woman's husband, whatever the *Daily Mirror* tells you." His big laugh filled the room. "I'm not the type to sit idle, though," he went on, looking around conspiratorially. "I've decided to write my memoirs. No sense in waiting until I'm old and my memory's going and I forget the good parts. I'm going to put it down while it's all fresh in my mind."

"I bet you've got some good tales to tell, Ifor," Harry-the-Pub commented.

"Tales that would curl your hair," Ifor said with a conspiratorial wink. "If I put down everything I've done, I'll need three volumes and my readers will need ice packs to cool them down, too." He laughed loudly. "I'll probably have enough lawsuits on my hands to last my lifetime. Not that they can touch me—everything I'm going to tell is true, however embarrassing it will be for certain people." He waved his empty glass at Betsy. "Another Jameson if you don't mind, my lovely."

The third and fourth Jamesons followed with no apparent ill effects, except that Ifor became friendlier by the minute. "So tell me, my friends," he said, draping a huge arm over Evans-the-Meat's shoulder, "what do you do around here for fun these days? Cricket is it this time of year? I rather fancy myself as a fast bowler."

"The local cricket team sort of fizzled out," Evans-the-Meat said. "Not enough young men in the village anymore."

"I remember when I was a boy, we had a splendid cricket team in Llanfair," Ifor said. "And football and rugby, too. All those men who worked in the slate mine. They were as fit as fiddles, weren't they? And the Côr Meibion—what a choir. That's what got me started in singing. I wanted to sound like them. Don't tell me the choir's dead, too?"

"Oh no, the choir's still going," Evans-the-Meat said. "It's not what it was, though. Austin Mostyn does his best but . . ."

"Austin Mostyn?" Ifor looked amused.

"That's what we call our choir director, Mostyn Phillips—"

"Mostyn Phillips?" Ifor exclaimed loudly. "Is he still going strong? I knew him. We were students together in London—fancy old Mostyn Phillips still being around. I must look him up."

"He was going to pay a call on you," Evans-the-Meat said. "We wanted him to ask you . . ." He paused with an embarrassed laugh. "To see if you'd . . ."

"Ask me what?" Ifor demanded.

There was embarrassed shuffling.

"Whether you'd have the time to help out with the choir," Evan finished for them. "The *eisteddfod*'s coming up and the choir really needs help."

"An *eisteddfod* coming up?" Ifor's face lit up again. All his expressions were giant-size, too, as if he was on stage at La Scala and not in the middle of the public bar at the Red Dragon. "That's wonderful news. I particularly wanted to go to an *eisteddfod* while I was here. I won my first singing competition at the little *eisteddfod* down in Criccieth. Is that the one?"

"This is the regional in Harlech," Reverend Parry Davies said. "Second in prestige only to the national."

"Wonderful." Ifor nodded. "So when does your choir rehearse? I'll be there."

Evans-the-Meat slapped Ifor on his broad back. "It's a great day for Llanfair, having you here, Ifor *bach*," he said. "Things are going to start looking up now, I know it."

SIX

"*NOSWAITH DDA*, GOOD EVENING ONE and all."
Mostyn Phillips came bustling through the door of the
village hall, clutching a sheaf of music to him. His normally immaculate hair was windswept from the walk up
from the road. "Sorry if I've kept you waiting. I was
going through the final selection of music and getting
copies made."

He put the music down on a music stand. "And I have
been doing some serious soul-searching. I'm afraid I
really cannot presume on my former friendship to ask a
singer of the caliber of Ifor Llewellyn to join our little
choir. I just wouldn't have the cheek. I mean, to think
that a world-renowned man like that would ever—"

"Would ever what, Mostyn?" A huge voice resounded
from the doorway.

Mostyn's jaw dropped. "Ifor," he said. "Is it really
you?"

"In the flesh, old friend," Ifor said, striding across the
floor so that the rickety floorboards creaked alarmingly.
"In the flesh as you can see, and plenty of it." He en-
veloped Mostyn in a huge bear hug, sending the music

stand and all the music flying. "Here I am, as you can
see, ready to do my part."

"Ifor, I don't know what to say. I am overwhelmed."
Mostyn dropped to his knees and started picking up the
music. "I don't know how to thank you. As Constable
Evans said, this is indeed a miracle."

"Come on then," Ifor said. "Don't just stand there,
man. Let's get to work. Show me what music you're
planning to sing for the *eisteddfod*."

Mostyn juggled papers on the music stand. He was
clearly flustered. "Well, look you, this is what I'd
planned to start with."

He nodded to Miss Johns at the piano and raised his
baton. Ifor sat without moving until they had finished the
song.

"And what was that supposed to be then?" he enquired.

"A Byrd motet. In praise of music."

"A Byrd motet?" Ifor exploded. "It sounded like a
flock of birds, if you don't mind my saying so—or the
Luton Girls' Choir. I've never heard such a dreary noise
in my life. You want to start with a good rousing chorus,
man. Make the audience sit up and listen. Something like
'Men of Harlech'!"

Mostyn's face was bright red. His little moustache
twitched nervously. "We can hardly start with 'Men of
Harlech' when we're singing in Harlech and half the audience will be men of Harlech, can we?" he demanded.
"That wouldn't make us any friends. And every choir
sings songs like that. If we want to make an impression,
we should sound different."

"Balderdash," Ifor boomed. "Give the audience something they know and like—'All Through he Night,' or
'Land of My Fathers,' or even a chorus from a popular
musical. *Oklahoma!* . . ."

"*Oklahoma!?*" Mostyn looked horrified.

"Too old-fashioned. Maybe you're right. Something
from *Les Misérables* then." He launched into "Do you

hear the people sing, singing a song of angry men." His huge voice filled the room and soon all the choir members were nodding in time.

"There you are," he said. "That's what a chorus should sound like. Not this pansy nonsense. It's not called a Choir of Daughters, is it? Well then, let them sound like men. I think I've got the score of *Lohengrin* with me. They could handle the Anvil Chorus. Or maybe the Soldiers' Chorus from *Faust*?"

"Everyone does the Soldiers' Chorus," Mostyn said through clenched teeth. "We don't have the numbers for a big sound, so I was trying for a different sound."

"Yes, but not bloody effeminate wailing," Ifor said, still smiling amiably. Evan got the impression he enjoyed baiting Mostyn. "You never did get it, did you, old chap? Remember that presentation you gave at college on medieval lute music? Half the audience fell asleep and even the professor fell off his chair!" He laughed loudly, slapping his tree-trunk thigh. "Well, you can forget all this rubbish. You've got a big sound now. You've got me!" He turned to the choir. "Do any of you boys happen to know the parts to 'Land of My Fathers'?"

By the end of the evening Evan had to admit that they sounded a lot better. Actually they sounded like Ifor singing with background noise. But that was preferable to the sound they had made before. At least it drowned out the out-of-tune baritones. But he noticed that Mostyn hastily put together his papers and scurried out to his car, without waiting to socialize. He was just getting into the car when Ifor appeared. "Is that what you're driving, Mostyn *bach*?" His voice resounded back from the hills. "That's the Austin? How does it go—a clockwork motor, or do you pedal it?

"Oh dear me," he muttered to the men standing around him as Mostyn drove away. "I think I've upset him. He always was quick to take offense. Unfortunately it was always too easy to tease poor old Mostyn. It was almost as if he was asking for it. He always did take himself too seriously. Just think what would happen if I drove off in a huff every time I got bad press! I just say publish and be damned and laugh it off." He draped his arms over the nearest shoulders. "Alright then lads, who's ready for a drink?"

The general consensus was that Ifor was a thoroughly good bloke who had arrived in the nick of time to save the *eisteddfod*. Evan wasn't so sure. He watched Mostyn, tight-lipped and increasingly nervous during rehearsals as they belted out "Land of My Fathers" and Ifor sang the drinking song from *La Traviata* with oompahs from the choir.

As the Llewellyns settled in, other villagers besides Evan started to wonder if having him in residence was a good thing.

"Would you listen to that, Constable Evans," Gladys, the Powell-Joneses' daily help, said as she came out of the grocer's shop and met Evan. "Imagine trying to do the dusting with that noise in the next room."

The sound of Ifor's huge tenor voice, practicing scales, echoed around the narrow valley.

"He's always singing, Mr. Evans. Morning, noon, and night," Gladys said, shaking her head. "And I thought he came here to rest his voice. I'd hate to hear what he sounds like when he's not resting it."

Evan grinned. "Some people pay hundreds of pounds and queue all night to hear him sing, Gladys. They'd think you were lucky to hear him for free."

"They can have my job anytime," Gladys said. "I'm thinking of writing to Mrs. Powell-Jones and handing in my notice. The minister and Mrs. Powell-Jones are no trouble at all—at least she can be picky and she always manages to find a spot I haven't dusted, but they let me get on with my work in peace. These people have no idea of time. They're just getting up at eleven o'clock in the morning and they want to use the bathroom when I'm trying to clean it and they want lunch at three o'clock in the afternoon. I tell you, Mr. Evans, I'm at sixes and sevens with them."

"It won't be for long, Gladys," Evan said. "And I expect they're paying you well."

Gladys smiled secretively. "If it weren't for the money, I'd have quit on the first day," she said. "The language, Mr. Evans. They use words I've never even heard before—not even on the telly and that's getting bad enough these days. And fight! They're always shouting and arguing—I'm just glad I don't always understand the bad names they're calling each other."

Evan was well aware of the fighting. So was every other resident of Llanfair. When the Llewellyns fought, which seemed to be most nights, the whole village heard it. Llanfair wasn't used to any noise after nine o'clock and the first time the Llewellyns fought, neighbors had called Evan right away.

"It sounds like they're killing each other up there, Mr. Evans," Mair Hopkins, Charlie's wife and the closest neighbor to the Powell-Jones house, had said breathlessly.

Evan hastily got dressed and ran up to the Powell-Jones house. As he approached he saw people in dressing gowns and slippers standing at their doorways. He could hear the noises long before the Powell-Jones house came in view—one of them a female voice just as loud as Ifor's. Then the sounds of crockery smashing and a slap and a scream.

Evan thundered on the front door. "Open up right away. It's the police," he yelled.

After a few minutes the door was opened by Ifor in a Chinese silk dressing gown. "What seems to be the problem, Officer?" he asked. His voice was slurred enough to hint that he'd been working his way through the Jameson again.

"I've received calls that domestic violence was taking place here," Evan said.

"Domestic violence?" Ifor threw back his head and laughed. "You hear that, my dear? Domestic violence is supposed to be taking place here."

Mrs. Llewellyn appeared behind Ifor. Evan expected her to look battered and bruised, but she looked serene and elegant in a turquoise satin robe, her face covered in cream and her hair in a turban. "We were just having a little disagreement, Officer," she said. "Nothing serious. We tend to disagree loudly at times. Thank you for your concern."

"But I heard the sound of blows," Evan said. "And something smashing."

Ifor laughed again. "My wife tends to express her anger by throwing things," he said. "Two of the Powell-Jones plates are regretfully no more, which means we'll have to buy them another set, I suppose. And when I nimbly dodged out of the way and laughed, she slapped me."

Mrs. Llewellyn looked slightly abashed. "It was only a slap, Officer. I do it all the time. It's impossible to hurt someone of Ifor's size."

"Felt like a fly landing on me," Ifor said and put his arm around his wife's shoulder. "I can't even remember what we were fighting about anymore, can you, my love?"

"I expect I'll remember it later," she said coldly. "Thank you for stopping by, Officer."

"Please try to keep the noise down after nine o'clock," Evan said. "People around here go to bed early."

"Don't they just," Mrs. Llewellyn said with a bitter laugh. "Godforsaken place. Why anyone would want to come back here when they'd had the chance to get out, I can't understand. When I left Colwyn Bay I swore I'd never go back there again."

"My wife doesn't have the Celtic soul, Constable

Evans," Ifor said. "Thank you again for coming so promptly. If she had been killing me, you'd have saved my life."

He escorted Evan firmly to the front door.

The evening fights didn't stop but the villagers gradually got used to them. They happened after Ifor had spent the evening at the Red Dragon, which he did most nights. Evan was also spending more time at the Red Dragon than he ever had before. Mrs. Williams's house was no longer the haven of peace and security it had been—there were dinners of stewed and pureed food followed by the Reverend Powell-Jones declaiming loudly from his room, or pointing out the evils of the modern world to Evan in the lounge as the latter tried to watch the news on the telly.

"Have you taken residence here, young man?" the other minister, Reverend Parry Davies, asked Evan as he stopped by for his evening pint. "Every time I come in here, you seem to be a fixture."

Evan sighed. "I wouldn't mind moving in here if they had a room for me. I can't take it much longer at Mrs. Williams's. All evening long he's reciting in his bedroom—all this woe-is-me stuff."

"Powell-Jones, reciting? What's he doing that for?"

"He's entering the *eisteddfod,* haven't you heard?" Evan asked.

"Entering the *eisteddfod*? The nerve of the man!" Parry Davies roared. "He's only doing it because he knows that I aspire to be crowned bard. Well, good luck to him. He is a newcomer who hasn't a chance, especially with his puny little voice."

"Who's got a puny little voice?" Ifor boomed as he came in. "Not talking about me again, are you?" His big laugh resounded and made the glasses on the shelves jangle in response.

"I'm dying to hear you sing, Mr. Llewellyn," Betsy

said, pouring his whisky without being asked. "I'm so excited about the *eisteddfod*. They say you're going to sing a solo with the choir."

"You should hear me sing in an opera," Ifor said. "I can't begin to give my full voice when I'm with the choir. I'd drown them all out. I'd probably bring the tent down."

"I've never seen a real opera," Betsy said wistfully. "I hear they're very romantic."

"Very," Ifor said. "It's always a story of an impossible love and the lovers die in each other's arms. That's how I intend to die—in the arms of a beautiful girl. But not until I'm ninety-eight of course." He had taken Betsy's hand and was idly playing with her fingers as he spoke. When he finished he put her fingers gently to his lips.

"I'd love to see you singing in an opera," Betsy said. Her cheeks were pink and she sounded flustered. "I bet you have all the girls in the audience sobbing when you die."

Ifor smiled. "If you're very good, I'll take you to an opera very soon. I've got the schedule for the Cardiff festival. We could drive down one day."

"You'd take me to an opera in Cardiff? I'd love it, Mr. Llewellyn."

"Call me Ifor," he said, still playing with her fingers. "I've got a feeling that you and I are going to be good friends."

Evan didn't sleep well that night. For all her flirting and exposed midriffs, Betsy was a naive child. How could she fall so easily for Ifor's line? Didn't she know his reputation? Evan knew it was none of his business but he couldn't just stand by and let her make a fool of herself. And he couldn't stand the thought of Ifor pawing at her.

Next morning he intercepted her on her way into work. "Betsy, you and I have to talk."

"Oh yes, what about?" Betsy was looking up at him expectantly.

"About Ifor Llewellyn. I don't want you going down to Cardiff with him."

"He's only taking me to an opera," Betsy said. "I think it's very nice of him."

"Betsy, wake up. Ifor's not the sort of man who takes young girls to operas with no strings attached. You should know that."

"And what if there are strings attached?" Betsy glared at him defiantly. "I'm a big girl, you know, and I happen to find him very attractive and I'm flattered that he seems to fancy me, too."

"And he also happens to be married and he gets through women at the speed most people get through their library books," Evan exploded.

Suddenly Betsy's face broke into a broad grin. "I've got it!" she exclaimed. "You're jealous, Evan Evans. Finally it's come out. You were just too shy to ask me before, weren't you? Pretending that you'd rather spend your time with that dreary Bronwen. Oh, you men are so funny." She ran her hands through her blond curls. "Tell you what then. If you're really starting to show the proper amount of interest in me, then I won't go down to Cardiff with Ifor. How's that then?"

Evan's brain was racing. Bronwen would understand that he was only doing it to save Betsy's honor, wouldn't she? Bronwen was a sensible, kind, caring person. She wouldn't want Betsy to go to Cardiff with Ifor Llewellyn, so she'd understand that he was only doing his duty.

"Well, Evan Evans," Betsy said. "Do you want to ask me out yourself or not? Are you going to take me out on Saturday night or shall I see if Mr. Llewellyn is free to drive me to Cardiff?"

Evan took a deep breath. "Okay, Betsy," he said. "We'll go out on Saturday night."

SEVEN

"SO YOU SEE I HAD no choice, Bron," Evan said.

She was standing with her hand on the gate to the schoolhouse, looking at him steadily. He imagined she'd practiced that look for times when her students came to school with excuses about not doing their homework. "I see," she said. She probably said the same thing to her students, too.

"Well, what would you have done?" he demanded.

"Oh, I'm sure you've made a very gallant sacrifice," she said. "Not every man would give up a thrilling evening at the pub for a hot nightclub with a half-clad Betsy. Maybe they'll give you a medal."

"At least I'm telling you about it," Evan said. "At least I'm asking your opinion."

"What I think doesn't matter, does it?" Bronwen's voice was still infuriatingly calm. "You and I are just friends, aren't we? That's what you tell everyone."

Evan fought to control himself. He had expected Bronwen to be reasonable. He had tried to be reasonable. Reason wasn't working. "Bronwen, you must know that I have no desire to go dancing with Betsy, but I couldn't let her go down to Cardiff with the Welsh Don Juan, could I? It seemed to be the easiest way to solve things, and I told myself that being a sensible, caring person, you'd understand."

Bronwen swung the gate to and fro then finally looked up with a half smile. "I suppose I do understand. And I don't really think you'll be seduced by one evening with Betsy, but you know how tongues wag in this village. You'll probably have her father showing up on your doorstep, demanding that you make an honest woman of her."

"Maybe that would have been the best way to solve this."

"Being pressured into a shotgun wedding with Betsy?"

"No." Evan had to smile now. "I mean the Ifor business. If I'd managed to catch old Sam Edwards when he was sober enough to listen to me, he could have gone after Ifor with that old shotgun of his and put the fear of God into him."

"I didn't think that policemen were supposed to recommend shooting people as a way of solving problems." Bronwen had relaxed. Her hands no longer gripped the gate.

"Sam Edwards has never hit anything yet with that old gun, or I wouldn't have suggested it."

"Ah well. Too late now," Bronwen said.

"At least I've managed to postpone the date until the eisteddfod's over," Evan said. "We've got practices every evening until we perform."

"How's it coming along? You sound alright from what I can hear."

"What you can hear is Ifor singing and the rest of us opening our mouths," Evan said with a grin.

"When are you performing?"

"Saturday night. We're going down to Harlech on Friday evening to rehearse in the pavilion, so we get a feel for the size of the place."

"I'll have to come and listen to you on Saturday," Bronwen said. "I've promised to take some of my children from school down to watch the folk dancing. Maybe we'll stay on to listen to your choir if it's not too late."

"I shouldn't bother if I were you," Evan said. He realized that the last thing in the world he wanted was for Bronwen to hear him singing.

"Oh, why?" Bronwen looked disappointed. "You don't want me to hear you sing?"

"We're not very good, Bron. Frankly I'll be glad when it's over," Evan said. "The atmosphere at rehearsals is getting uncomfortable."

"Oh? In what way?"

Evan sighed. "Mostyn Phillips takes the thing very seriously. Ifor thinks it's a huge joke. I think we're heading for a major blowup."

That evening Evan had just come home from the pub and was sitting in his room reading when the phone rang. It was Mair Hopkins, Charlie's wife. "They're at it again, Mr. Evans," she breathed into the phone. "I can hear shoutin' going on outside this time. I don't like to complain, but it's past nine o'clock."

"Don't worry, I'll go up there and see what's going on, Mrs. Hopkins," Evan said. "Thanks for calling me."

He put on his uniform jacket and hurried up the street. He could hear raised voices but he couldn't see what was happening because the chapel blocked his view of the speakers. Evan realized immediately that this time it wasn't just a domestic brawl. The voices were both male.

"I'm warning you!" The voice was clearly not English or Welsh.

"You think I'm scared of your warnings?" Evan recognized Ifor's big voice immediately. "Go back home and do your worst. I'm itching for a good fight. I'd just love to see you in court—best publicity I ever had!"

Before Evan had reached the chapel he heard something that sounded, in the clear night air, like a shot. With heart pounding, he realized it was only a car door slamming. An engine revved and a long, low car sped away. Evan could see that it had a foreign number plate. By the time he got to the Powell-Joneses' driveway, Ifor Llewellyn had gone back inside and everything was quiet. Evan hesitated for a moment, wondering if he should knock on the door, then decided whatever it was, it wasn't his business to interfere.

Ifor didn't show up for rehearsal the next day.

"Oh, this really is too bad," Mostyn said as the choir stood ready to start and Ifor hadn't made his entrance. "He knows how important it is to start rehearsals on time. He's doing it deliberately to annoy me, that's what it is. Alright. We'll start without him."

He nodded to Miss Johns at the piano. They worked their way through their program and still no Ifor. Evan sang along uneasily and was just about to volunteer to go and find him when the door burst open and Ifor strode in. "What was that meant to be?" he boomed. His speech betrayed a recent visit to the Red Dragon. "It sounded like a group of mice squeaking in a very large church. Give it some sound, for God's sake. Make it ring."

"You're very late, Ifor," Mostyn said in a clipped voice. "It's setting a poor example to these men."

Ifor grinned. "Ah well, I've just had some interesting visitors," he said. He looked around expectantly. "You'll never guess who just approached me—the boys from the Blaenau Ffestiniog choir! They've asked me to join them. It's a very fine choir, I hear. First class. They hope to win the gold medal and with me they'd definitely do it, wouldn't they?"

The color had drained from Mostyn's face. "You're not seriously thinking of backing out at this stage, and joining a rival choir?"

"Don't shriek, Mostyn. It's unladylike," Ifor said, still grinning. "I haven't signed a contract with you, you know. I was only doing this out of the goodness of my heart, and frankly I'm having second thoughts. I have my reputation to consider. I don't want Ifor Llewellyn to look a complete idiot in front of an audience, do I now?"

"It's just the sort of traitorous act I'd expect from you," Mostyn yelled. "I don't know why I thought you'd ever change. You always excelled at backstabbing, didn't you? Well, you're not letting us down now. Dress rehearsal in the pavilion, seven o'clock sharp tomorrow, and I expect you to be on time!"

He stormed out, pushed past Ifor and slammed the door behind him. Ifor looked at the stunned faces then he shrugged. "I really shouldn't do it, but it's too tempting," he said. "He asks for it, doesn't he?"

"Bloody 'ell," young Billy Hopkins, Charlie's grandson, exclaimed as he climbed out of the back of the van and got his first sight of the *eisteddfod* grounds. Evan seconded the thought. On what used to be the playing fields there were now three huge marquees, the middle one the size of a circus tent. Around them were tents of varying sizes, and around the perimeter hundreds of small booths were going up, ready to sell everything from Celtic jewelry to toffy apples. Everywhere was bustling with activity. Guy ropes were being tightened, frames assembled. People passed them carrying spinning wheels, garlands of flowers, bolts of cloth, stage prop pillars, boxes of paper cups. A young girl staggered past, clutching a Welsh harp as big as she was. Cars and vans wove cautiously in and out, hooting at pedestrians to get out of their way. The overall effect was that of an army setting up for a siege. This was heightened by the banner of the Red Dragon of Wales, fluttering from the tallest tent post and the towering form of Harlech Castle etched in black against a threatening sky.

"I didn't know it was going to be like this," Billy Hopkins muttered to Evan, who had just emerged from

Roberts-the-Pump's ancient limo. "I mean, this is something, isn't it?"

"Where's Austin Mostyn then?" Roberts-the-Pump asked, looking around him.

"He drove some students here straight from his school," Evans-the-Meat said. "They were in the boy soprano competition so Mostyn said he'd meet us here."

"Boy soprano, thet's what you should have entered, Evan bach," Charlie chuckled.

"And where's Ifor?" Roberts-the-Pump lowered his voice this time.

"Don't ask," Barry-the-Bucket muttered. "Let's just hope he shows up by seven o'clock or we'll never hear the last of it."

Mostyn came bustling over to them, clutching his conductor's baton and trying to look important. "Ah, there you are. I've had a chance to scout the place out and I know which pavilion we'll be singing in. So let's look sharp and get over there. I've been told they're on a very strict schedule." The words came out in a torrent. He set off at a brisk pace, causing the rest of the choir to break into a run to keep up with him.

"Look at all the TV vans," Billy Hopkins commented as they came to a halt outside the biggest tent. "Do you think my mam will be able to watch us at home?"

"It might even go out on the BBC national," Mostyn said proudly. "Especially since we've got such a great man singing with us."

"Where is he then?" Evans-the-Milk looked around nervously.

"He said he was driving down in his own car," Mostyn said. "That's understandable. You can't expect a celebrity to carpool."

This remark made the choir members smile. Inside the tent they could hear another Côr Meibion going through its paces. The strains of "Men of Harlech" competed with the tooting of car horns and the hammering of scaffolding.

Mostyn consulted his watch. "I hope they know they have to vacate the stage by seven," he said. "Our practice time is from seven to seven-thirty. I'm going in there on the dot of seven. I'm not sacrificing our practice time. Let's just hope that Ifor shows up right away."

As they entered the huge tent the choir on the stage finished their rehearsal and began to file off the stage. "The Ffestiniog Choir," Mostyn said with a disapproving sniff. "I see they didn't persuade Ifor to join them yet."

" 'Ello, Mostyn, old friend," the director called out as he came down the steps from the stage. "Going to give us a run for our money then, are you? I hear you've found yourselves a secret weapon."

"No thanks to you," Mostyn said coldly.

"What's that supposed to mean?"

"You know very well," Mostyn said. He passed the other man as if he didn't exist and started arranging his music on the stand. The choir director looked long and hard at Mostyn then shrugged and walked away. The Llanfair choir took up their positions.

"Five past seven," Mostyn said, checking his watch again, "and Ifor still isn't here. What did I tell him? I said seven o'clock sharp, didn't I? He really has no idea of time. We only have half an hour."

"He'll be here," Evans-the-Meat said. "We heard him warming up when we stopped to pick up Harry."

"He better get a move on," Mostyn said. "Warming up indeed. This isn't Covent Garden. What does he need to warm up for?"

Ten minutes later Ifor still hadn't arrived. Mostyn took them through their three songs, but it was only a half-hearted attempt as the men all had one eye on the door. Mostyn was getting angrier by the second. He yelled at the men who were setting up chairs and told them to go away until he'd finished. At last he threw down his baton.

"Oh, this is hopeless. Hopeless. He's ruined everything. How could I be so stupid to think that he'd help us? When did he ever help me? Ifor was always for himself and nobody else." He started packing music mechanically into his briefcase. "I know what he's doing, of course. He's realized how bad we sound and he doesn't want to lose face by singing with us. Understandable I suppose, but why did he say he'd do it, when he knew what we sounded like?"

"He'll be alright on the night," Harry-the-Pub said. "He's a professional. He knows what to do."

"That's right, Mostyn," Evans-the-Meat added. "Stars like Ifor don't need rehearsals. He'll be fine tomorrow.'"

"I wish I could believe that," Mostyn said. "If he doesn't show up tomorrow, we'll all look like fools standing up there with no soloist." He stalked down the steps and out of the pavilion ahead of the choir members, his eyes darting left then right, still searching for Ifor. He paused beside his Mini. "I've decided. I'm going to give him a piece of my mind," he said. "He's a professional and this is inexcusable."

"Don't go and upset him, Mostyn," Harry-the-Pub warned. "Then he might decide not to sing with us at all. As he said, he's not under a contract, is he? He's only doing us a favor."

Mostyn sighed. "You've got a point, Harry. But I still want to talk to him. He has to know how we all feel about being let down like this. It's just not right. It's not fair." His gaze fastened on Evan. "You come with me, Constable Evans. You know about handling people and saying the right thing. You can keep an eye on me and make sure I don't say something I'll regret. I know I have a tendency to fly off the handle."

"Alright, I suppose," Evan said hesitantly. He really had no wish to be trapped in a room while Ifor and Mostyn shouted at each other, but if it resulted in Ifor show-

ing up on time at the *eisteddfod* on Saturday, then he
supposed he should do it.

"I'll give you a lift in my car," Mostyn said. "Hop in.
We'll go straight there."

Evan tried to maneuver his long limbs into the Mini's
passenger seat. His head brushed against the roof and his
knees were almost up against his chest. He could see the
choir members grinning at his discomfort.

"We'll be there in no time at all," Mostyn said as they
roared out of the parking lot. "She might be old but she
hasn't lost an ounce of her zip."

Evan had never been more glad to see the lights of
Llanfair ahead of him. He had been flung from side to
side, unable to brace himself, as Mostyn took the bends
like a racing driver. His head hit the ceiling every time
they went over an uneven stretch of road and the seat
belt crushed his windpipe. He unwound his legs and
climbed out unsteadily in front of Ifor's house.

A light was on and Ifor's black Mercedes was parked
in the driveway.

"There you are. He just couldn't be bothered to come,"
Mostyn said, pointing angrily at the house. "Just don't
let me tell him exactly what I think of him. I'll try to
remain cool but it's not easy." He marched up to the front
door and lifted the knocker.

The front door swung open to his touch.

"That's odd." Mostyn looked up inquiringly at Evan.

Evan tapped on the half-open door. "Mr. Llewellyn?
Are you there?" he called.

There was no answer. Evan pushed the door wide
open.

"Do you think we ought to go in, Constable Evans? I
mean, he's probably over at the pub, drinking as usual
and we've no right to . . ." But Evan had already entered
the dark entrance hall.

"Mr. Llewellyn?" he called again. His voice echoed

from the black-and-white tiled floor and the ceiling high above the staircase. "Is anyone here?"

The only sound was the deep rhythmic tick-tock of a grandfather clock in the front hall. Then Evan noticed the shoe. It was a fashionable lady's dress shoe, black patent with an open toe and a high spiked heel. It lay directly outside the drawing room door.

"We should just leave, Mr. Evans," Mostyn said, grabbing at Evan's sleeve. "He's probably got a woman here. That's why he didn't show up. We can't just go barging in on God knows what."

Evan tapped on the drawing room door. "Are you in there, Mr. Llewellyn?"

Cautiously he opened the door. Immediately he was conscious of two smells. The first was alcohol, overpowering in the warm, closed room. He couldn't quite place the other smell.

He pulled at his collar. "Hot in here, isn't it?"

"He was used to Italian temperatures, wasn't he?" Mostyn said. "I expect he found this house too cold for him. He's probably turned the central heating on in the middle of summer!"

"There doesn't seem to be anybody . . ." Evan began. The heavy velvet curtains were drawn and the room had an aquariumlike quality. He reached for the light switch. Then he noticed the overturned table. It was a small round drinks table and it was lying in the middle of the floor. Evan started toward it.

Mostyn was skirting the edge of the room cautiously, as if not anxious to trespass. He reached the bow window and pulled back the heavy velvet curtains. "This radiator's on," he said.

Evan was well into the room when he noticed the foot, sticking out from behind the high-backed chintz sofa. Then he recognized the other smell. It was the smell of death.

EIGHT

IFOR LLEWELLYN WAS SPRAWLED ON the Axminster carpet, an empty glass beside his outstretched hand. An overturned end table and an almost empty bottle of Jameson lay on the hearth rug where they had landed. Evan heard Mostyn's horrified intake of breath as he dropped to his knees beside the body.

"Is it . . . him?" Mostyn could hardly get the words out.

Evan nodded. Without moving the body he could see the dark sticky patch on the right side of his head where the skull had been crushed. The dark stickiness had soaked into the carpet around his head, turning the red pattern brown. Cautiously his fingertips felt the neck for a pulse, with little hope of finding one.

"He's dead, I'm afraid," Evan said. Instinctively he looked around for a weapon. His gaze fastened on the old-fashioned brass fender, complete with curlicues and knobs, that surrounded the fireplace. The knob closest to Ifor appeared to have traces of blood on it. "He must have fallen and hit his head . . ." Evan said tentatively.

Mostyn came across and stood at a suitable distance behind the sofa, looking down on the body. "I told him

his drinking would be the end of him," he said in a
choked voice, "but I never thought it would be like this.
And here I was berating him for not showing up on time.
I feel terrible, Mr. Evans."

Evan got to his feet again. "How could we possibly
have suspected," he said.

"I think I'll wait for you outside, if you don't mind."
Mostyn's face was distinctly green. "I'm not feeling too
well."

"I'm coming, too," Evan said. "We shouldn't touch
anything until the CID squad gets here."

"The police?" Mostyn asked. "But surely, it was an
accident, wasn't it? You don't suspect . . ."

"It certainly seems to have been an accident, but I still
have to call them. I'm just the village bobby and we have
experts to handle things like this." He shepherded the
shaken Mostyn from the room.

"Should I wait, do you think?" Mostyn asked as they
stepped into the welcome freshness of the night air.

"You'd better. They'll want to take a statement from
you, seeing that we discovered the body together."

"Alright," Mostyn said. "I'll sit in my car, if you don't
mind. I'm feeling rather faint."

"Why don't you go across to the Dragon and get yourself a stiff drink. You look like you could use it."

"Oh, no thank you. After what I've seen tonight, I
don't think I'll want to touch alcohol again." Mostyn
shuddered. "No, I'd rather sit in my car, if you don't
mind."

"Alright, Mostyn." Evan put a reassuring hand on his
shoulder. "I'll call from the police station. They shouldn't
be too long."

It was half an hour later that the white police van drew
up at the Powell-Joneses' house.

"You certainly pick your times, don't you?" Sergeant
Watkins complained as he got out. He looked very much

the detective in a beige trenchcoat, but Evan noticed he was wearing jeans and a T-shirt under it. "I was in the middle of watching *Heartbeat*."

"Don't tell me you watch police shows in your free time," Evan said, holding out his hand to his old friend. "You're a glutton for punishment."

"The wife wouldn't miss an episode of *Heartbeat*," Watkins said. "And our Tiffany loves it, too. So what sort of accident was it that you've dragged me away for?"

"Nasty. It looks as if—" Evan began, then he broke off as he saw another man getting out of the van. This man was slim and elegantly dressed in a dark suit and tie. Evan took a quick look and then muttered to Watkins, "You didn't have to bring the big guns, you know."

"Good evening, Constable. The commissioner felt that I should come and see for myself, considering the implications." D.I. Hughes seemed to be answering Evan's question even though he couldn't possibly have overheard. "With a celebrity of this magnitude the press will need to be handled. Statements will have to be made."

Evan could tell that D.I. Hughes was looking forward to being the one on the telly, making those statements.

"This way." Evan led the detectives up the driveway to the Powell-Jones's residence.

"So who found the body?" D.I. Hughes fell into step beside Evan, leaving Sergeant Watkins to walk behind.

"Mr. Mostyn Phillips the choir director and I did, sir."

"You seem to make a habit of finding bodies," D.I. Hughes said dryly. He had never quite forgiven Evan for having solved a couple of murder cases that had stumped his department. "So tell me how you happened to be the one to find this one."

"Ifor Llewellyn was supposed to be rehearsing with our choir at the *eisteddfod* in Harlech and he didn't turn up so Mr. Phillips asked me to come with him and see what was going on."

"Ifor Llewellyn—singing with a local choir?" D.I.

Hughes didn't try to hide his astonishment or contempt. "What on earth for?"

"He was an old chum of Mostyn's. He was doing our choir a favor."

"I see. I'll need to talk to this Mostyn Phillips then, won't I?"

"He's right here in his car, sir." Evan was delighted to have scored a minor point. "I told him to wait for you."

"Splendid. We'll take a look at the body and then you can get a statement from him, Watkins." D.I. Hughes pushed open the front door with a gloved finger. "I hope you haven't been touching things, Constable."

"Oh no, sir. I opened the drawing room door, and I felt the body for a pulse, but that's it. I left everything else just as it was."

He indicated the door on his left. "He's in here."

D.I. Hughes stepped over the lady's shoe then reeled as he opened the drawing room door. "My God, what was he doing, bathing in the stuff?"

"He must have knocked over the bottle when he fell." Evan indicated the empty bottle beside the overturned table.

"It's awfully warm in here," D.I. Hughes complained.

"He's got the central heating turned on, apparently. He had just come from Italy."

"Then turn it off and open the windows, Constable. It really is most unpleasant in here. I can't work in these conditions."

The detective inspector bent to look at the body. "Very nasty," he said, turning the body slightly with his gloved hand to see the full extent of the wound. "Poor chap. What a way to go. Was he known to drink a lot, Constable?"

"I'd say he put away a fair bit," Evan said, struggling with the catch on the window, "but I never saw him incapacitated. He always seemed to hold it rather well."

"Of course we don't know how much of the bottle he

got through," D.I. Hughes said. "He might have been the type to go on occasional binges. Was anyone else in the house?"

"I haven't been in any other room, but I haven't heard or seen anybody else. I thought I'd better wait until you got here."

"Quite right, Constable. But in this case, it appears to be rather conclusive, doesn't it? The poor chap drank a little too much, tripped over, and hit his head on that fender—my God, what a wicked-looking piece it is. You'd think they'd have done away with it years ago, wouldn't you, especially with central heating in the house."

"If it were my house, it would be out in the shed," Sergeant Watkins commented.

"Well, the Powell-Joneses don't have any children," Evan said, "and I can't imagine that anyone was ever allowed to run around in this house."

D.I. Hughes squatted beside the fender. "Ah yes— there are clear traces of hair and blood on this knob. Poor chap. All the room to fall in and he has to fall in that direction." He got to his feet again and stood looking down dispassionately at Ifor's body. "Of course, Dr. Owens and the lab boys will have to verify the cause of death, but it does seem to be rather obvious, doesn't it? Anyway, there's nothing more I can do here tonight. Will you see about notifying next of kin, Sergeant? I'll make the phone call to HQ and then maybe I can get back for the tail end of my dinner party." He brushed his hands smartly against one another and began to walk out of the room.

"So was he living here alone?" he turned to ask Evan. "I thought he was supposed to have family with him."

"His wife has been here," Evan said. "We heard he has a son and daughter but I don't know where they are. They haven't shown up here yet."

"But we don't know where the wife is at the moment?"

D.I. Hughes turned back to Sergeant Watkins. "She'll
need to be contacted right away. Take a look around the
place and see if you can find out where we can get hold
of her. We'll go on down to your station, Evans. I'd
rather call the office from there. We'll need to get Dawson up here to take pictures and I suppose I'll have to
contact Dr. Owens at his yacht club. He always dines
there on Friday nights. And we should alert the chief
inspector that we'll need a detail of men posted up here.
The moment this story breaks we'll be besieged by the
media. Let's try and keep it to ourselves until we can get
the body to the morgue, shall we? I'd rather we didn't
have gory pictures splashed all over every front page."

Evan gave Ifor's body one last look as he followed the
inspector out of the room.

"You might just check out the rest of the house first,
Sergeant." D.I. Hughes paused at the front door. "Just in
case we find that—"

He broke off as the light tap of footsteps crunched on
the gravel outside and the door was pushed open. Mrs.
Llewellyn came in, dressed in a raincoat and scarf and
carrying an overnight bag. It must have started raining
because drops were dotted like pearls over her hair. Her
face was flushed and her eyes were bright.

"What on earth's going on here?" Mrs. Llewellyn de-
manded as she confronted the three men in her hallway.
"I saw the police car outside. Has there been a burglary?
I can't think what they'd have taken. There's nothing of
worth here. It's all junk and we left all our good stuff in
Italy except—"

"I'm afraid it's more serious than a burglary, Mrs.
Llewellyn," D.I. Hughes said, going over to her. "I'm
sorry to tell you there's been a nasty accident."

"Ifor's been hurt?" Her expression changed instantly
from annoyance to fear. "A car accident? But no, the
car's outside."

"Your husband fell and hit his head." D.I. Hughes

moved to stand between her and the drawing room door. "In there." He put out a hand to restrain her as she started forward. "He's dead, I'm afraid. I'd rather you didn't go in yet."

"Ifor? Dead?" She put her hand up to her mouth to stifle whatever sound had been about to come out. She looked bewildered. "But I must go to him." She started forward again.

D.I. Hughes stepped between her and the door. "If you don't mind, we're waiting for the police doctor to examine the body."

Mrs. Llewellyn stood staring at the closed door. "I can't believe it," she said quietly. "It doesn't seem possible, does it? Not Ifor . . ."

"Have you been away, Mrs. Llewellyn?" Evan asked, taking the bag she still clutched in one hand.

"What? Oh yes. I went up to London for a couple of days." She continued to stare at the door. "Was he drinking again? Damned drinking—I told him to lay off but . . ." She put her hand to her mouth again and fought to compose herself. "It was an accident, definitely, was it?" she asked suddenly.

"How do you mean?" D.I. Hughes looked up sharply.

It seemed as if she hesitated for a second before she said, "I mean, he didn't take his own life, Officer. I'm strong. You don't need to spare me unpleasant details."

D.I. Hughes looked surprised. "You think your husband might have had intentions of taking his own life?"

She composed herself and shook her head firmly. "Of course not. Ifor loved life. Everybody knew that. But he does—he did—occasionally get morbid when he'd been drinking."

"I can reassure you that this wasn't suicide, Mrs. Llewellyn," D.I. Hughes said. "It was a very unfortunate, tragic accident."

"Well, I suppose that's one blessing."

"Do you have somewhere you can go tonight?" D.I.

Hughes asked her, sounding almost human for once. "Any relatives or friends nearby?"

"Nobody," she said. "We know nobody around here anymore. I don't know why he wanted to come back here—godforsaken place. I told him he was mad. It was just a whim, of course. Ifor always got whims—like a large child really. I don't know what he ever saw in the place."

"You have children, I believe?" the D.I. enquired gently. "They're not here with you?"

"No. No, they're not. Neither of them are here. They're back in Italy." She looked around again as if she was in a strange place and had no idea where she was. "I must call them right away. How am I going to tell them? They won't believe it." She shook her head. "Just like me. I'm finding it hard to believe at the moment. I thought that Ifor was indestructible. He always boasted that he'd outlive us all, in spite of what his doctor told him . . ." This time she couldn't hold back the tears. "I'm sorry," she said after a moment. "I really must phone my children."

"If I were you I'd wait awhile, Mrs. Llewellyn." Evan put out a restraining hand. "Get a grip on things, right? Think out how you're going to tell them. You don't want to upset them more than necessary, do you?"

She nodded. "Perhaps you're right. I don't think I could be coherent at the moment. I don't exactly know what to do . . ."

"Maybe you should go and lie down for a while," Sergeant Watkins suggested. "This has been a terrible shock for you."

"How could I possibly lie down, knowing that my husband's body was in the house?" she demanded, her composure cracking for a moment.

D.I. Hughes turned to Evan. "Is there somewhere around here she could spend the night, Evans? She can't stay here. Our men are going to be coming in and out and she needs a good night's sleep. I'll have Dr. Owens give her a sedative."

"There's the Everest Inn, sir. You know, the new hotel up the road. It's very nice, I hear."

"Excellent. I'll have a woman P.C. come up to get her settled."

"Why don't I make her a cup of tea, sir?" Evan asked.

"Splendid idea. Give us the key to the station and we can get our phoning done down there so that Mrs. Llewellyn isn't disturbed more than necessary. Then I can be on my way."

"Oh and Mostyn Phillips, sir. He's sitting outside in a red Mini."

"I noticed that on the way in." D.I. Hughes laughed dryly. "I didn't think there were any of those running anymore. Alright, Sergeant. Go and get Mr. Phillips and bring him into the station. You can take his statement there."

"Right you are, sir," Sergeant Watkins said with a resigned look to Evan.

Evan walked down the hall and put a tentative hand on Mrs. Llewellyn's shoulder. "If you show me where the kitchen is, I'll make you a nice cup of tea. The best thing for shock, tea is."

She looked up at him and smiled. "You're very kind," she said and pushed open a swing door into a large tiled kitchen. Evan sat her at the kitchen table. She allowed herself to be positioned, like a doll. Then he put on the kettle.

"So you're from around here, too, are you, Mrs. Llewellyn?" he asked as he found the tea caddy and the sugar.

"From Colwyn Bay originally. I couldn't stand the place. When I left to go to college in London, I swore I'd never go back." She shuddered. "I should have followed my instincts."

"And you live most of the time in Italy?"

"I do. Ifor's at La Scala for part of the year, but then

he's always traveling and making guest appearances. I don't always go with him . . ." Those last words were heavy with meaning. Evan felt sorry for her. It couldn't have been easy being the wife at home, seeing pictures of her husband on a yacht with an Italian diva or a Danish princess.

Evan poured the milk and tea into a cup then added a heaped spoonful of sugar. He'd have added a heaped spoonful of brandy if he'd known where to find some—he was sure that even medicinal brandy was frowned on in the Powell-Jones household, and Ifor's medicinal Jameson now lay soaking into the carpet. Evan paused as he stirred the tea. Something about the whiskey and the carpet . . . something that wasn't quite right? His mind ran over the details of the scene again, then he shook his head and handed Mrs. Llewellyn the cup.

"There you are. You'll feel better after a good cuppa."

She managed a weak smile as she took it.

Evan perched on the edge of the kitchen table beside her. "Mrs. Llewellyn—what made you think that your husband might have killed himself?"

She seemed to wake up from a trance again. "I don't know what made me say that. Shock, I suppose. You don't talk rationally when you're shocked, do you? Ifor would be the last man in the world to inflict harm on himself. He thought the world of himself, didn't he?"

"But something must have made you say it."

"I suppose it was because he was rather put out at something I told him before I went up to London." Her clear gray-green eyes held Evan's in a steady, almost challenging gaze. "I told him I was considering leaving him. I was going to London to consult a lawyer." She paused and stirred her tea, the spoon tapping rhythmically against the bone china. "Ifor didn't take that too well. It came as a complete surprise, you see. He never thought I'd leave him, not after all this time."

"And would you have?"

"I don't know. When it came to it, he'd probably have talked me into staying again. He usually got his own way in the end—except for this time." She looked up from her tea again. "In spite of everything you've read, Constable, I think my husband needed me, maybe even loved me in his way."

She took a tentative sip of tea then got to her feet. "I must call the children now, before they get a garbled version from strangers. I'll do it in my room upstairs, if you don't mind."

"Of course not, I understand. You don't mind going upstairs by yourself?"

"Oh no," she said quickly. "I'd prefer it, thank you. I won't take long. Our daughter will be devastated, poor child. She adored her father. It was reciprocated, of course. He thought the world of her. Not an easy kind of love to take though—but that was how Ifor was. He either loved or hated. There was no in-between."

"And your son?" Evan asked quietly.

"Justin will be as shocked as I was to hear about his father's death," she said, gazing steadily at him.

NINE

MRS. LLEWELLYN SEEMED MORE COMPOSED when she came back down the stairs; in fact she looked almost relieved. "My son is going to try for the first flight out of Milan in the morning," she said. "He wants to be here for me as soon as possible. He has always been very . . . concerned for me. My daughter will come as soon as she can. She's not sure yet. She has work commitments, you know."

She sat down at the table again, picked up the teacup, then made a face.

"It must be cold by now," Evan said. "I'll pour you a fresh one."

He had just handed her the new cup of tea when there was a tap at the door and Sergeant Watkins came in, accompanied by a slim young redhead in police uniform.

"Mrs. Llewellyn, this is Police Constable Connie Jones," Sergeant Watkins said. "So if you'd like to get some things together, she can see you safely over to the Everest Inn for the night."

Mrs. Llewellyn stood up, again with that mechanical,

puppetlike quality. "Very well," she said. "I'll get some things together."

"Maybe you'd like me to come with you and help you pack," P.C. Jones suggested, taking her arm. "I'd imagine this house feels very big and empty at the moment."

"Thank you, but I can manage," Mrs. Llewellyn said stiffly. "I won't be long."

"Poor thing, she looks completely out of it, doesn't she?" P.C. Jones said. "It must be a terrible shock for her, coming home to find her husband dead." She started down the hall. "I think I'll go and keep an eye on her. I wouldn't want to be upstairs alone in this big house if that were me." She glanced at Sergeant Watkins, "And don't go making any remarks about women being scared. You said yourself in the car that this house gave you the creeps."

Watkins grinned. "I wasn't going to say a thing," he said.

P.C. Jones went out, leaving Watkins and Evan in the kitchen together. "So you sing in a choir," Watkins commented, a broad grin on his face. "I never knew that before. You've been hiding your light under a bushel, boyo. What do you sing—boy soprano?"

"Give over, Sarge." Evan wrinkled his face in embarrassment. "I got dragged into it because they didn't have any baritones who could even keep a tune. And it's only for the *eisteddfod*. After this weekend the only singing I do is in the shower."

He broke off as they heard the tap of high heels coming down the linoleum-clad stairs. "We're off then," P.C. Jones called. "We'll be up at the Everest Inn if you need us. Dr. Owens is supposed to be sending up a sedative for Mrs. Llewellyn when he comes. You'll remind him, won't you?"

"Right you are," Watkins called as Evan took the cup and saucer over to the sink and washed them up.

"Very domesticated," Watkins chuckled. "You'll make

some girl a lovely husband one day. Although if you'll
take my advice, boyo, you break a couple of bits of good
china the first few times you wash up and you'll never
be asked to do it again. It's worked like a charm for me."

Evan smiled and put the cup back on the dresser. "Did
you get a statement from Mostyn Phillips?" he asked.

"Yes. All done. I sent him home. He looked like death
warmed over. I thought he was going to pass out on me
any second. It took awhile because he was so upset, but
he just corroborated what you'd told us. Lucky you were
there to find the body or some idiot might have moved
it."

There was a tap on the half-open front door and P.C.
Dawson, the police photographer, stuck his head inside.
"Okay if I come in and start shooting?" he asked, then
grinned. "That's probably a tactless thing to say, isn't
it?"

"Yes it is, you cheeky bugger," Watkins said, going to
open the drawing room door. "It's in here."

"It's bloody cold in here," Dawson complained. "Do
we have to have all the windows open?"

Evan glanced at Watkins. "It's hard to please everyone, isn't it?" he asked as he went to close the window.
"When will Dr. Owens be here?"

"Soon, I hope. Of course the D.I. went back to his
dinner party and left me to take over. I've called in extra
men for first thing tomorrow morning. I'd imagine all the
press in Europe are going to flood into Llanfair once this
news breaks, so don't plan on getting a weekend off."

"That's okay," Evan said. "I don't suppose the choir
will be singing now, without Ifor. Maybe that's a good
thing. We sounded pretty awful. Poor old Mostyn—he
really thought he had a chance of winning for once with
Ifor as his star soloist."

Flashbulbs went off as Dawson photographed the body
from all angles. Evan stood looking down, trying to think

what had made him feel uneasy. Something was wrong but he couldn't think what.

"Jameson," Dawson commented. "Do you reckon he drank himself silly and passed out?"

A picture was forming in Evan's mind—Ifor standing at the bar beside him, knocking back tot after tot of Irish whiskey. He could see Ifor clearly, his face alive, his eyes sparkling with mirth as he threw back his head and laughed that big laugh and . . . the glass was in his right hand!

This glass lay only a few inches from his outstretched left fingers. Evan tried to recall again. Had he ever seen Ifor with the glass in his left hand? He was sure he hadn't.

"Right, that's me done," Dawson said. "Now if I hurry and get these developed, I can be in the Prince of Wales before closing time."

"Maybe I'll ride back with you," Sergeant Watkins said. "Evans is here to let the doctor in. There's nothing more for me to do here. We'll go and see if P.C. Jones has got Mrs. Llewellyn settled and then we can bugger off."

"Hold on a minute, Sarge." Evan was still staring at the body. *Just shut up. Don't say anything,* a voice was nagging in his head. He didn't want them to think he was trying to be clever again and make more of this than there really was. On the other hand, it was an important detail and he couldn't let it go unnoticed.

"What is it?" Watkins asked from the doorway.

"There's something that's not quite right here."

"Oh no," Watkins said, rolling his eyes. "Don't tell me you're going to say that this wasn't an accident and he's got some rare flower sticking out of his ear that proves he was really killed up the mountain and dragged here. No more murders in Llanfair, thank you kindly, Evans."

"I'm sorry, Sarge. It may be nothing," Evan said, "but I felt I should bring it up because it doesn't make sense."

"Okay. I'm going to take the bait and I'll probably regret it—what doesn't make sense?"

"I stood beside him in the pub several times. He held his drink in his right hand. So why is his glass lying next to his left hand?"

Watkins snorted. "I really don't think that's a biggy," he said. "Any number of reasons. He had the bottle in his right hand so he picked up the glass with his left."

"But it looks as if the bottle was on the table and he knocked it over when he fell," Evan said.

"He was probably blind drunk," Watkins said. "When you're totally blotto you'd grab the glass with the nearest hand, wouldn't you?"

Evan shrugged. "Maybe. I just thought it was odd, that's all."

"Not odd enough to stop me from popping off home," Watkins said. "I've been working late all week. I'm going to get it from the wife as it is for spoiling her Friday night. At least now I'll be in time to make her a cup of cocoa."

"Very domesticated." Evan couldn't resist a smile.

After Watkins and Dawson had gone, Evan remained in the room, staring down at the body. If you were right-handed, didn't you automatically reach for anything with your right hand? Evan tried to reconstruct the scene in his mind. What had made Ifor fall into the fireplace? If he'd been staggering around and bumped into the sofa, he wouldn't have fallen in that direction at all. If he'd tripped over something, he'd have needed something to trip over—the edge of the hearth rug, a sofa leg and in either case he'd have fallen parallel to the fireplace, not directly into it. And if he'd passed out, it was unlikely he'd have been standing. He'd merely have slumped in his seat. There had to be a secondary cause.

Evan's brain was now working in high gear. There could have been an added medical factor. "In spite of what the doctors told him." That was what Mrs. Llew-

ellyn had said, wasn't it? Maybe Ifor had a major health
problem that they didn't know about. He could have suf-
fered a heart attack. He'd been sitting on the sofa with
the little drinks table in front of him. He'd felt the chest
pain coming on, stood up, and pitched forward. That
would make sense, apart from the glass in the wrong
hand. No doubt Dr. Owens would be able to clear it all
up when he arrived.

The resident Home Office pathologist was a colorless
middle-aged man with thinning gray hair and a perpetu-
ally sad face. Evan imagined you'd get a face like that
if all you did was to examine recently dead people.

"Evans, isn't it?" he asked, walking briskly past Evan
into the house.

"That's right. This way, sir."

"So what have we got here, Constable?" he asked as
Evan showed him into the room. "Ah, very nasty," he
commented. "Vicious-looking fender, isn't it? I'll get Forensic to take samples from that knob in the morning,
just to confirm." He knelt down and began to examine
the body, jotting down notes in his little book.

"Severe trauma behind the right ear. Skull fracture . . ."
he muttered as he wrote. "Been dead about two, two and
a half hours, I'd say." He looked up at Evan. "You were
the one who found the body, were you, Evans?"

"Yes sir. That was around eight-fifteen."

"And how did he look to you then?"

"I didn't like to touch him more than necessary," Evan
said, "but he didn't look as if he'd been dead long, if
you know what I mean. His skin was still pinkish, not
white like it is now. His arm moved easily."

"That confirms what I'm seeing here. Off the top of
my head I'd say seven to seven-thirty, not much earlier
than that."

He got to his feet and tucked the notebook back into
his pocket. "I'll have the body taken down to the morgue,

then you can lock up this place for the night. Nothing more we can do here until the morning."

"Excuse me, Doctor," Evan began tentatively.

Dr. Owens looked up.

"Can we definitely tell that this was an accident?"

"In what way?"

"There's something about the way he's fallen. I can't reconstruct it in my head. I can't see what he would have tripped over, for one thing. I wondered if we'd know if there were any other factors—a heart attack, for example, that would have caused him to pitch forward like that."

"Oh we'll know right enough," Dr. Owens said. "We always do a full autopsy in cases like this. We need to see if he was mixing drugs and alcohol or if, as you say, it was a medical condition. If he was an ordinary chap, we'd probably put him on ice until Monday, but we've got orders from the powers that be to come up with a definitive cause of death as soon as possible. So I'm going to be working on him first thing in the morning—which puts paid to my sailing plans for the weekend. Ah well, goes with the job, doesn't it? I'd imagine we'd know conclusively what killed him by midday tomorrow."

"That's good," Evan said. "That's a load off my mind."

The doctor patted his back. "You're a village constable, young man. You're not supposed to carry the worries of the world on your mind. We'll call the morgue van up here and then you can go and get a good night's sleep."

It was a little after 11:00 P.M. when Evan finally let himself into Mrs. Williams's front hall. He realized that he'd had no dinner and he was starving. Mrs. Williams would have gone to bed by now but it was possible she'd left him something in the oven, but the thought of dried-out vegetable puree was not an appealing one. He went into the kitchen and cut himself a couple of slices of bread and a wedge of Caerpfilly cheese. Then he poured himself a glass of milk to go with it. Beer would have been better, but Mrs. Williams came from a long line of teetotalers.

Evan was definitely feeling more human as he tiptoed up the stairs, pausing every time a stairboard creaked. Reverend Powell-Jones had stressed to him more than once that he was a light sleeper and could never get back to sleep if woken.

Evan had just reached the top step when the door at the front of the hall flew open and the minister stood there, like an avenging ghost in his long white nightshirt. Evan began to feel that he'd plunged into the middle of *A Christmas Carol.*

"Young man," Reverend Powell-Jones declaimed, evidently not caring if he woke Mrs. Williams in the process. "You and I have to talk."

"About what?" Evan eyed him warily. With his knobby knees sticking out from below the nightshirt the minister was not the most attractive figure Evan had seen recently, and that counted the corpse.

"Your drinking problem."

"My what?" Evan couldn't have been more astounded. "Where did you get the idea I had a drinking problem?"

"I should have thought it was fairly obvious," Reverend Powell-Jones said. "You are down at the public house every evening of your life. You stagger up the stairs at—" he consulted his watch—"eleven-twenty-five and you deny you have a drinking problem. Come now, young man. Be brave. Face up to it. You'll feel better if you do."

Evan fought back a strong desire to punch him. "Mr. Powell-Jones," he said, trying to keep his voice calm and even. "Has it ever occurred to you that I spend every evening at the pub because you have taken over my house and I've had my fill of lectures and tasteless food?

And as for tonight—I have just returned from an accidental death scene where I was on duty until twenty minutes ago. I missed my dinner. I missed my drink at the pub. I'm tired and exceedingly bad tempered and I'm going to bed."

He started in the direction of his bedroom. He heard Reverend Powell-Jones mutter, "Well, I never did!" Then he remembered something and turned back at his doorway. "Oh and one more thing, Reverend. It was your house the person was killed in. You might find yourself being questioned as an accessory!"

With that he strode into his bedroom and shut the door. Once he was behind the closed door, a big grin spread across his face.

"Now I feel a lot better," he said out loud and just wished that the pub were still open.

TEN

"TREADFUL, ISN'T IT? TREADFUL JUST." Mrs. Williams stood over Evan's bed with a morning cup of tea. "Treadful," she said again. It was one of the few English words she chose to use, being more expressive than the Welsh in the circumstances. "That poor man, cut off in the prime of his life."

Evan often wondered why the government hadn't looked into using the occupants of Llanfair as international spies. They had an uncanny way of finding out exactly what was going on, long before the authorities did in most cases.

Evan took the tea from her. "How did you hear about it?"

"Evan-the-Milk told me. He got it from Mrs. Hopkins, who watched the whole thing."

"Watched the whole thing?" Evan sat up. Was it possible there was an eyewitness?

"Well, she could hardly help seeing all those police cars, could she? And then the poor man being carried out to the ambulance," Mrs. Williams clarified. "And his poor wife arrived back to find her husband dead, so they say."

Evan nodded. Mrs. Williams wasn't going to get any more juicy details out of him.

"I expect you'll be needed early, to control the crowds," she said.

"Are there crowds already?" He attempted to get up.

"Only local people from the village. No reporters yet, but I expect there will be. He was a very famous man, after all. They say he fell and hit his head. I never did like the looks of that fender in the minister's house."

Evan got up and grabbed his shaving kit. This was one morning when he had to make the bathroom before Mr. Powell-Jones.

"I hope his family lets him be buried here," Mrs. Williams called after him as he hurried down the hall. "We haven't had a decent funeral for ages now, have we, and they could afford to put on a lovely one with all the trimmings. Maybe that famous Italian lady will come and sing at it."

Evan thought that Ifor's widow would hardly be likely to invite his famous mistress to sing at his funeral. He also doubted that she'd want Ifor buried in a place she so disliked.

He was on his way out of the bathroom when his way was barred by the Reverend Powell-Jones. "Who was killed in my house? I have a right to know," the minister demanded. Evan had ignored the persistent taps on his door the night before. "I've been awake all night worrying," the minister went on, "and it's not good for me. I need my rest if I'm to be at my best tomorrow."

"I'm sure you'll do just fine in the poetry competition, Reverend," Evan said. "You've already learned how to rhyme. Rest and best. That's good for starters."

"This is no time for facetious jokes, young man." The reverend's face was stony. "Who was killed in my house? It wasn't in my bed, was it? My wife could never sleep in a bed in which someone had been murdered."

"Who said anything about murder?" Evan said calmly. "It was an unfortunate accident and it wasn't in your bed. Mr. Llewellyn fell and hit his head, in the drawing room. It looks as if he hit your fender."

"Terrible. How tragic." The reverend's face had brightened up considerably. "I must call my wife at once. I wanted to spare her unnecessary worry until I knew all the details, but I'm sure she'll want to be here. And I must get up there right away. The grieving widow will need someone to console her."

He scuttled off to his bedroom like a large crab. Evan thought that the last person Mrs. Llewellyn would want around her at the moment was the Reverend Powell-Jones, quoting Scripture and offering her plates of prunes.

He hurried back to his own room to get dressed. He wanted to make sure he was up at the house before any Powell-Joneses showed up.

"I've got your breakfast ready, Mr. Evans," Mrs. Williams called as he ran down the stairs.

"Sorry, Mrs. W. Can't wait," Evan said. "I'll just grab a slice of your bara brith. That will keep me going."

"Bara brith for breakfast. 'Deed to goodness, what is the world coming to?" Mrs. Williams demanded.

"Not bran and prunes, we hope," Evan said as he exited the kitchen.

The weather had dawned bright and fine for the *eisteddfod*. Evan remembered it as he came out of the front door. With all the excitement of the last night, he had forgotten that today he was supposed to be a member of the Llanfair Côr Meibion, taking part in his first *eisteddfod*.

A brisk wind was rushing up the pass from the ocean, ruffling the coats of the sheep on the hillside. *A good day for walking,* Evan thought, and his gaze strayed to the gray stone schoolhouse. He hadn't spoken to Bronwen since their misunderstanding about his date with Betsy, but he remembered that she would be down at the *eisteddfod* today with her schoolchildren. Now he wouldn't even have a chance to join her. He'd probably be too busy fending off pushy journalists.

Evans-the-Post was coming toward him, his eyes wide with excitement, his lanky limbs flapping so that he looked like an oversize rag doll. "They say they found a body, *Plisman*," he called to Evan. "They say he had his head all bashed in. I tried to take a look, but they wouldn't let me."

"The body's already gone," Evan said.

"Who did it then?" Evans-the-Post asked, his limbs twitching with suppressed excitement. "Is it another murder?"

"It was just an accident," Evan said. "He fell and hit his head, that's all."

"Oh. That's all, eh?" The smile faded. "My brother Tomos fell and hit his head once. He was never rightly the same after."

He went on his way, fingering the letters he hoped to read if Miss Roberts, the postmistress, didn't catch him. Evan wondered if he, too, hadn't fallen on his head at some stage.

A small crowd had gathered outside the chapel, where today's text read "Let your light shine before men." Across the street the biblical text read "Blessed are the meek."

A police car was already parked in the Powell-Joneses' driveway beside the black Mercedes. Evan wondered briefly how Mrs. Llewellyn had come up from Bangor station last night. Taxi, he supposed. People with their kind of money probably never thought twice about taking taxies.

Jim Abbott and another officer were standing beside the police car.

"Morning, Evans," Jim Abbott called. "Is this the time

you usually show up for work? Cushy job." He grinned
to his partner.

"I shouldn't be showing up at all today," Evan said.
"It's Saturday, isn't it?"

Jim Abbott nodded. "I suppose they don't get crimes
on the weekends up here. If someone's going to be drunk
and disorderly, they show consideration and do it during
your working week."

"So what's happening?" Evan asked, indicating the
house. "Has Mrs. Llewellyn come back here yet?"

"No. The place is empty. We've got Forensic coming
to take samples from where he bashed his head and nobody's to be let in. If Mrs. Llewellyn wants to go in,
she's to be escorted and she's not allowed into the room
where the body was."

"Oh, and Evans," Abbott's fellow officer said. He was
a skinny young man with sandy hair. Evan thought his
name was Harris. "We're not to answer any questions.
When the media shows up we're to tell them that we
know no details and refer them to D.I. Hughes at HQ."

"Fine with me," Evan said. "Do you want me to stand
here and help you control the crowd?" He kept a straight
face as he indicated the ten to twelve people who were
loitering respectfully a few yards away.

"They'll be here, don't you worry," Abbott said with
a momentary frown of annoyance. "Just as soon as the
word gets out, they'll be pouring in from all over Europe."

Evan went over to the group of villagers. Charlie's
wife, Mair, was in the middle of recounting her story
again. "And then I looked out of the window again and
bless me if they weren't carrying the poor man out on a
stretcher. He must have been a load, too. They were staggering all over the place. I thought they were going to
drop him once and I said to Charlie, You better go out
and give them a hand . . ."

Evans-the-Meat came out of his shop to join them and

soon most of the members of the Llanfair choir were assembled there.

"What they're saying is true, then, is it?" the butcher asked Evan. "Ifor Llewellyn is dead?"

Evan nodded. "I'm afraid so, Gareth."

"What do you think will happen then, Mr. Evans?" Harry-the-Pub asked. "About the *eisteddfod*, I mean. We surely won't be singing after this. It wouldn't be right."

"I think we should go ahead and sing," Evans-the-Meat said. "In tribute to our famous native son. Remember what he said to us? He said the grandest thing a Welsh-man can do is to sing in an *eisteddfod*."

"I think he said win an *eisteddfod*, Gareth," Roberts-the-Pump said dryly. "And I don't think we're likely to do that without Ifor, do you?"

"At least I think we should give it our best shot," Evans-the-Meat said.

"I think it would be up to Mostyn," Evan suggested. "He's the choir director, isn't he? I don't know if he'll feel like singing today. He was very shaken up last night."

"Well he's got a very weak stomach, Austin Mostyn has," Evans-the-Meat said. "He's not exactly what you'd call robust, is he—in fact I can't imagine him rooming with Ifor Llewellyn when they were students. They must have driven each other mad."

"Ifor certainly enjoyed baiting him, that's for sure," Harry chuckled. "You know there never were any men from Blenau Ffestiniog here that night he claimed that they'd been to see him. He was just making that up to get a rise out of Mostyn—he told me so."

"Well, he won't be getting a rise out of anyone any-more," Roberts-the-Pump said dryly. "It just shows you. You can never tell when your number's going to be up."

The men nodded. Having worked in the precarious conditions of the slate mine, they knew this to be true. Life wasn't always easy in a mountain village.

"So should we plan on going down to the *eisteddfod* this afternoon or not?" Harry-the-Pub persisted.

"Why don't we wait until we've heard from Mostyn," Evan said. "I'm not sure that they'll let me get away to sing. They're anticipating crowds later."

At that moment the bus came groaning up the steep grade, belching a cloud of black diesel fumes, and stopped outside the pub. Several hikers got off and headed straight for the Mount Snowdon trails, hitching up their packs as they went. They were followed by a tiny, sparrowlike woman in a well-worn black coat, clutching a shopping basket that seemed too large for her. She started up the street toward the chapels, then saw the crowd standing around and broke into a brisk trot.

" 'Deed to goodness—what's happening here then?" she asked, pushing her way into the middle of the crowd.

"Oh, it's you, Gladys," Mair Hopkins said. "I didn't think you worked on Saturdays."

"I don't usually, but they asked me to come in, seeing that the mistress has been away." Her eyes strayed to the police car in the driveway. "What's going on here then?"

Evan stepped forward before anyone could give her an amended version. "There's been an accident, Gladys. I'm afraid Mr. Llewellyn's dead."

Gladys's jaw dropped open. "Mr. Llewellyn dead, is it? No! It can't be. He was right as rain when I left him last night, talking and laughing as if he hadn't got a care in the world."

Evan's ears pricked up. "Last night? You were here last night—until what time?"

"I was working late, see," Gladys said, frowning to remember, "on account of the mistress being gone. I thought I'd stay on and make them some dinner, so she had a good meal when she got back—not just that cold salami stuff that they seem to eat. It must have been around six when I left. Yes, it must have been, of course, because I got the six-ten bus, didn't I?"

"And Mr. Llewellyn had someone with him then?"

"He had to have, didn't he? I could hear them chatting away in the living room."

"Do you know who it was?"

Gladys shook her head. "I couldn't rightly say. I was in the kitchen with the door shut, look you, and I don't think the master knew I was still there. I usually go by four, but I thought I'd just make a nice shepherd's pie so they'd get something warm in their stomachs." She paused and looked around at the crowd. She was clearly enjoying being the center of attention for once. "Well, I'd got the pie out of the oven, look you, so I thought that maybe I should go and tell him that it was on the table ready, whenever he was hungry. But when I got to the living room door, I heard him talking and laughing and I didn't like to disturb him. He doesn't always take kindly to being disturbed, especially when he's singing, poor man."

"So you've no idea who the other person was?" Evan asked. "A man or a woman?"

Gladys frowned. "I couldn't rightly say. Not a high woman's voice but it could have been either. I couldn't hear the other voice as well as the master's. He's got a very big voice, hasn't he? The other one was very faint through the door and Mr. Llewellyn was doing most of the talking, and laughing, too. I didn't hear what they were saying though. I just went on home."

"Thank you, Gladys. You've been very helpful," Evan said.

"Can I go in and do my dusting now, sir?" Gladys asked.

"I'm afraid nobody's allowed in yet," Evan said.

"But I came all the way here. It cost me seventy pence on the bus and there won't be one back until ten."

"You can come across to the police station," Evan said. "I'll make you a cup of tea and maybe I can take down everything you've told me. Who knows, it might be important."

"Might it now?" Gladys looked delighted. "Well, who would have thought it?" She trotted beside Evan on her little bird legs, taking five steps to every one of his.

"You know, I might recognize the voice again if I heard it," she said as they moved away from the crowd. "It was kind of unusual like."

They had just reached the police station and Evan was about to unlock the door when a shrill voice froze him in his tracks. "Constable Evans! I need your assistance this minute, if you please."

Evan turned around to face Mrs. Powell-Jones, storming down the street with a look of thunder on her face. "Constable Evans. Will you please go and tell those impudent young men who are currently lounging around the police car in my driveway who I am? They are refusing me entry to my own house. They informed me, very rudely indeed, that they had orders to admit nobody and that included me."

Evan began to think more kindly of Jim Abbott and his partner. Anyone who could get the better of Mrs. Powell-Jones, even temporarily, deserved a medal.

"I'm afraid what they said is true, Mrs. Powell-Jones," Evan said soothingly. "We can't have anyone in there until the lab boys have had a chance to take their samples."

Mrs. Powell-Jones's face was incredulous. "Take their samples? I understood this was a tragic accident. Are you saying it's something more sinister?"

"Not at all. But in the case of any accidental death, we have to establish the exact cause, and that means taking samples from objects in the room."

"I've never heard such rubbish," Mrs. Powell-Jones snapped. "If I don't get access to my house soon, I shall have to telephone my friend the chief constable. I need to see if any of my furniture has been damaged in the accident. It's very old and valuable, you know."

"I'm sure it won't take long once the Forensic team arrives, Mrs. Powell-Jones," Evan said. "It should be all clear by later today. I wouldn't worry."

"Valuable ornaments might have been knocked over," Mrs. Powell-Jones said. "Not that I am one to place a monetary value on things, but my ornaments have great sentimental value for me. Some of them have been in my family for generations."

"There was nothing broken as far as I could tell," Evan said.

Mrs. Powell-Jones's ears pricked up. "Ah, so you actually saw the body?"

"Yes, I was the one who found him."

"And?"

"I really can't tell you anything yet. The D.I. will be issuing a statement. I've been told not to talk about it."

Mrs. Powell-Jones shook her head in annoyance and made tsk-tsk noises. "I knew it wasn't a good idea to let the house to that man, however much money he offered," she said. "If I'd realized he was the same Ifor Llewellyn who used to carry the coal scuttles up to our rooms . . . breeding will tell, you know. Or lack of it." She leaned closer to Evan. "I understand he drank, like a fish?" She paused. Evan said nothing. "Drinking is the cause of so much grief in the world, isn't it?" she went on. "That's why I—" Suddenly she noticed Gladys standing in the shadows of the doorway. "Gladys, what are you doing here?"

"I was coming to do my work, ma'am. They asked me to come in today."

"On a weekend? They were paying you extra, I hope?"

"Oh yes, ma'am. Quite a bit more than you give me." Gladys looked smug.

"Such extravagance." Mrs. Powell-Jones shook her head again. "Ah well, I suppose I must do my duty and go to offer words of comfort to the bereaved widow. She is in the house, I take it?"

Very clever, Evan thought. Mrs. Powell-Jones certainly wasn't stupid. "No, she's up at the Everest Inn," he said, watching her face fall. "I think your husband's already up there with her."

Having dispatched Mrs. Powell-Jones, Evan seated Gladys, made her tea, and was just getting her statement from her when he saw the white shape of the Police Incident van come to a halt outside his open door.

"I'll be right back, Gladys. Don't go away," he said.

"It's up the street where those people are standing, by the chapel," he called to the van. To his surprise it was not one of the lab technicians but Sergeant Watkins who got out of the van first.

"I'll be with you boys in a minute. You know where to go, don't you?" Watkins waved to the van driver and the van then continued on up the street.

"I'm surprised to see you here, Sarge," Evan began. "I thought you'd got today off and—"

Sergeant Watkins cut him short. "Okay, how do you do it, that's what I want to know?" he demanded, striding toward Evan.

"Do what?"

"Is it something about your nose? It's not a particularly big nose. It's a very ordinary nose, when you come to look at it, so it must be something else."

Evan was looking at him as if he'd suddenly started speaking Serbo-Croatian. "Excuse me, Sergeant. I don't follow you. Why are we talking about my nose? What's that got to do with anything? Am I supposed to have smelled something?"

"You know very well you are. Smelled a rat, that's what." Sergeant Watkins tapped the side of his own, more generous, nose as he gave Evan a knowing wink. "You sensed it, didn't you, right from the start. You picked up on the glass for one thing. And those subtle

questions to the doctor about heart attacks. You didn't
suspect for one minute that he'd had a heart attack—"

"Wait a second, Sarge," Evan interrupted again. "Are
you telling me that it wasn't an accident?"

"Accident my foot," Sergeant Watkins said. "Someone
coshed him on the head."

ELEVEN

EVAN STARED AT HIM. "HE was murdered? They're sure of it?" Had he suspected it all along, he wondered. Had that been the uneasy prickling of his skin when he was in that room? Was it the presence of evil and not the heat that had made him feel clammy, and made Mostyn Phillips look as if he was about to faint?

Sergeant Watkins moved closer to him although there was nobody within hearing distance. "Pretty conclusive, I'd say. There was no alcohol in his system, for one thing. So he hadn't been drinking. The killer just splashed it around a lot to give that impression. And whatever killed him wasn't the knob on the fender. It had at least one sharp edge."

Evan tried not to be glad that his hunch had been right. An accident was one thing. This opened up a whole new can of worms.

"The D.I. is down in Caernarfon, playing host to the press and loving every minute of it. So I've got instructions to come up here and do the spadework before he shows up. Are you in the mood for some digging?"

Evan smiled. "Ready when you are, Sarge."

"Right, let's go into your office and you can start me off with the background facts."

"I've got the cleaning lady in there right now," Evan said. "You could start with her. She was one of the last people to see and hear Ifor Llewellyn alive. I've just been taking her statement, in fact."

"One of the last people, was she? That's useful."

"It certainly is," Evan agreed. "And according to her, it seems that Ifor had a visitor yesterday evening, not too long before he was killed."

He ushered Sergeant Watkins into the one-room station. "Gladys, this is Sergeant Watkins," he said. "I think he'd like to hear your story."

"Very well, sir," Gladys said, smiling shyly.

"Before we start, Gladys," Sergeant Watkins said. "You've been working in the house all the time Mr. Llewellyn's been there?"

"Oh yes, sir, and for years before that. I've been house-keeper to the minister and Mrs. Powell-Jones since nineteen seventy-nine. I know that house like the back of my hand."

"Good." Sergeant Watkins nodded. "We'll probably want you to come on a tour with us later, after the men from my headquarters have finished with the room. Now, Gladys," he perched on the edge of Evan's desk, smiling down at her, "what can you tell me about working for Mr. and Mrs. Llewellyn?"

"Well, sir, it wasn't always easy, as I was telling Constable Evans here. I never knew whether I was coming or going. When the minister was there, everything went like clockwork. They always had lunch twelve-thirty on the dot. I always laid the little table for tea before I went at four. And it was always washing on Monday, ironing on Tuesday, polishing on Wednesday—"

"Yes, we get the picture," Watkins interrupted. "And it wasn't like that with Mr. Llewellyn?"

"Oh no, sir. Like I said, I never knew what was supposed to be happening. I'd get there at nine o'clock and they'd still be asleep. I'd be in the middle of my dusting and they'd want breakfast. Sometimes they had lunch at three o'clock in the afternoon and . . ." She lowered her voice and leaned closer to the two policemen. " . . . they wanted me to use garlic, sir. I told them I'd never seen a need to use that smelly stuff before and I wasn't about to start now."

"So the hours were all mixed up. What else? What was the atmosphere like there? Happy?"

"Noisy sir. Awful noisy."

"Yelling, you mean?"

"Mostly singing, sir."

Watkins tried not to smile. "Some people actually like that noise, Gladys, but I can't say I'm one of them myself. I'd rather have the Beatles. So Mr. Llewellyn sang a lot. What about Mrs. Llewellyn?"

"She was moody like, sir. Didn't say much—of course it was hard to say much when he was around. Sometimes she lay in bed with a book most of the day, then she'd go out for a drive, but she didn't seem to enjoy life, if you get my meaning, sir."

"Did she have many friends?"

"Oh no, sir. Nobody came to see her, the whole time she was here, as far as I know. She was on the telephone a lot though. I think she talked to her children. Her face looked quite different when she was on the telephone."

"But the children weren't here at all?"

"No, sir. We heard that the whole family would be coming, but the children never came after all. Mrs. Llewellyn said she'd left them in Italy. Of course they're both grown up and able to take care of themselves, so I understand."

"And Mr. and Mrs. Llewellyn—how did they get along?"

"Not always so well, sir." Gladys looked uncomfortable, as if she didn't want to be disloyal to her employer.

"In fact when he wasn't singing he was shouting. There was a lot of shouting going on in that house, sir."

"So they fought a lot. About what?"

"Oh, sir!" Gladys looked shocked. "It wasn't my business to listen in on their conversations. Besides, they did most of it in English—and the language they used, sir! I've never heard a lady use words like that before. I used to go and shut myself in the kitchen when they started."

Sergeant Watkins jotted in his notebook. "And what about visitors, Gladys. Did they have many?"

"None at all while I was there, except for Mr. Phillips stopping by with some music a couple of times, and Evans-the-Meat delivering—but that was tradesmen's entrance, not the front door."

"So nobody came to call in a month?"

"Mrs. Llewellyn told me that Mr. Llewellyn's doctor told him to get away somewhere peaceful and have a complete rest. He'd been overdoing it, she said, and his blood pressure was very bad. But if you ask me, sir, I don't think he was helping his blood pressure very much, the way he acted."

"And did they get many phone calls, Gladys?" Evan asked. "Did you have to answer the phone for them?"

"Oh no, sir. It wasn't my place to answer the phone." She leaned closer again. "I'm a wee bit scared of the telephone still, sir. It doesn't seem natural, sending voices down a wire, does it?"

"So you've no idea who might have called them?"

Gladys shook her head.

"Tell the sergeant about last night before you left," Evan said.

Gladys recounted the story, almost word for word as she had given it to Evan. Sergeant Watkins made notes. "So you didn't go to the front door and let the person in, Gladys? And you couldn't tell who it was?"

"No, sir. Like I told the constable, I was back in the kitchen with the door shut, making the pie. And when I

went to the drawing room door, I only heard little
snatches of the other voice. Mr. Llewellyn did most of
the talking as usual, and a lot of laughing, too. But the
other voice was much softer—a gentle voice like."

"Woman or man?"

"That's what I can't say, sir. I told Constable Evans.
Not a very high woman's voice, look you, but it could
have been either."

"And when you left to catch your bus, Gladys," Sergeant Watkins asked, "did you happen to notice any
strange cars parked nearby?"

Gladys frowned. Then she shook her head. "I was in
a hurry because I was worried the bus might go without
me," she said, "but I think I would have noticed if anyone
had parked outside the house."

Sergeant Watkins got up again. "Thank you, Gladys.
You've been very helpful," he said. "Would you mind
sticking around for a while? I'd like you to get a look at
the room where the cri—the accident—happened. You
could tell us if anything had been moved since you saw
it last."

"I'd be happy to, sir," Gladys said. "The next bus
doesn't go until ten anyway. I'll pour myself another cup
of tea, if you don't mind."

Evan followed the sergeant out into the bright sun-
shine. "Very interesting. He fought with his wife. She
wasn't very happy."

"But she also wasn't there," Evan said. "She only just
got back from London when we were there, remember?"

"We can easily check up on that, can't we?" Watkins
asked. "London can be a very convenient alibi. I think
we should go and talk to her now, before any word gets
to her that we're looking on this as a suspicious death."

They walked up the village street. "Lovely day isn't
it?" Evan said.

Sergeant Watkins frowned at him. "Don't rub it in. I'd
promised my wife and daughter that I'd take them to the

eisteddfod. Our Tiffany's keen on seeing the dancing competition. Why do these things always happen on fine days—and on my days off, too? I was looking forward to hearing you sing tonight!"

Evan gave him a look that stopped the grin. "I don't know if we'll be doing it now. Ifor was the one thing that made us sound halfway decent. Some of the men want to go ahead as a sort of tribute to Ifor, but I suppose it will all be up to Mostyn."

"He seemed to be taking it very hard last night," Sergeant Watkins said. "I can't imagine he'd want to be up there in front of people today with his star performer dead."

"Probably not," Evan nodded thoughtfully, "although there was little love lost between those two. I can't say Mostyn would grieve over Ifor Llewellyn's death."

Sergeant Watkins looked up expectantly. "Are you hinting at something?"

Evan laughed. "Oh no, I'm not hinting that Mostyn might have killed him. He was certainly angry enough the night before when Ifor threatened to join another choir, but I don't think he's the type to go coshing people over the head, do you?"

Watkins smiled, too. "You're right about that. Positively green he looked last night, didn't he, poor little bugger. And I don't think he could reach Ifor's head, unless he got a step-ladder!"

"There's no way Mostyn would have killed off his star performer," Evan said. "He actually thought we had a chance for the gold medal with Ifor singing the solos. He'd have waited until after the *eisteddfod* to do anything to him."

"That's probably true," Watkins agreed. "You don't give up your one chance for a gold medal, do you?"

"Anyway, he couldn't have killed Ifor, even if he'd wanted to," Evan pointed out. "He was down in Harlech waiting for us when we arrived last night. He'd been there all evening with some of his pupils from school. And Ifor was still alive and singing when the last of the choir members drove out of the village."

"Oh? They heard him, did they?" Sergeant Watkins looked with interest at the group of villagers still hanging around the crime scene. "Are any of them here now?"

"Most of them," Evan said. "Harry-the-Pub and Evans-the-Meat said they'd heard him."

"Maybe we should talk to them on our way past, while we've got them together here. We'll be able to pin down the last time he was seen or heard alive, and who knows, someone might just have noticed something important."

"They don't miss much around here," Evan agreed.

"Good. Then why don't you start asking the questions?" Watkins patted him on the arm. "They're liable to tell you more than me. And you know my Welsh is a little rusty. I'll just go in and check on the lab boys."

He ducked under the white police tape that now blocked off the driveway, passed the van that was parked outside the house, and disappeared into the building. The Llanfair locals crowded expectantly around Evan.

"What's going on then, Evan *bach*?" Charlie Hopkins asked, nodding in the direction of the house. "What's all the fuss about?"

"They're just trying to make sure of all their facts before they make a press statement, I'd imagine," Evan said evasively. "You know how newspapers always get the wrong end of the stick."

"Either he hit his head or he didn't," Evans-the-Meat said belligerently. "I don't see what's so hard that they need to send up half the county's experts wasting good taxpayer money."

"It's all routine procedure in cases like this, Gareth," Evan said. "When someone winds up with a bloody great hole in his head, we have to check it out thoroughly." He moved closer to the group of men, who were standing a little apart from other small groups of women, children, dogs, and bikes.

"One of the things we need to do is to establish what time he died," Evan said. "You said you heard him singing when you left Llanfair last night, Gareth?"

"That's right. Warming up his voice, the way he always did."

"You could hardly miss it, could you?" Harry-the-Pub added. "Not the way he belted it out."

"And what time was that?" Evan asked.

The men looked at each other. "The six o'clock news had already started, I know that much," Harry said. "But we were down in Harlech and parked just before seven, and that trip has to take forty-five minutes, so I'd have to say about six-ten, wouldn't you, boys?"

The other men who had ridden with Harry nodded. "Must have been six-ten, six-fifteen," Evans-the-Meat concurred. "And we were the last to leave, I think. Your van had already gone, Charlie."

"Yes, we left around six, but it took me longer to find a parking space," Charlie said.

"Did you hear him singing, too, Charlie?" Evan asked.

"I can't say I did, but maybe I'm so used to all the noise by now that I didn't even notice," Charlie said. "It's not easy living next door to it, you know, Evan *bach*. Morning, noon, and night, singing and fighting and singing."

"You didn't hear any fighting the last couple of days, did you?" Evan asked.

"The last time was when the missus called you," Charlie said. "After that it's been real peacefullike, apart from the singing."

"Oh yes, I'd almost forgotten about that incident the other night," Evan said. "Did you happen to overhear what was going on when your missus called me?"

"I can't say I was that interested," Charlie said. "I just turned up the sound on the telly. She was the one who always got upset." He looked across at a tight knot of women standing at the Hopkins's cottage door. "Mair, remember that night when you called the constable?" he asked. "Did you happen to hear what they were fighting about?"

"Which night was that then?" Mair Hopkins asked as the group of women parted for her. "There have been so many, haven't there."

Evan went across to join the women. "You called me one evening last week, Mrs. Hopkins. Ifor was yelling at a strange man."

"Ooh yes, that's right. I remember now. Very sinister it was, too. I pulled back the curtain and got a look at him—ooh, and he looked like a very shady character." She hugged her arms to her and gave a dramatic shudder. "All dressed in black and dark flashing eyes and hadn't shaved. I said to Charlie, what's the betting he's one of those Mafia who's tracked Mr. Llewellyn down here? Charlie told me I was talking nonsense but he looked like a gangster to me right enough. And he spoke foreign, too. Not English, I mean, but real foreign."

"And you didn't happen to hear anything that was said?"

"Only Mr. Llewellyn yelling that he wasn't scared. The whole street heard that, I'd imagine."

Several women nodded.

"And he drove a foreign-looking car, too," one of the women said. "I heard the yelling as well, when I was putting our Gwen to bed."

"What about last night," Evan said. "Did any of you see or hear anything going on at the Llewellyns' house? Any visitors? Anything unusual?"

There was silence, then Mair Hopkins shook her head. "I can't say I noticed anything at all out of the ordinary, like. I saw him outside putting things in his car about five-thirty, it would have been. I heard him doing his singing exercises when I was in the kitchen peeling potatoes for dinner. That would have been after six."

"How much after six?"

"Let's see. I went in the kitchen right after Charlie left with the lads from the choir. It could have been as late as six-thirty before I went back into the living room to see the weather forecast on the telly. I don't know why I bothered. They're never right, are they? I always say to Charlie, I wish I could get paid for a job where I was wrong most of the time—"

"So Ifor was alive and singing at six-thirty." Evan interrupted her discourse on the weather-forecasting profession. He looked around the crowd. "Did anyone happen to see or hear him at any time after that?"

Another silence. Several people shook their heads.

"Anyone seen leaving his house after that or any strange cars driving down the street?"

More silence then Harry-the-Pub said, "Here, what are you getting at then? There's something more to this death than just a man falling and hitting his head, isn't there?"

"See, what did I tell you, I knew it," Evans-the-Meat said triumphantly. "I said they wouldn't make all this fuss over an accident. Someone bashed him on the head."

"It was that Mafia man, of course. What did I tell you?" Mair Hopkins yelled back.

Evan could feel the whole situation slipping away from him.

"Hold on a minute, everyone," he said in a voice to rival Ifor's. "Let's not jump to any conclusions. When the lab technicians have given the place a thorough going-over, maybe we'll know a little more. Right now we're just trying to work out exactly when he died and who was the last person to see him alive."

"That would have to be Gladys, wouldn't it?" Mair Hopkins said. "I saw her coming out of the house when I was doing the potatoes. She almost missed her bus."

"What was Gladys doing there that late?" one of the other women asked.

Mair Hopkins shrugged. "I've no idea. She's usually gone by four, but it was after six last night."

Sergeant Watkins appeared from the house. "They're still working away in there. I don't imagine they'll be done for a while. Why don't we go up and talk to Mrs. Llewellyn?"

Evan accompanied him up the street, away from the chattering group of villagers. The last of the houses was left behind and only the giant gingerbread shape of the Everest Inn blocked the clear view of the pass and Mount Snowdon's peak beyond.

"Any conclusive evidence turned up yet?" Evan asked.

Watkins glanced back to make sure they were far enough away from eavesdropping ears. "One thing's interesting. There are no prints at all on the fender knob. It was wiped clean, then the killer smeared traces of blood and hair on it with something like a handkerchief."

"Either it was well planned out or we've got a killer who thinks on his feet," Evan said.

"Or her feet."

"You reckon a woman could have been strong enough to kill Ifor?" Evan asked. "He was a big bloke. He told me once that when his wife hit him, it was like a fly landing on him."

"His wife hit him, did she?" Watkins looked interested.

"And threw plates at him, I understand. But he treated the whole thing as a joke."

"Not much of a joke now," Watkins said. "I'm looking forward to talking to Mrs. Llewellyn. Her weak and helpless act last night doesn't seem to me like a woman who throws plates and hits her husband. Did he hit her, too, do you reckon?"

"I didn't see any evidence of it, but she kept herself to herself while she was here. We hardly ever saw her and Gladys said she often stayed in bed. I must remember to ask Gladys if she ever saw signs of Mrs. L. being knocked around."

"That would give us a good motive, wouldn't it?" Watkins said thoughtfully. "Abused spouse snaps and kills him. I've seen it before."

"Another thing you should know first, Sarge," Evan said. "She told me that the reason for her trip to London was to see her lawyer about a possible divorce."

Watkins's eyebrows shot up. "She was divorcing him?" Then he shook his head. "But that wouldn't help us at all. If she was getting rid of him legally, she wouldn't have needed to kill him. It would have made more sense if he'd killed her."

"She told me Ifor was shocked and took it very hard. That's why she suspected he might have taken his own life. She said he'd probably end up by talking her out of it. He usually got his own way in the end. Maybe she was scared she wouldn't be strong enough to go through with it."

"Fascinating," Watkins said. "At least we've got someone with a motive. Let's hear what she has to say now."

———————— TWELVE ————————

"IT'S LIKE A POSH MAUSOLEUM, isn't it?" Sergeant Watkins murmured to Evan as they stepped into the foyer of the Everest Inn. Leather sofas and armchairs were dotted around on a floor made of polished slate. A floor-to-ceiling river-rock fireplace took up most of one wall. There was no fire in the fireplace at this time of year and the whole area was deserted apart from the girl at the reception desk. Their feet clattered, unnaturally loud, on the slate floor, causing the girl to look in their direction.

"Welcome to the Everest Inn. May I help you?" she asked in an attempt at an upper-class English accent with definite Welsh undertones.

"Watkins held up a warrant card. "Sergeant Watkins. North Wales Police here to see Mrs. Llewellyn," he said.

The girl looked flustered and reverted to Welsh. "Police? Oh dear. Maybe I should get Major Anderson?"

"That won't be necessary," Evan said. "We only want a little chat with Mrs. Llewellyn. What's her room number, please?"

"I think she just left," the girl stammered. "Yes, see, here's her key hanging up."

"Left? How long ago?" Watkins gave Evan an anxious glance. They were both imagining what D.I. Hughes might say if they'd lost an important witness, if not a prime suspect.

"Only a few minutes," she said. "I'm surprised you didn't pass her."

Watkins was one pace behind Evan as they fought their way through the revolving door again.

"Where can she have got to?" Watkins demanded. "She can't have gone on up the road to the top of the pass. There's nothing there."

Evan was scanning the scene. "She could have taken the back way," he said. "There's a footpath that goes behind the Powell-Joneses' property." He broke into a run. Watkins followed, breathing heavily after a few steps.

There was a gap in the drystone wall around the parking lot and as they approached it, they could see a figure moving between the larch trees that had been planted to shelter the inn. Evan quickened his pace, taking the rocky path in sure strides. Watkins followed, running more cautiously.

"Bloody 'ell," he muttered. "You need to be a mountain goat up here."

"Mrs. Llewellyn!" Evan called. "Hold on a minute."

The hurrying figure stopped, looked around and hesitated—*almost as if she was trying to assess whether to make a run for it,* Evan thought.

"Oh, it's you, Constable," she said. Her face was composed and she was smiling graciously as he reached her. "I thought for a moment it was those horrible people again."

"Horrible people?"

"That minister and his awful wife. There is nothing I wanted less this morning than spiritual comfort from them, especially her. She more or less told me that my husband's death was judgment from heaven for his sinful ways. I had the greatest desire to hit her."

Evan nodded. "That reaction is not uncommon with Mrs. Powell-Jones," he said and got an answering smile. "So where were you off to?"

"I was just on my way to get my car and go to pick up my son. He called first thing this morning. He's managed to get a flight into Manchester. I said I'd pick him up so that he didn't have to go to the trouble of renting a car."

Sergeant Watkins caught up, red faced and breathing heavily.

"Mrs. Llewellyn was going to meet her son, Sergeant," Evan said. "He's flying into Manchester."

"If you could just spare us a few minutes first," Sergeant Watkins managed to say. "We've got a few routine questions to ask you."

"Couldn't they wait until I get back?" She barely masked her annoyance.

"I'd prefer to get them over with," Watkins said. "We need to check on all the facts in this case, including your trip to London."

"My trip to London—what on earth does that have to do with Ifor falling?"

Either she was in the clear or she was a good actress, Evan thought. The surprise sounded genuine enough.

"Mrs. Llewellyn, you know what the press will be like when they get hold of this story, don't you?" Evan said before Watkins could come up with an answer. "They're bound to want to know where you were when it happened."

She nodded. "Yes, I suppose you're right. They do love digging up scandal where Ifor's concerned."

"Shall we go back to the hotel to talk?" Watkins asked.

"Can't we talk as we walk?" she asked. "I'd imagine this footpath is about as private as you can get and I don't want to keep Justin waiting at the airport."

"Alright. You went to London. For how long?"

"Let's see. I left on Tuesday, came back on Friday night."

"Train or car?"

"Train. I won't drive in London. It's a madhouse."

"So you've still got the ticket stubs?"

"Of course. I caught the nine-twenty down on Tuesday and I arrived in Bangor last night on the seven-thirty train that left Paddington at two."

"And the purpose of your visit was what?" Watkins asked genially.

She shot a quick glance at Evan. "I explained it to the constable last night. I went down to consult my solicitor. I was thinking of getting a divorce."

Watkins had opened his notebook and was scribbling away. "Solicitor's name and address please?"

"Oh really, this is too much," she snapped. "Why am I being treated as a criminal? Can I help it if my husband falls down in an alcoholic stupor when I'm away?"

"Solicitor's name, please?" Watkins said passively.

"Dutton, Faber and Dutton. Queen Anne Street."

"And what did Messrs. Dutton, Faber and Dutton advise?"

"They talked me through the steps I'd need to take to file for divorce. It's rather more complicated because our principal residence is in Milan."

"At least you won't have to go through that anymore." Evan was intending to say something kind. He realized as he said it that it sounded all wrong and she gave him an annoyed glance.

"My husband might have made me very angry at times and driven me crazy often, Constable, but believe me, I would never have wished him dead."

"Did he ever hit you, Mrs. Llewellyn?" Watkins asked.

Another look of genuine surprise. "Who on earth told you that? Ifor was a big old softy. He used to cry at *Bambi* and *Dumbo*. The only person I ever remember him hitting was a paparazzi photographer who was following our daughter too closely. Ifor was very protective of our daughter, even though she can take care of herself quite nicely."

"Your daughter's not coming over with your son, then?" Watkins asked.

"She'll be over for the funeral, which we can't arrange until you people release Ifor's body to us. Naturally she is very upset by all this, poor child. And this is a bad time for her—she has a lot of pressure at work right now. She's in the fashion industry, you know. Her father didn't approve at all. There was only one career as far as he was concerned and that was music. He wanted her to be the world's greatest soprano. He fantasized about them singing duets someday. But that was Ifor—always the dreamer." She sighed heavily.

"And your son—does he have a musical career?" Watkins asked.

"Hardly." She looked amused. "Justin is completely unmusical," she said. "He claims to be tone-deaf, but I think he just pretends to annoy his father."

"So he and his father didn't get along?" Evan asked.

"They—didn't see eye to eye about a lot of things. Justin was a very sensitive child and Ifor has—had—a way of devouring those weaker than him. Take poor Mostyn Phillips—he always loved to tease Mostyn. Mostyn took everything so seriously and Ifor hardly took a thing seriously in his life."

"We were talking about your son, Mrs. Llewellyn," Evan reminded her. "Had he and his father quarreled?"

She stopped walking and eyed the two policemen steadily. "Just what are you getting at, Constable? Is there something you haven't told me about my husband's death?"

"We won't know that until the lab work's complete, madam," Sergeant Watkins answered for Evan. "For the present we are piecing together the details of an accident."

"In answer to your question, Constable," Mrs. Llewellyn said, starting to walk on again ahead of them, "my husband and son agreed to disagree. They led separate lives. My son has his own life. His own circle of friends, in Italy."

"I see." Sergeant Watkins nodded. "Well, we'll be able to ask him ourselves when you bring him back from the airport, won't we?"

"I'll be free to take my car then?"

They had reached the back of the Powell-Jones house. There was a gap in the tall yew hedge that led to the back lawn. Mrs. Llewellyn stepped through ahead of the two men.

"I'll have to check with Forensic," Watkins said, "but I can't imagine they'd have any interest in the car, seeing that it wasn't used last night."

"Mrs. Llewellyn." Evan hurried to catch up with her. "Had your husband ever had any dealings with the Mafia?"

This time she laughed out loud. "You've been reading too many tabloids, Constable. Ifor and the Mafia? What on earth for?"

"Someone came here last week and threatened him. I overheard part of it. The man had a foreign accent. He drove a foreign car and your husband yelled after him, 'I'm not afraid of your threats.' Any idea what that might have meant?"

She stopped in her tracks, in the middle of the Powell-Joneses' back lawn. "Last week, you say?" Then she shook her head. "I've no idea. It certainly wasn't when I was in the house."

"So you can't think of anybody who has threatened your husband or wanted him dead?"

She laughed again, a short brittle laugh. "Hundreds of people, Constable. Ifor had a great talent for making enemies. I should imagine that half the husbands and boy-friends of Europe wanted him dead." Then the smile faded. "You do think it wasn't an accident, don't you?" she said in a low voice.

"Maybe we'll know more by the time you get back with your son," Sergeant Watkins answered. "And please come straight back here. I expect my D.I. will want to talk to both of you."

"I'm not likely to leave until I can take my husband's body for burial," she said coldly.

She stood, tapping her foot impatiently, while Sergeant Watkins disappeared into the house. He returned almost immediately and nodded. "They see no reason that you can't take the car, but they'd like you to step inside first and take a look around the living room. It should only take you a moment."

Mrs. Llewellyn made a visible effort to compose herself. "Very well. If you insist," she said. "My husband's body is not there any longer, I understand. I expect I can handle bloodstains."

"Thank you, Mrs. Llewellyn," Evan said. He escorted her down the driveway and in through the front door.

The smell of stale alcohol faintly lingered. The smell of death had gone, to be replaced with the chemical odors that accompanied the lab team. Mrs. Llewellyn stood in the front hall and waited for Sergeant Watkins to go ahead.

"What we'd like you to do, Mrs. Llewellyn, is to look around the room and see if anything is missing, or anything has been moved from its usual place. It should only take you a moment and then you can be on your way."

"Very well." She took a deep breath and was about to walk into the room when Evan pointed to the black shoe, still lying in the front hall. "By the way, Mrs. Llewellyn," he said. "Any idea what this shoe's doing here?"

"It's mine," she said. "I hate wearing heels. I always kick them off the moment I get through the door. I expect you'll find the other one somewhere around. Now, if you'll lead on, Sergeant."

Evan stood in the hallway, watching her with interest. Was it really her shoe? She had admitted ownership so quickly but he didn't think that littering the front hall with discarded shoes went along with her character. He thought of the spotless kitchen. Gladys wasn't the sort of housekeeper who would leave shoes lying around for several days. He was pretty sure of that, too. He'd have to ask her when she came back.

He followed Mrs. Llewellyn into the room, where two police technicians in white coats looked up and nodded a greeting. "Just take a look around, please," one of them said. "Let us know if you notice anything that has been moved, or is missing or shouldn't be here."

Mrs. Llewellyn cast a quick gaze over the surfaces. Evan thought she paused momentarily at the top of the heavy carved sideboard, decorated with a fruit bowl, two candlesticks, and several lesser ornaments, before she said, "No, everything looks the same as far as I can see." Her gaze went down to the floor where the patch of brown stained the red carpet. "Is that . . . where he was?"

"That's right," Sergeant Watkins said. "It appears that he hit his head on the fender."

"What a ridiculous object it is," she said angrily. "Completely useless and ugly, too, like most things in this house. Ifor used to have to polish it when he was a child. Strange that it should have been the end of him." Suddenly she shivered. "Is that all?" she asked.

"For now, yes. We might need you to go through the rest of the house more thoroughly later, when these boys have finished," Sergeant Watkins said. "But we won't detain you any longer at the present."

Evan went over to the mantlepiece and picked up a silver-framed photo. It was the sort of snapshot that might be in any home—two parents, two children sitting together in a motorboat, hair blowing out in the wind, squinting in the fierce sunlight and hamming for the camera. "Your family?" he asked.

She nodded. "Taken some years ago now, of course, but it reminds me of a very happy summer we spent together."

As she left the room Evan held up the photo. "You don't mind if I borrow this, do you?" he asked the nearest lab technician. "We might need to show her picture around."

"Go ahead," the man said. "That certainly wasn't what killed him." Evan put the photo into his jacket pocket and hurried after Watkins.

"You'll be gone a couple of hours, I'd imagine," Watkins said as he opened the car door for Mrs. Llewellyn. "You'll probably find that they're finished with your house by then, although I think we'd prefer that you stay another night at the inn."

"Don't worry," she said with a shudder. "Nothing would induce me to sleep in that house again. I never liked it from the start, creepy place. Why Ifor had fond memories of it, I'll never know."

"Excuse me, Constable Evans." Evan spun around at the tap on his back.

"Oh Gladys. What can I do for you?" he asked as the diminutive person stood there, clutching her shopping basket. "Run out of tea, have you?"

"No, the tea was very nice, thank you," Gladys said, bobbing her head like a bird. Suddenly she noticed Mrs. Llewellyn. "Oh, good morning, madam. I didn't see you there. I was very sorry to hear about your husband. God rest his soul, poor man. If there's anything I can do for you . . ."

"Thank you, Gladys. You're very kind."

"I made you a lovely shepherd's pie last night," Gladys said with a hint of accusation. "I expect it's all spoiled now, sitting there in the kitchen. Oh well. Can't be helped. The thought was there."

"So what did you want, Gladys?" Evan asked again.

"How much longer do you think I'll be hanging around here, Constable Evans?" she asked. "Because my bus goes soon and I'd like to get my shopping done before the shops shut at one. If I don't catch this bus, the next one gets me down to Caernarfon too late."

Evan looked at Watkins.

"Why don't you go on down and do your shopping, love," Watkins said to her. "Constable Evans has got your address, hasn't he? We'll send a car to get you when we're ready for you to take a look at the house."

"Send a car for me?" Gladys's face flushed with pleased embarrassment. "That sounds very nice, thank you. Only I'll have to explain to the neighbors first. I wouldn't want them to think I was being carted off in a police car."

"I'm driving down," Mrs. Llewellyn said. "Why don't I give you a lift, Gladys?"

"Thank you, madam. That's most kind of you." Gladys beamed. She was clearly imagining the neighbors' faces when she arrived home in a big black Mercedes.

"Well, come along. Let's get going then," Mrs. Llewellyn said. "I'd like to be there at the gate when his plane gets in."

Gladys hopped into the car and sat erect and haughty as Mrs. Llewellyn drove away.

"Well at least that's made somebody's day," Watkins said with a smile. Then the smile faded. "Don't look now, but we've got company," he said. The first of the press cars was pulling up outside. "Amazing how news travels, isn't it?" he muttered to Evan. "Now just as long as we can keep them thinking it was only an accident, we'll give ourselves breathing room. I need to have someone check out Mrs. Llewellyn's London jaunt right away . . . and what was all that about the Mafia back there?"

Evan related the shouting match he had overheard. Watkins nodded. "Interesting, but don't think it's going to be easy to track the bloke down. That's one of the problems with the bloody EEC—everyone comes and goes as they please without having to show their passport. We've no way of knowing what bloody Italians are here, have we? Do they still keep records of car license plates on the cross-Channel ships?"

"I've no idea," Evan said.

"I'll put in a call to the Yard. They know that sort of stuff. Oh, and I should ask the D.I. to get in touch with the Italian police, too. They'd probably know if Ifor Llewellyn had been involved with the Mafia in Italy." He looked up from his notebook and grinned. "This is going to make the D.I.'s day—talking to the media and chatting with the Italian police about possible Mafia connections—he'll be giving himself ideas that he's somebody important."

THIRTEEN

BY MIDMORNING, CROWD CONTROL HAD become a necessity and even Jim Abbott was having to work hard. Several TV vans with crews trailed cables across the Powell-Jones driveway. Humbler journalists got out of cars almost as old as Mostyn's, and the foreign media had arrived, talking noisily into mikes with a lot of arm waving.

Evan stood in the street, directing traffic while the other two policemen fielded questions and kept inquisitive journalists away from the house. The inhabitants of Llanfair hung around, hoping to be interviewed for the telly or the front page of a London daily. Evan listened to several exaggerated accounts of how the speaker and Ifor had been best mates and shared pints in the pub.

"I've called Austin Mostyn," Evans-the-Meat announced as he wormed his way back into the crowd. "I've told him how we feel about honoring Ifor's memory so he's agreed that we should sing tonight. But he says please excuse him if he doesn't come up to the village today. It's too upsetting for him."

"I can understand that, seeing that he found the body and all," Charlie Hopkins agreed.

"Poor man. What a shock for him. His best friend, too," Mair added.

Reporters from the international press stood, perplexed and frowning, as the conversation went on around them in Welsh.

"Could you translate for us, Constable?" an elegant young man from the *Daily Express* asked Evan. "We're rather at a loss here, you know. It's very inconsiderate of people to speak Welsh when they know we don't understand it."

"Why shouldn't we speak Welsh?" Evans-the-Meat demanded in English. "It's our language, isn't it—and the finest, oldest language in Europe, too. If I had my way every schoolchild in England would learn Welsh instead of French or Latin."

He frowned as he saw the smile on the *Daily Express*'s face. "If you care to ask us a question in English, we'll be happy to answer it," he said. "We are perfectly bilingual, you know, which is more than any of you so-called educated types are."

Evan noticed that Harry-the-Pub had now disappeared, obviously opening early today with the hope of doing a good trade. Journalists were known for putting away the beer. As he turned to look at the pub he saw Betsy come running out, her tiny lace apron flapping in the breeze, her arms waving distraughtly.

"Tell me it's not true!" she yelled as she ran up the street. Her face was tear stained. Her mascara was running. She was not looking her best.

"They said he's dead," she gasped as she neared Evan. "I was sleeping in late because it's Saturday. I've only just heard. Please tell me it's not true!"

"I'm afraid it is, love," Evan said.

"Oh, no. Not him. He was so alive, so sexy," Betsy wailed and flung herself into Evan's arms. "Hold me,

Evan. Hold me tight," she gasped. Evan stood there, feeling embarrassed and awkward, conscious of all those eyes on him and realizing that these outsiders hadn't understood a word of Betsy's outburst in Welsh.

"I'm sorry, Betsy love." Evan patted her hair. "It's been a shock for all of us."

"And I could have gone to the opera with him," she sobbed. Then she raised her head from his chest and gazed up hopefully. "Still, at least I've got you, haven't I, Evan *bach*? You and I will have a grand old time on our date and who knows . . ."

Evan had just been considering this ramification—with Ifor dead, would that let him out of his obligation of a date with Betsy? "I think we should put off talking about dates for a while, don't you, Betsy," he said. "Now that Ifor's gone and—"

She read his thoughts. "Hold on a minute, Evan Evans. Are you trying to tell me that you don't want to go on a date with me anymore?" Her large blue eyes opened even wider. The resemblance to a Barbie doll was remarkable. "You don't want to go on a date with me!" she cried. "You just asked me to stop me from going with Ifor. You don't really like me after all!" Tears began to cascade down her cheeks. The journalists had moved closer. Some were even holding microphones in their direction, in case Betsy turned out to be one of Ifor's bereaved girlfriends.

"Betsy, this isn't a good time to talk," Evan said, putting his hands firmly on her shoulders. "You're upset. Everyone's upset. I'm supposed to be doing my job, controlling the crowd. Now please, be a good girl and let me get on. Traffic's backing up, look you."

"You really don't care, do you?"

"Of course I care," Evan said. "Why do you think I wanted to stop you from going down to Cardiff with Ifor if I didn't care?"

"You mean it?" A hopeful smile spread across her

face. "Oh Evan. That's wonderful just." She flung herself into his arms again, reached up, and gave him a noisy kiss on his cheek before running back to the pub.

Evan gave an embarrassed grin to the watching crowd. Then the smile froze on his face. Bronwen was standing only a few feet away, watching him.

"I was comforting her," he said, as Betsy disappeared into the Red Dragon.

"So I see."

"She was upset about Ifor's death, poor kid. I just happened to be the nearest person . . ."

Bronwen nodded. "Of course." She smoothed down her full skirt that was blowing out in the wind. "Well, I'm on my way down to Harlech to the *eisteddfod*. I promised the children and it's a good idea to get them away from all this." She started to walk away.

"I might see you there," Evan called after her.

She looked back, surprised. "You're not going to be singing, after what happened, are you?"

"I thought we should bow out, personally, but some of the men think that Ifor would have wanted it. I don't think Mostyn's too keen either, but he said he'd meet us there if we wanted to go ahead. Not that we've any chance of getting a medal now."

"I might come and hear you," Bronwen said, "if I haven't anything better to do." It was delivered like a slap in the face. Evan forced himself to go back to his traffic directing. *Women,* he thought. Life was complicated enough without having women to complicate it even further!

Sergeant Watkins came out of the house again. "It looks as if they're almost done in there," he said to Evan, drawing him aside from the crowd.

"Have they found anything interesting?"

"Could be," the sergeant muttered. "They've established one thing. He was definitely dragged to the position we found him. Traces of blood all across the carpet.

But no sign of a murder weapon. Any idea where the Powell-Jones woman got to? It wouldn't be a bad idea to let her have a look at the crime scene. She'd know if anything was missing."

"I could go and find her for you, but I'm stuck here directing traffic," Evan said.

"I've got reinforcements coming up any moment now," Watkins said. "Then we can take their car. The D.I. is putting all his energy into tracking down our Mafia visitor. So that will keep him nicely out of our hair. He wants me to check out Mrs. L.'s London trip. Do you want to help?"

"You're driving up to London?"

"No such luck," Watkins said. "The Met police are going to be making calls for us to the solicitor and to the hotel where she said she stayed. I've just got to check on trains. See if anyone noticed her last night. Anyone can buy a ticket and not use it, can't they?"

A few minutes later Evan and Watkins successfully negotiated the crush of reporters and drove away in the newly arrived police car.

"I rather wish we'd put a tail on the wife now," Watkins said. "We've only got her word that she's going to Manchester airport, haven't we? I don't know what I'd say to the D.I. if she did a bunk on us. Realizing that you can cross the Channel without showing a passport has made me nervous."

"I wouldn't worry too much, Sarge," Evan said. "She's driving a pretty distinctive car, isn't she? And why would she need to run, if her alibi holds up?"

Watkins drew out a clean white handkerchief and mopped his forehead. "I hope so," he said. "Why didn't I think? We could have sent a squad car to get the son. I suppose it's because I'm not used to crimes this important. It's not too often that world-famous opera singers are killed in Llanfair, is it?"

"You could always get on the phone to HQ and have

them alert the airlines at Manchester—just in case she changed her mind and decided to fly out."

"Good thinking," Watkins said. "I don't know why you don't apply for transfer to detective training. You're a natural for it—as well as born bloody lucky."

"I think about it sometimes," Evan said, "but I had my fill of excitement and violence when I was on the force down in Swansea."

"Saw too much, did you?" Watkins nodded with understanding. "I know. It gets to me like that sometimes. When a little kid turns up murdered or an old lady has her head bashed in for her pension book—then I ask myself why I'm doing it."

"I saw my dad gunned down," Evan said.

Watkins looked at him. "I heard something about that," he said.

Evan stared straight ahead. "I don't think I'll ever get that sight out of my mind. At least life makes sense in Llanfair—most of the time, anyway."

"So who do you think could have done it?" Watkins wisely changed the subject. "Coshed Ifor Llewellyn, I mean."

Evan frowned. "As Mrs. Llewellyn said, he must have had a lot of enemies. It doesn't seem to me that it was a Mafia type of killing. From what I've read they're always neater—bullet to the back of the head. Coshing is too risky. Sometimes the person lives."

"What about the wife?"

"Why would she have needed to kill him, if she was going to divorce him?" Evan asked. "A divorce gets her free of him and a fat alimony check to go with it. Besides, do you really think she'd have had the strength to do that kind of damage?"

"You're right. It's a tough one, isn't it? I'll be interested to hear what the son has to say. I get the feeling there was plenty of hostility between him and his father."

As they talked the road was dropping steadily between

steep green hillsides. The bleating of sheep came in through the open car windows. They had to slow through Llanberis, which was full of tourists. Hikers and climbers wandered across the road, heading for the mountain trails. Day trippers lined up for the next train up Snowdon and children dragged their parents in the direction of ice-cream shops. It seemed strange to Evan that this kind of life was still going on with death so close by.

Bangor railway station was also busy on this summer Saturday. The car park was full and Watkins had to park in a No Parking zone.

"Let's just hope they don't have the nerve to tow the police car," he muttered to Evan. "I'd hate to have to explain that to the D.I."

They crossed the parking lot and pushed through a busy booking office to the ticket collector at the gate. A train had just come in and they waited until he had collected the last of the tickets before approaching him.

"Were you on duty here last night?" Watkins asked him.

"What if I was?" He was a little man and he looked up belligerently.

Evan got out the photo. "It's not a particularly good picture, but do you think you saw this woman? She was wearing a gray-green raincoat last night and had an expensive silk scarf around her head. She looks elegant and fashionable and slightly foreign, I'd say. I think she'd stand out among the usual crowd."

The ticket collector took the photo and studied it intently. "Can't say that I remember her," he said, "but there was a big crush of people getting off last night, on account of it being Friday. Was she on the five o'clock train?"

"No, the one after it—it got in around seven-thirty, I think she said."

The little man shook his head triumphantly. "Is that what she told you? There wasn't a seven-thirty train last night. It was delayed—points failure at Crewe. It didn't get in until after nine."

"Is that so? Thanks a lot. You've been very helpful." Watkins turned to Evans with a knowing look. "So she didn't get back from London last night," he muttered, as they moved out of earshot of the now-curious ticket collector. "Now I'm dying to hear whether she was ever there at all. Great. That gives us one person with motive and opportunity. We're getting somewhere, Evans."

"Excuse me, mate." The ticket collector tapped Evan on the arm. "You were here a few weeks ago, weren't you. You put a young girl with black hair on the London train."

"You've got a good memory," Evan said.

"Ah well, in my line of work, I've sort of trained myself to notice things." The ticket collector was now bursting with importance. "I noticed her because there was something odd. She had wet hair for one thing. And you were all wet, too, weren't you. That's what stuck in my mind."

"Quite right," Evan said. "Her car went into a lake. I pulled her out."

Watkins looked surprised.

"Hiding your light under a bush . . ." he began but the ticket collector cut him short. "You know she came back, sir."

"What?"

"That girl came back. Earlier this week. I recognized her right away."

"Did she now," Evan said. "Do you remember what day it was?"

"Could have been Tuesday. There was a go-slow down in London on Tuesday and the train got in late. Yes, I think that was it."

"And do you remember anything else? Was anyone here to meet her? Did she get into a car?"

The man shook his head. "I didn't see. I had to take the tickets, didn't I?"

"Well, thanks very much," Evan said. "That's very interesting."

"Is she a wanted criminal?" the man asked excitedly. "One of those drug pushers? She looked shifty to me."

"No. Nothing like that," Evan said. "Thanks again for your help."

"What was that about?" Watkins asked as they headed back to the car.

"Oh, just something that happened when Bronwen and I were on a hike. A car went into a lake. I got the girl out and put her on a train to London."

"Oh, nothing to do with this business then?"

"I don't see how . . ." Evan began, but then he paused, his mind racing to connections he hadn't considered before. "The strange thing was that the first time I saw her, she was coming out of the Powell-Joneses' house, right before the Llewellyns moved in. I suppose it was just coincidence . . ."

"We've got one good lead to go on already today," Watkins said. "Let's get back to Llanfair and wait for Mrs. Llewellyn to show up with her son. I'm interested to hear how she's going to explain this."

They were back in Llanfair half an hour later but there was no sign of Mrs. Llewellyn's car. Sergeant Watkins's face fell. "I'll put in a call to HQ," he said. "They were checking the departure lists checked at the airport. Lord, I hope she hasn't run for it."

"Give her time, Sarge," Evan said. "She couldn't have made it to Manchester and back yet, and you know what airports are like, especially on a summer weekend. If she's not back by two o'clock, then you can start worrying."

"I don't care what you say, I am worrying now," Watkins said. "We'll have the D.I. showing up any moment."

"Now might be a good time for Mrs. Powell-Jones to take a look at the house," Evan said. "And Gladys, too."

"Good idea. You go and find the Powell-Jones woman. I'll put in a call for a car to pick up Gladys. I'd say that neither of them miss much. Between them we'll know if anything was moved or removed."

Evan unlocked the police station for the sergeant to make his call and then went in search of Mrs. Powell-Jones. It was possible that she'd gone back to her mother, but he didn't think so. He suspected that Mrs. Powell-Jones was as curious as anyone about a suspicious death in her house.

Gladys hurried along Pool Street, clutching her basket in front of her. What with all the summer visitors, Caernarfon was getting too crowded these days. They should leave the residents in peace to do their shopping, not clutter up the pavements buying postcards and ice creams!

At least she had a little more time before the shops shut, thanks to the lift Mrs. Llewellyn had given her. A nice lady, after all. She'd always seemed a bit quiet and standoffish before. She'd left Gladys to get on with her work and never stopped to chat or gossip, but today she had been quite talkative, asking Gladys the same kind of questions the police had asked her. That was understandable, of course. She wanted to find out exactly what had happened to her husband. It was only natural, wasn't it?

Gladys wished she had been able to tell her more—like who the late visitor was, for instance. That was bothering her—there was something about that voice. She hadn't heard any of the actual words spoken, but the way the voice rose and fell—she was sure she'd recognize it if she heard it again.

The clock on the castle struck twelve. Gladys glanced up. She just had time to pop into the greengrocers and pick up a nice bunch of leeks and some fresh peas for

Sunday lunch. She wanted to be back when the police sent a car for her. A satisfied smile spread across her face. What would that snobby Mrs. Thomas at number thirty-one think now? Gladys hoped, not for the first time, that she'd been seen arriving in a Mercedes this morning.

She stood impatiently on the corner where Pool Street came into Castle Square. So much traffic these days. She could remember when she was a girl and they didn't even need to have zebra crossings or lights saying WALK NOW. A coach had disgorged its passengers and they swept toward her in a talking, laughing tide. Gladys glared at the DON'T CROSS light. Really, pedestrians had no rights these days. She inched forward, ready to dart across before the tourists the moment the light changed.

As she glanced down the street a flash of color caught her attention and recognition lit up her face. So that's who it was! Of course. It made sense now. Across Castle Square a policeman blew his whistle and the traffic surged forward in a roaring jumble of cars, buses, and lorries. Gladys moved impatiently from one foot to the other and shifted her basket to her hip. Suddenly something struck her in the middle of her back. She went lurching forward. She was conscious of a big dark shape in front of her, then, ridiculously, of flying . . .

Evan was met by a very harassed-looking Mrs. Williams at his landlady's front door. "Oh, there you are, Mr. Evans," she said. "I've got both Powell-Joneses here, in the sitting room. I hope it's not much longer before she can get into her house again. She's already found dust on my picture frames and now she's asked to borrow my best sheets and pillowcases."

"What on earth for?"

Mrs. Williams leaned conspiratorially close. "She's got to make him new robes for the *eisteddfod*. The ones she made him are too tight."

"Oh, the *eisteddfod*—right." So much had been going on that he'd forgotten about it. He was supposed to be performing tonight, wasn't he? "The bard's competition is tomorrow, isn't it. I'm surprised he's going to enter a competition on the Sabbath."

Mrs. Williams's eyes twinkled. "It's a very holy kind of competition, Mr. Evans," she said.

"Nonsense. You know as well as I do that the tradition of crowning the bard goes back to the Druids and pagan times. It couldn't be more unholy."

Mrs. Williams chuckled. "Don't you go telling him that now. Set his heart on winning, he has. This year he's determined to beat Mr. Parry Davies."

She pushed open the living room door. "Here's Mr. Evans back now."

The Powell-Joneses looked up in annoyance at the interruption. The reverend was standing with a white sheet pinned over his shoulders, looking like an amateur production of *Julius Caesar*. His wife was in the process of pinning a tablecloth around his head.

"Very fetching, Reverend," Evan couldn't resist saying.

Edward Powell-Jones merely scowled.

"Should I make us all a nice pot of tea?" Mrs. Williams asked brightly.

"We've only just had lunch," Mrs. Powell-Jones said with annoyance. "Too much eating and drinking is unhealthy."

"Especially drinking." Her husband glanced in Evan's direction. "And gluttony is one of the deadly sins."

"How much longer am I to be kept here, Mr. Evans?" Mrs. Powell-Jones demanded. "I have many important things that I should be doing today. I had hoped to go down to the *eisteddfod* this afternoon and see if the judging has taken place for the craft events yet. I entered one of my tapestries, you know. A fine rendition of Caernarfon Castle, worked in local Welsh wool."

"If you're ready to accompany me now, Mrs. Powell-Jones, I think you'd be able to do your tour of the house."

"Finally," she said, giving a triumphant smile. "I won't ask you to accompany me, dear." She patted her husband's hand. "You have your speech to work on, as well as your sermon for the morning. Besides, men are quite useless. They never notice anything."

"But what about . . ." Edward Powell-Jones began as Mrs. Powell-Jones made for the door. She swept out of Mrs. Williams's cottage like a ship in full sail. Evan followed.

"Mrs. Powell-Jones has come to do a tour of the house," he said to the new shift of policemen at the gate. Bulbs flashed, microphones were thrust in their direction. "Hey, lady. You own the place, right?" a transatlantic voice demanded. "See any hanky-panky while they were here? Did he bring in any babes?"

Mrs. Powell-Jones turned to give him such a withering glance that the microphone seemed to droop in his hand. Then she went on her way, unhindered.

"Hmmph," she said as she was shown into the drawing room by Sergeant Watkins.

"You've seen something, madam?" he asked.

"They've been moving the furniture around, for one thing."

"Really?"

"That little desk was always against the far wall. It really doesn't go at all where they've got it now. The cheek of some people. I specifically said that I wanted everything left as it was . . ."

Watkins nodded to the lab technicians to move the desk.

"Aha," one of them exclaimed, dropping to his knees. "She's right. This is probably where he fell. These look like blood spatters, don't they?"

"It would tie in with the way he was dragged," the other agreed. "Hold on while I take some samples. Then we need to get photos of the spatter pattern, but I'd say he fell here right enough."

Mrs. Powell-Jones looked at them with astonishment. "Are you now telling me that he didn't fall and hit his head on my fireplace? Somebody dragged him over there? Why?"

"No doubt it will all come out in good time, madam," Sergeant Watkins said evenly. "Now, please take a good look around. Has anything else been moved. Is anything missing?"

She studied the room in silence then she let out a horrified cry. "Something most definitely is missing, Officer. One of my prized possessions—a bronze statue of an eagle in flight. It used to sit here, on the sideboard." She pointed dramatically at the spot where there was now an innocuous bowl of fruit.

Watkins glanced at Evan. "A bronze statue. We better search the garden and the area outside."

Evan didn't like to say that the area outside extended to a hundred or so square miles of rugged mountains. Anyone who wanted to dispose of a bronze statue could do so in any number of streams or gullies, over cliffs, under bracken, even down abandoned mine shafts. Some areas were so hard to reach that there was a good chance a hidden object might never be found.

"Make sure it is recovered immediately, Sergeant," Mrs. Powell-Jones said. "It belonged to my grandfather. It is a priceless family heirloom."

"We'll do our best, madam. I promise you," Watkins said. He broke off as he became aware of a disturbance outside. Voices were raised. A car door slammed. Evan ran outside to see the black Mercedes waiting at the police cordon. A young man in jeans and a black T-shirt had just got out.

"We're his family," he was saying to the unmoving policeman. "They sent my mother to the airport to pick me up and we were told to come straight back here. Well, here we are."

Evan stared at the newcomer. He was a slim young man with hair cut very short in the European way. He had an angular, boyish face and an air of arrogance. Evan had seen him before, he was sure of that. But where?

The young man's voice had risen until he was yelling over the background noise. "Now for God's sake move the damned tape."

The voice was familiar—a young voice raised in anger. A car door slamming and a young girl shouting, "Bugger off, Justin!"

That was it! He had seen Justin twice before—once fighting with a young girl outside the Powell-Joneses' driveway where he now stood, and once at the edge of a lake when a car went into the water.

FOURTEEN

EVAN MANAGED A WELCOMING SMILE as he went to meet the newcomer. "Mr. Llewellyn? We've been expecting you. Please come in. Sergeant Watkins is waiting."

"This way?" the young man asked indicating the house. He moved aside as his mother drove her car back into its parking space. "Will they need to talk to my mother anymore? She's very tired. Naturally she didn't sleep well last night."

"Just a few more questions, sir."

A spasm of anger crossed Justin Llewellyn's face. "I can't see why we're being put through all this. Aren't the news media bad enough? We've been hounded for years, you know. My poor mother—she couldn't go anywhere without someone letting off flashbulbs in her face."

"I'm very sorry, sir," Evan said. "We're only doing our job. Following instructions."

Justin looked at him scornfully. "I don't see what my mother or I have to do with a really unfortunate accident. We were both far away, minding our own business."

Evan opened the door and ushered the young man inside. He stood in the hallway, waiting for his mother to catch up.

"It happened in the drawing room," Evan said.

Justin looked around. "The drawing room?"

"You've never been here before, sir?" Evan asked.

"Good God, no. I've stayed well away. My father and I were on different planets, Constable. He led his life, I led mine."

"So you didn't come to visit your mother?"

"I just told you." Justin's voice had risen again. "I arrived from Milan this morning. Do you want to look at my boarding pass?" He turned to his mother. "Really, this is too much. Why don't we just get out of here and go to a hotel somewhere?"

"This won't take long, sir," Evan said, "but I know the detective sergeant has a couple of questions." He pushed open the drawing room door. "In here, please."

Mrs. Powell-Jones, Sergeant Watkins, and the two lab technicians looked up with interest as the Llewellyns were ushered in.

"Oh good, you've arrived at the right moment," Sergeant Watkins said. The relief that Mrs. Llewellyn had shown up again was noticeable on his face. "Maybe there's something you can clear up for us. This is Mrs. Powell-Jones." The minister's wife nodded her head graciously in a sort of regal greeting. "She owns the house and she has noticed that a valuable object is missing."

Justin looked around the room with amusement. "Does she think you've been pinching the silver, Mother? Doesn't she realize that you could buy her and her house many times over?"

Mrs. Llewellyn gave him a warning frown. "What kind of object, Sergeant?"

"A bronze sculpture," Mrs. Powell-Jones said. "Of an eagle in flight, presented by the grateful employees to my grandfather on his fiftieth anniversary as owner of the slate quarry."

"It sat there on the sideboard, apparently." Sergeant Watkins pointed. "Where the fruit bowl is now."

Unaccountably Mrs. Llewellyn began to laugh. "That thing?" she said. "Is that what all the fuss is about?" She started for the door. "Please come with me," she said. "I think this is one mystery I can clear up for you." She led them to the big oak cupboard under the stairs and opened the door. "Is that what you're looking for?" she asked.

Mrs. Powell-Jones gave a cry and darted in to retrieve the bronze bird from among the rags and brushes. "My valuable sculpture, tossed into a broom cupboard!"

Sergeant Watkins took it from her. "Just a moment, madam." He turned to Mrs. Llewellyn. "Any idea how the statue wound up in there?"

Mrs. Llewellyn was still trying not to smile. "I can tell you exactly when it was put in there, Sergeant. It was placed there the day we arrived, by my husband. He said it was a god-awful Victorian horror and he couldn't stand to look at it on a daily basis."

"Well, I never did! The cheek of it!" Mrs. Powell-Jones clutched at her throat, stricken. "If you've quite finished, Sergeant, I think I'll be going now. I promised my mother I'd check in on her and I want to see if they've finished judging my tapestry . . . besides which it's too painful to stay here any longer."

"I understand, madam," Sergeant Watkins said. "Thank you for your assistance. We have your phone number, don't we? We may be calling on you again."

"Not to tell me that more valuable pieces of artwork have been flung into cupboards, I hope," she snapped. Then she made a grand exit.

"Whoops," Justin said, grinning at his mother. "You really put your foot into that, didn't you?"

"Well, for once I agreed with Ifor. It is truly hideous," Mrs. Llewellyn said. Then her eyes widened as she focused on the bronze bird. "Why were you so interested, Sergeant? You can't think . . . are you suggesting that my husband might have been hit with . . . that?"

"We're not ruling out any possibilities, madam."

"Let the poor man rest in peace, Sergeant," she said. "Why try and find a mystery when there isn't one?"

"No, madam. Just trying to get to the truth," Watkins said. "Now if we could go somewhere to talk where we won't be disturbed?"

"I think the minister's study is across the hall," Evan said. He led the way to a dark, book-lined room. Watkins took the chair at the desk and offered the two leather armchairs to the Llewellyns. Evan stood at the doorway. Mrs. Llewellyn was no longer smiling.

"Well. Get on with it," Justin said.

He was tense, Evan noticed, perched on the edge of his chair, his fingers plucking at the fabric of his trouser leg.

Watkins cleared his throat. "You arrived in this country only this morning, is that correct, sir?"

"That's correct. I got in at ten-thirty. Nine o'clock flight out of Milan. You gain an hour coming this way, you know. I've got my ticket and boarding pass somewhere . . ." He started fumbling with his jacket pocket.

"That won't be necessary for the moment," Watkins said. "You were in Milan when you got the news?"

"In Bellagio. We have a summer home on Lake Como. That's where I was."

"Were you alone in the house?"

"Apart from the servants."

"You have a sister, I believe," Watkins asked. "She wasn't there with you?"

"My sister is a career woman," Justin said with something close to a sneer. "She is very busy in Milan, arranging fashion shoots. She pops up to the lake when she gets a chance but I haven't seen her in a while."

"So how long since you were in England, Mr. Llew-ellyn?" Evan asked.

Justin spun around to stare at him, as if he had com-pletely forgotten his presence. "In England last? Gosh, that must have been awhile ago now. Last spring some-time? I've forgotten. Can you remember, Mother?"

"I think you came over when Dad did that gala per-formance at Covent Garden back in March," Mrs. Llew-ellyn said evenly. She was looking steadily at her son.

"Oh, that's right." The young man sounded relieved. "Of course. I remember now."

"And you haven't been over since?" Evan asked. He noticed Watkins's querying look.

"Not that I can remember," Justin said.

"So you've never been here before?"

"Good God, no. Why would I want to come to a dump like this? Especially if my father was here. I'd keep well away, believe me."

"As a matter of course, sir," Watkins said, making Jus-tin turn back to him, "can you detail for us your move-ments this week?"

"My movements this week? Do you think I killed him by remote control from Milan?" He gave a brittle laugh, paused, and then said, "That is what you're getting at, isn't it? The reason for all these questions—you don't think it was an accident at all."

"No, sir," Watkins said. "We have reason to suspect that it wasn't an accident."

"Then I suggest you start looking further afield, Ser-geant," Justin said. "There were many people in the world who wished my father dead, but my mother and I weren't among them. There were times when he annoyed us, but we had plenty of reasons for wanting him alive . . . including a very generous allowance in my case."

"You must be tired after your flight," Sergeant Watkins said. "If you'd just be good enough to write down for us your complete movements during the week, with the names and addresses of people we could contact as witnesses . . ."

Justin rose to his feet. "I just told you, Officer," he said in a shrill voice, "I had no reason to kill my father. None at all. Now will you stop hounding me!"

"We haven't even started hounding yet, sir," Watkins said pleasantly. "We'll be asking the same questions of everyone who was connected with your father. Show him out, will you, Evans?"

Mrs. Llewellyn rose to accompany her son.

"Not you, madam," Sergeant Watkins said. "We have a few more details to go over with you."

"But I thought I answered any possible questions earlier," she said. "Really, I'm very tired and I'd enjoy being able to relax with my son . . ."

"Only one question," Sergeant Watkins said as Evan came back into the room. "Where were you, really, yesterday?"

Evan saw her visibly start. "What do you mean? I told you. I was in London. I came back on the seven-thirty train."

She saw Watkins look across at Evan.

"What are you trying to tell me?" she demanded.

"There was no seven-thirty train last night, Mrs. Llewellyn," Evan said. "It was an hour and a half late, due to a points failure at Crewe. It hadn't even got in to Bangor when you showed up at this house."

"So I'll repeat the question, Mrs. Llewellyn," Watkins said. "Where were you yesterday?"

"Oh, very well." She gave a dramatic sigh. "I suppose I should have told you right away and saved all this unpleasantness. I came back from London a day early and I spent the day with friends in Llandudno. I didn't want Ifor to know where I was. He didn't like these particular friends, so I had to arrange meetings around other trips."

Watkins opened his notebook. "The name and number of these friends in Llandudno, if you don't mind."

"They're not in Llandudno any longer. We just found it a convenient place to meet. The home address is actually in Cheshire. But I can look the number up for you."

"And the place you stayed in Llandudno—they'll have a record of your stay, will they?"

For the first time she looked really flustered. "I—didn't actually sign the register myself. My friend's name will be there, of course."

"Of course," Watkins said.

Evan's opinion of Watkins's interviewing techniques was steadily rising. He was being quiet and genial and yet succeeding in getting Mrs. Llewellyn rattled.

"We have a picture of Mrs. Llewellyn that we can show for identification purposes, don't we, Evans?" Watkins asked, looking over her head.

"That's right, sir." Evan produced the picture from his pocket.

"That's my personal property. You've no right . . ." she began.

"Don't worry. I'll take good care of it," Evan said. "You'll get it back, good as new. Unless you'd like to supply us with a better one. This one's rather old now and it doesn't show you clearly."

"Oh, keep it," she snapped. "I don't suppose you can do much harm to it."

"What did you want me to do, sir?" Evan asked.

"I thought we'd take a spin down to Llandudno—see if anyone at the hotel could vouch for Mrs. Llewellyn being there."

The woman's face had flushed bright red. "Is that really necessary?" she asked.

"You've nothing to worry about if you're telling us the truth, have you?"

"Well, the truth is . . . Sergeant. I was there with . . . a close friend . . . a married, close friend. I'd hate him to be dragged into this."

"Let us have his name and address and we'll be discreet, madam," Watkins said. "We're trying to find out who killed your husband. I'm sure you'd want to give us your full cooperation, wouldn't you?"

"Yes, I would," she said.

She took the piece of paper Watkins offered her. "Very well. His name's James Norton. He lives in Cheshire. I'm not quite sure of the post code . . ."

"The phone number would be helpful," Watkins added.

She scribbled quickly and handed him back the paper. "He really doesn't need to be brought into this, you know. It's not fair on him."

"As I said, madam, the police are trained to be discreet."

She gave him a disbelieving stare. "Am I free to go now?"

"For the moment, yes. But please stay within reach at the inn. And make sure your son gives us the details we wanted."

"Very well," she said.

Evan escorted her to the front door. Watkins followed. As they crossed the front hall, Evan noticed her glancing down at the floor.

"What happened to my shoe?" she asked. She was trying to make it come out casually.

"The shoe? Oh, I think the lab boys have got it bagged ready for fingerprinting."

"A shoe?" She attempted a laugh. "Surely nobody can think that Ifor was killed with a lady's stiletto?"

"Just routine, ma'am," Evan said. "Any suspicious object needs checking out. You'll get it back. Do you remember where you left the other one?"

"I . . ." she looked around. "I expect Gladys must have tidied it up by now. She must have missed this one."

Right, Evan thought. She was hardly likely to miss a shoe right outside the drawing room door.

He opened the front door for her. "We'll be in touch," he said.

"And . . . you will be . . . tactful?"

"Yes madam. We will be tactful."

He watched her hurry to join her son, who was standing by the car.

"Do you think there's something strange about that shoe?" Watkins asked as he closed the door.

"I'm not sure. That's something we can ask Gladys when she gets back here—whether she noticed the shoe yesterday."

Watkins glanced at his watch. "She should be here by now. I think I'll give them a call and see when they're likely to get here."

He disappeared into the study. Evan heard him say, "Not there? Are you sure they went to the right address?"

He was frowning when he came back to Evan. "The stupid woman wasn't there. The constable knocked several times."

"She probably took longer to do her shopping than she'd planned," Evan said.

"Or she decided she didn't want to be mixed up in this," Watkins added.

Evan didn't agree. He thought that Gladys was relishing her role as star witness.

"Ask the neighbors," he said. "Maybe she just popped next door to tell them all the juicy details."

Watkins nodded. "You could be right. Okay. Let's follow up on the Llandudno business, shall we? That was a turn up for the books, wasn't it? Went to meet her lover?" He winked at Evan. "What's sauce for the gander is sauce for the goose, eh?"

"And it gives her a motive for killing her husband," Evan pointed out. "If he'd found out about the relationship and refused to give her the divorce . . ."

"She might have been desperate enough to get him out of her way," Watkins finished. "I wish we could turn up the murder weapon, or I don't see how we'll ever be able to tie her to the crime."

Evan nodded. "Nobody that I questioned saw her sneaking back earlier. Of course I haven't been house to house yet."

"And, as we know, it's easy enough to park up at the Everest Inn and come down that footpath without being seen at all," Watkins agreed with a sigh. "She used that way herself this morning." He put his hand on the drawing room door and went in. "Are you still here?" he demanded. "What do they do—pay you double time on Saturdays? Or are you trying to get out of the weekly shop with the wife?"

"We're about to leave, Sarge," one of the technicians said with a grin. "I think we've given everything a good going-over." He was carrying a tray full of plastic bags, all neatly labeled.

"Found anything new and interesting?"

"Only this." He held up a small Ziploc bag. It contained a black hair about six inches long. "We found it on the carpet beside him. It might be his, of course. He wore his hair long for a man, didn't he? But his hair was curly and this is dead straight. And it seems finer than his, too."

Wheels were turning inside Evan's brain. Successive pictures flashed through his head . . . a girl's black hair plastered to her face as he dragged her to shore. That same girl saying emphatically, "He's not my boyfriend!"

He took the photo out of his pocket and stared hard at the two children . . . a skinnier version of Justin was smiling up at the camera and beside him a shy, scowling face, half-hidden by black hair.

Evan grabbed the sergeant's arm and pulled him aside.

"I think we should go after Mrs. Llewellyn and tell her we'd like to speak to her daughter," he said.

FIFTEEN

"SO YOU MANAGED TO GET away after all, Constable Evans." Roberts-the-Pump greeted Evan as they met in the *eisteddfod* car park that evening. "We thought we'd have to go ahead and sing without you."

"Yes, they took pity on me and let me off for the night," Evan said.

The choir members looked serious and self-conscious in their black Sunday suits and stiff white collars—*like a lot of overgrown boys,* Evan thought.

"The crowd of reporters has thinned out," he said. "They lost interest when we wouldn't let them speak to Mrs. Llewellyn or see inside the house. Now there's just one or two diehards camped out for the night. The rest are pestering the D.I. in Caernarfon."

"So it's true what we heard, is it, Evan *bach?*" Charlie Hopkins moved closer to Evan. "Someone really coshed him on the head?"

"It looks that way, Charlie," Evan said. "The D.I. hasn't said so officially, so I can't say any more."

"We saw them out searching along the riverbank and in the fields," Harry-the-Pub said with excitement in his voice. "Was it the murder weapon they were looking for?"

"Possibly," Evan said. "I'm just the village bobby. They don't let me in on their detective work."

"Go on with you!" Evans-the-Meat gave him a hearty shove. "Thick as thieves with that sergeant, you are. Everyone knows they couldn't solve crimes without you, so they just call you in secretly, like."

"That's not true," Evan said uncomfortably.

"Well they can't be onto anything or they'd never have let you come down here and sing," Evans-the-Meat said firmly. "Charlie's wife reckons it was that Mafia hit man who did it. Have the police found him yet?"

"Not that I know of," Evan said. "They're making enquiries."

Evans-the-Meat snorted. "Making enquiries! That's what they always say when they've bloody well gone and lost the suspect."

Evan decided it was high time they changed the subject. He looked around. "Where's Mostyn then?"

"We're supposed to be meeting him at the pavilion. He wanted to listen to the other performances," Evans-the-Meat said. "He's certainly a glutton for punishment, isn't he?" He broke off and stood there, listening. Over the other sounds, the strains of a male voice choir singing "Men of Harlech" floated on the breeze toward them. "He'll probably have to hear "Men of Harlech" sung a hundred times today."

Evan smiled. "He loves his music, doesn't he?"

"Loves his music? It's the only thing he lives for," Evans-the-Meat agreed.

"I think it's very good of him to agree to go ahead with our performance tonight." Evan was remembering Mostyn's ashen face as he looked down at the corpse. "He must know we won't sound as good as the other choirs without Ifor."

They left the trampled grass of the car park and

showed their passes at the competitors' entrance into the main field. A strong, salty breeze from the ocean was flapping all the banners and bunting. The setting sun had tinted all the tents with a rosy glow. Good smells greeted them from the many food booths around the periphery. Sizzling sausages and frying onions, the more exotic scent of curried chicken kebabs, fish and chips, donuts, toffee apples, and candy floss all competed to lure the hungry traveler. There were also stalls devoted to pure Welsh produce—bowls of thick steaming lamb cawl, or grilled lamb chops, laver bread made from seaweed, local oysters and crab sandwiches, and local baked goods like Welsh cakes and bara brith.

Evan was reminded painfully that he hadn't had a good meal in weeks and no proper meal at all today. After their performance he'd stop and treat himself to a big helping of fish and chips—and a pint of Brains beer.

They were passing the tents that housed the crafts exhibits now. Suddenly he heard the sound of shouts and screams. A scuffle seemed to have broken out in a pavilion designated "Handicrafts Made from Local Wool." He could see arms flailing in the middle of a crowd of people. He looked around for police or security guards, then decided he had better intervene himself.

The tent seemed to contain displays of knitted baby clothes, crocheted afghans and sweaters, woven rugs— nothing that could possibly attract a thief or a vandal. He pushed his way through the crowd that had gathered. "Alright. Calm down everyone. North Wales Police," he announced. "What's going on here?"

"Fighting like wildcats they were," an elderly official said, taking out his handkerchief to mop a perspiring bald head.

"She started it," an angry woman's voice cut in.

"You had no right to try to copy me!" another voice retorted. Evan knew that voice instantly. He saw that the two fighting wildcats, now being held apart by obliging

spectators, were none other than Mrs. Powell-Jones and
Mrs. Parry Davies.

"You two should be ashamed of yourselves. Ministers'
wives, too!" He stepped in between them.

"I was pushed beyond my limits, Constable Evans,"
Mrs. Powell-Jones said. "I am a Christian, God-fearing
woman, but that woman riles me to the extent that I can
no longer control myself." She grabbed Evan's arm.
"Look you, what she had the nerve to do this time!"

She indicated a table full of tapestry work. Side by
side were two tapestry pictures, one labeled, "Caernarfon
Castle," by E. Powell-Jones. The other "Caernarfon Castle at Sunset" by J. Parry Davies.

"How was I to know the stupid woman was also doing
a tapestry of Caernarfon Castle?" Mrs. Parry Davies demanded.

"Because you spied on me, that's why," Mrs. Powell-
Jones said. "You know I always work on my tapestry in
the living room and I don't always draw the curtains."

"How do I know that you didn't spy on me?" Mrs.
Parry Davies asked. "I always work on my tapestry in
my living room and that gives directly onto the street."

"Of course your house, or should one say cottage, is
visible to all and sundry, not set back in its own grounds,
that is true," Mrs. Powell-Jones said. "But I can assure
you that I have never had the desire to peek in at your
windows. I have been working on this particular tapestry
for almost a year now."

"What do you think I did with mine—run it up last
night?" Mrs. Parry Davies demanded. "I've been working
on mine for over a year."

"Hmmph. Obviously a slow worker," Mrs. Powell-
Jones shot back.

Evan held out his hands as the two women were about
to start again. "Ladies. There's no law that says you can't
do the same subject, is there? Why not let the judges
decide who has done the better work?"

"Because mine is worked in the true subtle hues of North Wales and hers has the lurid glow of a Caribbean sunset," Mrs. Powell-Jones said. "Naturally those over-bright colors will attract the judge's eye first."

"Thank you. I'm glad you admit that mine is more outstanding," Mrs. Parry Davies retorted.

Evan glanced at the worried-looking official, then frowned at the two women. "If this gentleman wishes to press charges of disturbing the peace, I shall have to con-fiscate these two works of art as evidence," he said. "Then neither of you will have a chance in the judging."

"You couldn't . . . you wouldn't!" Mrs. Powell-Jones's face flushed brick red.

"I most certainly would." Evan couldn't resist a smile. "So are you going to promise to behave, or do I take the pictures with me?"

"Really!" Mrs. Parry Davies glared at Mrs. Powell-Jones. "I don't see why my chances of winning should be spoiled by a jealous imitator."

"Me, the imitator?"

Evan picked up the two pictures and tucked them un-der his arm. "Do I take these with me or do you promise to go away and not come back until the judging is over?"

"Oh, very well, Constable," Mrs. Powell-Jones said at last. "Put them back. I expect the judges will be able to detect superior needlework when they see it."

"I want you both to leave first," Evan said.

The two women glared at him, then swept out of the tent like two ships in full sail.

"*Diolch yn fawr,* Constable," the official said, tucking his handkerchief back into his breast pocket. "Thanks very much. I didn't know what I was going to do with them. Proper pair of wildcats they were."

"I know. I have to live in the same village as them," Evan said. He left the tent and hurried to catch up with his choir.

Applause was spilling from one of the larger pavilions.

Evan glanced inside and was rooted to the spot. A young woman sat on stage, holding a harp to her. Her long blond hair spilled over her shoulders like spun gold. Her dark blue skirt was spread out around her so that she looked like an exquisite white nymph in the middle of a pool of blue water. For a second Evan's heart flip-flopped. He thought it was Bronwen. Then he realized that this girl was younger and a stranger.

He walked on, still shaken by what he had seen and by his reaction. He hadn't realized it before, but Bronwen was beautiful. She had that same otherworldly quality of the young harpist, a special something that made people turn and stare . . . and that made his heart lurch.

He looked around hopefully. Was it possible that she was still here? Hardly. It was getting late. She would have taken her young schoolchildren home by now. And she hadn't displayed any great enthusiasm for coming to his performance tonight. He had spoiled everything by agreeing to go on a meaningless date with Betsy. How could he have been such a fool? Of course Bronwen misunderstood. As soon as he got back, he'd tell Betsy that the date was off. He had to stop trying to please everybody. It never worked. If only he could find Bronwen and . . .

He wondered for a second if he was hallucinating. She was coming toward him through the crowd, her long braid over one shoulder, wearing a red cape that flowed out behind her and made her look ridiculously like a children's book illustration of Little Red Riding Hood.

"Bron!" he called.

Her face lit up as she spotted him. "Evan! I didn't think you'd be here, after all the goings-on in the village."

"They didn't need me anymore. D.I. Hughes has taken over," Evan said.

"Taken over what?" Bronwen looked puzzled.

"You hadn't heard. It wasn't an accident at all. Ifor

Llewellyn was killed and afterward it was made to look like an accident."

"Well, I never!" She sounded like Mrs. Williams. "Was it a robbery?"

"No. Nothing was taken. There was nothing worth stealing. They had left all their good stuff in Italy."

"Do they have any idea who might have done it? And, more to the point, do you have any idea who might have done it?"

"I've got some ideas," Evan said. "The D.I.'s inclined to go along with the Mafia theory at the moment. It makes him feel important to keep getting calls from Interpol." He grinned at her and she smiled back. "I'm glad you're still here," he said. "I thought you would have had to take the children back home by now."

"One of the fathers took them back in his van," she said. "I wanted to stay a little longer and get a look at the exhibits for myself . . . and listen to some of the singing."

"Don't expect too much from our choir," Evan said. "We're not exactly Covent Garden material without Ifor."

"Don't worry, I've brought my earplugs," she said, smiling.

"Do you want to get something to eat after we've finished," he asked, "and walk around a little?"

She nodded. "I'd like that—if you're not planning to meet Betsy at the rock concert."

"Rock concert? That's too tame for us. We only go to raves," Evan said. Then he grew serious. "Look, I'm sorry about Betsy. I just didn't want to hurt her feelings. You know that."

"Yes. I know that. Evan the Boy Scout."

"I'm getting better. I just told Mrs. Powell-Jones to pipe down and behave herself."

"Evan, you didn't!"

"I certainly did. Enjoyed every moment of it, too."

Bronwen slipped her arm through his. "Are you heading for the choir pavilion right now?"

"I should be. We're on soon. Mostyn will get in a state if I'm not there."

"I'll walk over with you."

The crowd was thicker here in the middle of things. People streamed from one marquee to the next as new events started. A children's dance troop had just finished performing in one of the main pavilions. They came running out, twelve little girls all dressed in white with flowers in their hair, like little angels from a Renaissance painting.

"Now can we get hot dogs?" they demanded of their chaperon.

Evan and Bronwen exchanged a smile.

"I'm sorry I overreacted about Betsy," she said. "I must be an insecure person. It comes from a failed marriage, I suppose."

"You've no reason to feel insecure," Evan said. "I'm a reliable kind of chap who—"

A loud scream made him break off in midsentence. "Evan Evans! Oh my goodness. It is you!" A young woman flung herself into his arms and kissed him full on the mouth.

SIXTEEN

"MAGGIE!" EVAN GASPED WHEN THE girl finally released him. "What are you doing here?"

"I'm helping a friend with her dance troop," she said, still beaming up at him delightedly. "She wanted someone to help chaperon the children so I said I'd come along for a bit of a lark. Makes a change from Swansea, doesn't it? And who knows, I might even get interested in culture." She ran her fingers through dark curls. "So where are you these days? You're not still in that godforsaken little village, are you?"

"That's right. Still in the same place."

"I couldn't believe it when your mother told me that you'd gone back to North Wales. Whatever for, I said. There's nothing but rain and sheep up there—and people who look like sheep."

Evan felt a light tap on his arm. "Would you like to introduce me, Evan?"

"Oh Bronwen. Of course. This is Maggie Pole. We knew each other down in Swansea."

"We knew each other very well, down in Swansea,"

the girl said, eyeing Bronwen's long hair and swirling cloak. "Are you performing here?"

"No, just a supporter."

"Oh, I thought because of the costume." She herself was wearing jeans and a Swansea Rugby Club sweat shirt saying FOR RUGBY PLAYERS A TRY IS A SCORE.

"This is Bronwen Price," Evan said quickly. "She teaches at the village school in Llanfair."

"A schoolteacher?" Maggie shook her head. "I reckon you deserve a medal, having to put up with the little brats every day. One trip up in the bus was enough to convince me that children and I don't get along." She smiled up at Evan. "So do you have time for a chat? My little angels have just gone off to get food so I'm free for a while and I'd love to give you all the news from back home. Have you heard about the rugby club? It's gone pro. They're paying their best players now. How about that— if you'd stuck around, you could have quit being a policeman and made your fortune at rugby."

"Hardly," Evan said awkwardly. "I was never that good."

"You were bloody good and you know it," Maggie said. She looked past Evan to Bronwen. "He always was too modest. That was one of his very few deficiencies, wasn't it, Evan love?"

"Look, Maggie, I'd love to talk but my choir is about to sing and the choir director will have a fit if I don't show up."

"Singing? You? That's a new one!" Maggie laughed loudly. "The only time I heard you sing was in the bus on the way home from rugby games and you couldn't sing those songs at an *eisteddfod,* could you?" She looked around then leaned closer to Evan. "What a bloody boring thing this is, isn't it? All in Welsh, too, and you know how bad my Welsh is. I mean—"

"Look, Maggie. I'm sorry but I have to go," Evan interrupted. He could feel Bronwen's eyes boring into him.

"You won't be singing that long, will you?" Maggie asked. "Let's go for a drink afterward. They've got decent South Wales beer, I notice. You, too, if you'd like, Miss Price," she added.

"Oh, that's okay, thanks," Bronwen said. "I should be getting back home. I'm sure you and Evan have a lot to talk about."

"Don't go, Bron," Evan said but she shook her head solemnly. "I think this is one case where three is definitely a crowd." She moved off into the crowd before Evan could stop her.

"Oh dear, have I upset her?" Maggie asked, turning big surprised eyes on him. "I didn't mean anything— only I was so surprised to see you and I have to hear how you're doing. I'll meet you at the beer tent shall I?"

"If you like," Evan said.

He could feel the sweat trickling down the back of his neck as he went into the choir pavilion. Of all the people in the world, why did she have to be here tonight?

"Here he is now," Evan heard muttered in the darkness as he joined his choir backstage.

"Sorry, Mostyn. I got waylaid by an old friend," Evan said. "How are you doing?"

"I am not sure I can go through with this," Mostyn said. "This has been a great shock to me. I really don't know . . ."

"You'll be fine, Austin Mostyn." Evans-the-Meat clamped a big hand on the fragile shoulder of the choir director. "We're going to get out there and give a slap-up performance as a tribute to our old friend Ifor. Right men?"

Evan didn't think the reply sounded overenthusiastic.

"But what are we going to sing?" young Billy Hopkins asked nervously. "Ifor sang all the solos, didn't he? We can hardly have big gaps where we hum."

"We'll have to go back to our old program, won't we?" Roberts-the-Pump said.

"No, we'll stick to the songs we have practiced," Mostyn said, as if every word was a great effort for him. "I'll take the solos myself."

He straightened his bow tie then motioned them to follow him into the wings.

Evan could feel the tension around him and he felt tenser than most. He wished that they'd canceled their performance tonight. If he hadn't been here he would never have known that Maggie Pole was in North Wales. He still felt clammy and in shock. He could picture her so clearly—same bubbly personality, unruly dark curls, big dark eyes, talking a mile a minute—was it possible that he still had feelings for her after all this time, after all that had happened?

Rubbish, he said to himself. He would go and have a quick drink with her and tomorrow he'd tell Bronwen the whole story. He should have told her sooner. They had been wrong to keep so much of their pasts hidden from each other.

The choir before them ended with a rousing rendering of "All Through the Night."

"And now, *annwyl gyfeillion,* dear friends," the announcer's voice boomed through the large tent. "The Côr Meibion from Llanfair under the direction of Mr. Mostyn Phillips."

They filed out onto the stage, hair slicked down, black boots shining, faces shining with sweat. Evan took his place in the back row. Mostyn raised the baton and they started to sing.

They opened as planned with the drinking song from *La Traviata.* Their voices resonated, loud, clear, and rich in the packed marquee. Evan thought they had never sounded so good. Then Mostyn's voice took up the solo part. He had sung through passages for them before during practice, to show what he wanted but Evan had never

heard his full voice before. Obviously neither had any of
the other choir members. They forgot that they were supposed to be staring straight ahead and glanced at each
other or gave each other subtle nudges. Mostyn had a
nice voice—not of the power or quality of Ifor's but a
high, sweet tenor.

An amazed thought shot through Evan's mind—they
might just make it to the final after all! Then suddenly,
abruptly, Mostyn stopped singing.

"I'm sorry," he said, both to choir and audience. "It's
no good. I can't do this. A very great man was supposed
to be singing this solo . . . he was struck down unneces-
sarily, before his time—I was stupid to think that I could
ever fill his shoes. Please excuse us . . ." He fled into the
wings, leaving the choir to march offstage alone, amid
the rising murmur of the audience.

The announcer quickly took over the mike and explained the full details of the tragedy. "We understand
what Mr. Phillips and his choir must be going through
right now. They have our deepest sympathy. The music
world and Wales in particular have lost a giant in the
field."

Evan followed the other choir members out into the
open air. The sun had now set and lights were twinkling
from half-open tents and booths. The sound of sweet children's song, of harps and flutes and drums, the smells of
wood smoke and roasting, the glow of fires and the fluttering of flags gave the whole scene a distinctly medieval
feel that contributed to Evan's sense of unreality.

He didn't see Sergeant Watkins until the latter grabbed
his arm. "Too bad," he said. "I was looking forward to
hearing you sing."

"What are you doing here, Sarge?" Evan asked, shaking himself back to reality and the present.

"Looking for you. I thought you'd like to know that
the wife has confessed. She's down in Caernarfon with
the D.I. right now."

Evan stood rooted to the spot. "Mrs. Llewellyn? She's confessed to the murder?"

Watkins nodded. "She turned up in Caernarfon, cool as a cucumber. 'I have decided to come forward and straighten this whole mess out before my family and friends are dragged into it.' She said, 'I want you to know that I killed my husband.' "

Evan gave Watkins a stunned look. "She's certainly a cool customer, isn't she?"

"And a good actress, too. I would have bet my pension she didn't do it, even though she had the motive and the opportunity."

"Me, too," Evan agreed. "I could imagine her putting a neat little bullet into her husband or poisoning him slowly, but bashing him over the head? Has she told you what she used as the weapon?"

"She hadn't told us anything by the time I left. She probably won't if the D.I. uses his subtle methods of interrogation. Did you come here in your own car?"

"Yes, but . . ."

"You can follow me then."

"You want me down at HQ in Caernarfon? Surely the D.I. hasn't requested my presence?"

Watkins chuckled. "No, but I have. I told him you'd been the one who knew the most about her, so it made sense to have you there. He wasn't very interested either way. He's still onto his Mafia theory. Now he's trying to prove she had Mafia connections and hired a hit man—don't laugh—that's his current line of thinking. He's dying to fly to Europe to testify in an international case."

They had reached the perimeter of the field. "See you down there," Watkins said. Evan headed for his own car, his heart beating fast. So it was Mrs. Llewellyn after all! Why hadn't he suspected it? He'd felt all along that she was tense and hiding something, but her visit to her "friend" would have explained that. They would have accepted that explanation, too. In the absence of the murder weapon, they'd have had a hard time pinning the crime on her. So what would have made her come forward and confess voluntarily?

Evan drove out of the car park and headed across the toll bridge, spanning the estuary to Porthmadog and the less mountainous route to Caernarfon. He wasn't entirely sure that he was doing the right thing, butting in on the D.I.'s interrogation. Sergeant Watkins might want him there but he was pretty sure the D.I. would tell him to bugger off. But he had to admit that he was very curious to hear what Mrs. Llewellyn had to say.

Police HQ in Caernarfon had that empty, out-of-hours feeling as their feet echoed along a half-lit hallway. Watkins tapped on the interview room door. Detective Constable Mathias came out. "You needn't have rushed," he said, closing the door swiftly behind him. "She's had second thoughts. She talked to her lawyer and he told her not to say any more until he drives up from London. He'll be here in the morning. The D.I.'s sending her home for the night."

As he saw Evan register surprise he went on. "It's okay. She posted bail. She's not going anywhere and we've no cells suitable for someone like her, have we?"

"Are they going to build a high-class jail when she's convicted?" Watkins asked dryly. "So there's no point in Evans having a chat with her, is there?"

"The D.I. suggested he could drive her home, since he's going that way. Who knows, she might get more friendly in the car."

"I'd be happy to drive her," Evan said, "if she doesn't mind riding in my old bone shaker. They don't provide village constables with police vehicles, you know."

"Just as long as it gets her home, it saves one of us having to run her up there on a Saturday night," D.P.C. Mathias said. "I personally had a date and—"

"Oh no!" Evan put his hand to his forehead.

"What?" Watkins asked. "You were supposed to be on a date, too?"

"I was supposed to be meeting someone down at the *eisteddfod*. She'll think I stood her up." He sighed. "Oh well, nothing I can do about it now."

"Your bird-watching young lady?" Watkins asked. "She'll understand. She has to know what a policeman's life is like by now."

"No, it wasn't her," Evan said. "It was an old girlfriend from Swansea. I bumped into her at the *eisteddfod*. We'd arranged to meet after I'd finished singing . . ." he saw the exchange of smirks and gave Mathias a warning frown . . . "don't even ask."

"Meeting an old girlfriend on the sly?" Watkins grinned at him. "Asking for trouble, that's what you are."

"It was all harmless, Sarge. Just catching up on Swansea news, that's all. Now I've no way of getting in touch with her." As he said it he realized that he felt relieved. Now Maggie would go back to Swansea and he'd get on with his life up here and never think of her again.

"I'll tell the D.I. that you'll drive Mrs. L. home then, shall I?" D.P.C Mathias asked.

"By the way," the thought suddenly struck Evan, "what ever happened to Gladys? Did they finally locate her?"

"No. She never showed up at home. I went round to her house several times," Mathias said. "I checked with the neighbors, too. They didn't know where she was."

A woman P.C. was coming down the hall with two cups of tea on a tray. "Did I hear you asking about Gladys somebody?" she said. "An old lady, was she? Gladys Rees?"

"That's right," Watkins said.

"Then I can tell you why she never showed up when she was supposed to. I went with her to the hospital this afternoon. She got hit by a car crossing Pool Street, poor old dear. It's always the same with these old people, isn't it? She was in a hurry to get her shopping done before the shops closed and her eyesight wasn't too good. I've seen it before. And the cars drive too fast around that corner, too."

"So she's in the hospital, is she?" Evan asked. "We should get down there—"

"No need for that," the woman P.C. cut in. "She died soon after the ambulance arrived."

"Was she conscious? Did she say anything?" Watkins demanded sharply.

"Say anything about what?" The P.C. looked puzzled. "Yes, she was conscious. Quite alert, in fact. That's why I was surprised to hear that she'd died."

"Did she see the car that hit her?" Evan asked.

"Oh, I don't think so," the P.C. said. "She was hit from behind, looking the wrong way. They said she was tossed in the air like a rag doll."

"And the car didn't stop?" Evan asked.

"It was all rather confused. The driver that hit her got the impression that another car had hit her first. He said one minute she wasn't there, the next she landed on his bonnet. He was very upset, poor man. You know how it is when it's crowded on Saturdays." She paused and stood there, frowning. Then she gave them a sad little smile. "I mustn't let the D.I.'s tea get cold or he'll shout at me. You could check with the hospital casualty room. She might have said something there, but I'm not sure what you expected her to say?"

"Who tried to kill her, of course," Evan said.

Watkins drew Evan to one side as the woman P.C. disappeared into the interview room and D.P.C. Mathias followed her.

"You think it wasn't an accident then?" he asked.

Evan shrugged. "It could have been, I suppose. She was in a hurry to do her shopping and she was old and her eyesight wasn't too wonderful, maybe. But it's too much of a coincidence, isn't it? She was about to take a look at the house where she had cleaned and dusted for years. She'd know instantly if something was missing, or was in the wrong place. And she heard Ifor Llewellyn talking to someone shortly before he died, didn't she?"

Watkins's eyes lit up. "You know what else is interesting—the way Mrs. Llewellyn came forward very quickly and volunteered to give Gladys a ride home. She could have pumped her for information on the way and found out what she knew."

"I'm going to get someone onto this right away," Watkins said. "I'm going down to the hospital and find out the exact time the accident took place and see if Gladys said anything relevant while she was there. Then tomorrow I'll get people out to Pool Street and talk to the witnesses. Someone must have seen what hit her, and if it was a big black Mercedes . . ."

"It would be easier for the killer to be doing the pushing, not the driving," Evan said. "You know how crowded Pool Street is on a Saturday. You follow Gladys. You stand behind her when she's about to cross. A large vehicle comes and you give her a little push. If anyone notices, you say you were pushed from behind and pitched forward into her. It's a no-risk way of getting rid of someone."

Watkins nodded. "That's true enough. Oh well, at least we don't need her testimony anymore, now we've got a confession. But why would Mrs. L. go to the trouble of getting rid of Gladys if she was going to confess?"

"Because something has happened since that has made her change her mind. Maybe the friend in Llandudno made it clear that he wasn't going to give her an alibi."

"Yes, we'll have to question him tomorrow, whether she likes it or not."

"I'll go and see if the D.I. has finished with Mrs. L. for the night, shall I?" Watkins said. "You two might have a nice chat on the way home."

Evan gave him a sideways glance. "Come on, Sarge.

You think she'll warm up to my charm and tell me all the details? And if she did, her solicitor would say that she was coerced and I'd be in big trouble."

"I didn't mean that you should pump her for information. But a harmless little chat might tell us something we didn't already know."

"I'd say that Mrs. Llewellyn isn't the type to give anything away by mistake," Evan said. "She kept her affair secret from her husband, didn't she?"

"Maybe, maybe not," Watkins said. "I'm beginning to wonder if he'd found out about it and that's what made her get rid of him. Still, we'll know in the morning, if her lawyer lets her talk."

He disappeared into the interview room and reappeared with an ashen-faced, tight-lipped Mrs. Llewellyn. She was wearing a dark suit and sensible black shoes. Evan got the feeling that Mrs. Llewellyn was the type of woman who instinctively knew what to wear for any occasion. She'd find it hard having to wear a prison uniform.

"It's good of you to drive me home, Constable," she said as he opened the car door for her.

"Sorry about the car. It's not exactly like your Mercedes," Evan said.

He started the engine. Mrs. Llewellyn sat very straight and stared ahead of her as they drove out of town and into the blackness of the countryside. For a long while neither of them spoke. Then she said, "You summoned my daughter here. I don't know what made you do that. How can she help you—she was in Milan." Evan remained silent. He changed gear with a grind as the car began to climb up the Llanberis pass.

"I particularly wanted to keep her out of it," Mrs. Llewellyn went on. "She's a very emotional child and . . . and she worshipped her father. This will be very distressing to her."

"Yes, I expect it will," Evan said.

"I had hoped to keep the truth from her. But I suppose it is already plastered on every newsstand around the world by now. God, how I loathe the media. They wrecked my life."

Evan nodded. *That would probably be a good line of defense for her,* he thought. Driven over the edge by living in a media spotlight and constantly hounded by paparazzi. Any jury would have sympathy with that.

She didn't speak again until he pulled up in the Everest Inn car park.

"Will you be picking me up in the morning?" she asked as if she was arranging a car pool for a normal occasion.

"I think they'll send a car for you when your solicitor arrives," Evan said.

"I see." She sighed as he opened the door for her. "Now I've got to face my son. I'm not looking forward to it."

"Then don't tell him anything until you really have to." Evan felt sympathy for this remote, composed woman. How many years had she had to hide her true feelings while her husband was photographed with beautiful women?

"My son and I have no secrets from each other, Constable," she said coldly. "We have never had secrets from each other."

She gave him a polite nod then walked toward the lighted doorway of the inn.

Evan watched until she had disappeared inside, then he went home. It had been a long day.

SEVENTEEN

EVAN OPENED HIS EYES TO the rumble of thunder. *Too bad,* he thought, *that will put a damper on the* eisteddfod's closing day. The thunder became more persistent and he realized that it was knocking on his door.

"Mr. Evans?" Mrs. Williams's shrill voice punctuated the thunder. She opened the door and peeked around it. "Sorry to disturb you and on the Sabbath, too, day of rest and gladness, isn't it? But there's someone on the phone for you and he says it's very urgent."

It must be very early, Evan decided. Mrs. Williams was still in her dressing gown and slippers and she never slept in much past six. He reached for his own robe and followed her downstairs to the phone.

"Sorry to wake you, but the D.I. told me to." Watkins's voice came cheerfully on the line. "And if I have to be up at six-thirty on a Sunday morning, then there's no reason why you shouldn't be, too."

"Thanks a lot," Evan muttered, only half joking. "What's happened?"

"Mrs. Llewellyn just called," Watkins said. "She wants to talk now, before her lawyer gets here. She says she's scared he'll stop her from telling us everything and she needs to get it off her chest. The D.I. wants you to pick her up from the hotel and bring her down to HQ."

"What's wrong with sending a squad car for her?" Evan grumbled. "It's my own car and my own petrol, you know."

"So put in a claim. I think it's an excuse to get you here. I don't think the D.I.'s willing to admit it, but he'd like to have you around, just in case."

"I'll be down right away," Evan said. "She's ready and waiting, is she?"

"So she said. Anxious to get on with it."

"Right, Sarge. I'll pick her up as soon as I'm dressed. Any more news about Gladys?"

"I went round to the hospital after you left last night, but it wasn't any use. They say she died on a gurney before they could get her into an operating room. No one had time to talk to her."

"So now we'll never know," Evan said, trying to control the rising anger he felt at the death of the old woman.

"Unless we can find a witness who saw something. I'm putting men out there today," Watkins said. "But if nobody comes forward, I'm not too optimistic—unless we can get Mrs. L. to confess to Gladys as well?"

"Wouldn't that be nice." Evan put down the phone. He was almost back to his room when the front bedroom door opened and a tousled Reverend Powell-Jones stuck out his head.

"What is all this unearthly commotion in the middle of the night?" he demanded.

"Sorry, Reverend, I've just had an emergency phone call," Evan said.

"Most inconsiderate," the reverend muttered. "I needed my sleep, today of all days. This is my big day, you know—my first bardic competition. By the end of today I hope to be crowned and chaired as bard. That fool Parry Davies will be eating his words."

Evan was about to say something on the subject of Christian charity but changed his mind. There were already enough complications in his life.

"I suppose it was something to do with Llewellyn's death?" Powell-Jones asked. "I knew it was a mistake to let the house to those people, but my wife insisted, and when she gets a bee in her bonnet, there's no stopping her."

Evan knew what that was like. He almost felt sympathy for him. "Oh well, I expect you can have your house back very soon," he said. "I don't think the family will want to move back into it, after what happened."

"I'm not sure that we will," Powell-Jones said. "My wife is a sensitive woman, Mr. Evans. She says that the aura of violent death will linger . . . I hope they'll have the decency to pay to have the carpet cleaned."

"I'm sure they'll do that," Evan said. "I have to go now, Reverend. Mrs. Llewellyn's waiting for me. Good luck with your poetry."

"It's in the hands of God." The Reverend Powell-Jones raised his eyes piously to heaven. "Only He knows who best deserves the honor."

His modest expression didn't manage to disguise who he thought that person should be. Evan smiled to himself as he went back to his room.

"I'm sorry to drag you from your bed so early on a Sunday morning, Officer," Margaret Llewellyn was the third person to apologize to him within half an hour, Evan noted, "but I couldn't wait any longer with this thing hanging over me. I've hardly slept all night." Her appearance confirmed this. She looked pale, haggard, and at least ten years older—but she had still taken trouble over her appearance, fresh lipstick, not a hair out of place.

"I'm afraid there are a few newspapermen still hanging around outside," Evan said. "I've parked the car as close as I could and I've left the passenger door open. All we have to do is make a run for it."

"Thanks. You're very thoughtful." She smiled at him. "Alright. I'm ready. Let's go."

Evan held open the big central door and she ran swiftly to the car, pushing aside microphones and cameras. She did it so casually that Evan realized this was something she was used to. He shut her door, got in, and nudged his way through the persistent flashbulbs and microphones.

"At least I'll be away from them soon," she said, leaning back and closing her eyes. "God, how I hate them."

She hardly said another word all the way down to Caernarfon and Evan didn't interrupt her silence.

D.I. Hughes looked up from his conversation with Sergeant Watkins as Mrs. Llewellyn was ushered in. The interview room was small with walls painted institutional green. It had once had a window but it had been painted over and the room was lit with a single stark central light. The large electric clock on the wall moved forward in rhythmic jerks accompanied by loud ticks. Hardly the sort of environment to make a suspect relax.

Watkins got to his feet and pulled out a chair on the opposite side of the table for Mrs. Llewellyn. Evan waited by the door, expecting the D.I. to dismiss him. Instead the inspector said, "Come in and close the door, please, Evans. I think we're ready to get started."

Evan closed the door and stood by it, since there were no more chairs in the room. D.I. Hughes leaned over to the tape recorder, which was in the middle of the table. "This is Detective Inspector Geraint Hughes. I am in interview room B with Detective Sergeant Watkins and Constable Evans. It is seven-ten, on Sunday August the second. Would you state your full name please."

"Margaret Ann Llewellyn."

"Mrs. Llewellyn, before we begin, would you affirm

that you have been read your rights, including your right
to have a lawyer present?"

"That is correct." She answered mechanically.

"You understand that anything you say in this room
could be used against you in a subsequent trial?"

"I understand."

"And yet you don't want to wait for your solicitor to
arrive?"

"No. I want to tell you everything that happened in
my own words. My solicitor would only try to stop me."

"Very well, then let's get started," the D.I. said.
"Would you please describe for us the relevant events
this week, leading to the death of your husband on Friday
evening."

"Alright." She seemed composed and not unduly worried. "I went to London on Tuesday morning."

"For what purpose?"

"I went to visit my solicitor. I wanted to see about
getting a divorce from my husband."

"Did your husband know about this?"

"I had mentioned it to him. He never thought I'd go
through with it. I had made similar threats before when
I was upset."

"And would you have gone through with it this time?"
D.I. Hughes asked gently.

"I . . . I'm not sure. Probably not. Ifor could be very
persuasive."

"So you went to London on Tuesday. When did you
see your solicitor?"

"On Wednesday morning."

"But you didn't return home until Friday?"

Mrs. Llewellyn looked down at her hands. "I've already explained to these officers that I went to visit a
friend in Llandudno. I spent Thursday night there."

"This was a male friend?" The D.I. acted as if this was
news to him, which it wasn't.

"That's right."

"And your husband thought you were still in London?"
She nodded.

"Would you answer the question with a yes or no, please."

"Yes," she snapped into the tape recorder.

"So you arrived home when?" D.I. Hughes continued.

"Early Friday evening. My . . . friend drove me as far as Bangor. Then I got a taxi. I arrived home a little after six to find Ifor very drunk. He had been brooding about the divorce. He said there was no way he'd ever let me go." She paused and brushed an imaginary hair out of her face. "I said if he'd treated me better, I wouldn't be thinking of leaving him. That was probably a stupid thing to say. He could get belligerent when he was drunk. He said he'd treated me far too well. What I needed was a damn good spanking and he was going to give me one. I'd been knocked around by him before—he didn't know his own strength. I'd wound up in the hospital once." She gave a deep shuddering sigh. "He had a glass in his hand. He turned to put it on the table. That's when I grabbed the whiskey bottle and hit him."

"You hit him?" the inspector asked.

"Yes. I hit him on the back of his head. I had to stop him before he attacked me, you understand."

"Did you hit him very hard?"

The words were coming more breathlessly now. "I only meant to knock him out for a while, so that I'd have a chance to get away until he sobered up."

"But you hit him harder than you intended?"

She swallowed hard. "I don't think so. He was drunk, remember. He pitched forward and he hit his head on that damned fender. I knew right away that he was dead."

"Excuse me for interrupting, but why didn't you call the police right away?" D.I. Hughes asked.

She was playing with her engagement ring, a large square-cut emerald, twisting it round and round her finger. "I panicked, I suppose. I wanted to avoid a situation

like this. I just wanted to get away. So I left the house
by the back door and hid out for a while up on the hill.
When you were all at the house, I made my entry."

"Thank you, Mrs. Llewellyn," the inspector said.

Evan noticed she gave an almost audible sigh of relief.
The inspector turned to Watkins. "That all seems very
straightforward. Any further questions, Sergeant?"

"Just a couple, sir," Watkins said. He leaned forward
in his chair. "Was the whiskey bottle full or empty, Mrs.
Llewellyn?"

"I'm not sure. Ifor had been drinking so maybe it was
empty. I didn't notice."

"It was fairly light then. You'd have to hit someone
very hard to knock them out with an empty bottle."

A spasm of annoyance crossed her face. "Maybe it
wasn't completely empty. I really didn't notice."

Watkins glanced at Evan. "You say your husband had
been drinking, Mrs. Llewellyn. Was the top on the bottle?" he asked.

"I really don't know . . . is this relevant?"

"Only that the whiskey would have splashed all over
you if you'd hit him with an open bottle."

"Then the top must have been on it."

"It wasn't on it when we found it," Evan said. "And
there was whiskey spilled all over the carpet. You must
have got some on your clothes, Mrs. Llewellyn. Did you
change your clothes before you left?"

"No . . . I . . . there was no whiskey on me. He pitched
forward, you see. Away from me."

"Which hand was your husband holding his glass in?"
Evan asked, then suddenly realized that he was not officially part of this interrogation. "Sorry, sir," he muttered.

D.I. Hughes waved his hand. "No, go on, Evans. It's
a relevant question."

"I still don't see . . . his right hand, of course. Ifor was
right-handed."

"And he hit his head on the fender knob?" Evan went on.

"He must have. It all happened so quickly and I was in a state of shock."

"And what happened to the bottle?" Watkins asked.

"I . . . put it on the floor."

"With your fingerprints on it?"

"No. I wiped it clean first."

"With what?" Evan asked.

She was having to look from one to the other and this was clearly upsetting her. "With my handkerchief."

"And what did you do with the handkerchief afterward?"

"I threw it into a dustbin." She got to her feet. "Look, I've told you what happened. I didn't mean to kill him. I was defending myself. Why are you hounding me like this?"

"Nobody's hounding you. We're just trying to get our facts straight, madam," D.I. Hughes said. "I'm not quite clear where you hit your husband?"

"On the back of his head."

"And then he fell forward, striking the front of his head?"

She nodded eagerly. "Yes, that's right."

"So there would be two areas that showed trauma?"

This made her hesitate. "You know, I really didn't hit him hard and Ifor had a skull like iron. Maybe only the wound from the fender was visible."

During the pause that followed the clock on the wall moved forward with loud one-second ticks.

"Any more questions?" The D.I. looked at Watkins then at Evan.

"Did anyone in the village notice you arriving in a taxi just after six, Mrs. Llewellyn? Was anyone out in the street at that time?" Evan asked.

"I have no idea," she said sharply. "I know the villagers liked to spy on us, but I had no interest in what they were doing. You'd have to ask them."

"What taxi cab company did you use, from Bangor, Mrs. Llewellyn?" Hughes asked, glancing up from his notes. "Would you recognize your driver again?"

"Oh really!" She got to her feet. "One taxi looks very much like another; so does one taxi driver."

"And you picked the taxi up where?"

"At the station, of course. Isn't that where one always picks up taxis?" She stood up. "Look, I've changed my mind. I'm going to wait for my lawyer before I answer any more questions. This is all getting too stressful. You're treating me like a criminal when no crime was committed. I was only acting in self-defense."

D.I. Hughes rose to his feet as well. "It is now seven twenty-eight in the morning. This session is now being suspended, pending the arrival of Mrs. Llewellyn's solicitor from London," he said into the machine and switched it off. "I'll take you to the cafeteria, Mrs. Llewellyn. You can get a cup of tea while we wait." He escorted her from the room with a chivalrous gesture.

Watkins and Evan were left alone. Watkins let out a long breath like a deflating balloon. "Well, that was interesting, wasn't it? How long do you reckon it took her to think that one out?"

"Meaning that she didn't do it?"

"Pretty obvious, wasn't it?"

"One thing was obvious," Evan said slowly. "She'd never seen the room with the body in it. She went entirely on what she'd heard."

"But why?" Watkins asked. "What made her confess, do you think?"

"Two possible reasons," Evan said. "Either she's covering up for somebody, or she's pretending to be stupid and she's really very clever."

"How do you figure that one out?"

"She knows she's a prime suspect so she comes in and

confesses, but her confession makes it clear that she knows nothing about the crime. So we dismiss her as a suspect. If we don't ever come up with the murder weapon and nobody saw her sneaking into Llanfair at the right time, we'd never be able to pin it on her."

Watkins nodded. "That's true," he said. "I always thought she was a clever woman. But what if she's doing this because she knows who really did it and she wants to save him."

"Or her?"

"Her?"

"I don't think we should rule out the daughter until we've heard her story."

Watkins frowned. "The daughter? But she was in Milan."

"It's easy enough to pop across to Europe and back these days. They don't even check your passport most of the time, do they? In fact you don't even need a passport between here and Italy."

"But why would the daughter want to kill her father? By all accounts she adored him."

"That's what Mrs. Llewellyn wants us to believe. She's told us several times."

"So you mean she might not have been that fond of him?"

Evan shrugged. "We'll know when she gets here. I'm anxious to see her again. I've got a feeling we've met before."

"The girl whose car went into the lake?"

Evan nodded. "It would tie in, wouldn't it? She pops over to scout out the place before her old man arrives. So did the son."

"If it wasn't the daughter then it would have to be the son, wouldn't it?" Watkins asked. "I've got my suspicions about him. He's very wound up, isn't he?"

"He's certainly jumpy," Evan said. "When will we get confirmation that he was actually in Italy, do you think?"

Watkins grinned. "I don't think the Italian police work at our speed. Maybe next year. If we don't hear something soon, you and I will just have to drive to Italy to get statements."

"I can see the D.I. authorizing that." Evan chuckled. "We'll know more when she gets here. It will be interesting to interview them separately and see where their stories differ."

"That would explain why Mrs. L. was lying, too," Evan said. "A mother will do anything to protect her kids, won't she?"

"Even go to jail for them? I suppose it's possible." Watkins nodded thoughtfully. "Yeah, come to think of it, my wife would throw herself in front of a speeding train to save our Tiffany. But then so would I, so that doesn't explain anything."

He grinned sheepishly at Evan. "Come on," he said, opening the door. "I'm dying for a cup of tea. The wife wouldn't get up on a Sunday morning, so I had to leave without breakfast."

"Tough life," Evan said dryly.

They walked down the empty hall.

"You know what," Evan exclaimed as they reached the swing doors leading to the waiting area. "One person we haven't really looked into yet—her boyfriend. He had the motive and the opportunity. She admits he drove her as far as Bangor. What if he came all the way here—maybe to confront Ifor and tell him she was getting a divorce. He and Ifor quarreled and he hit Ifor? Gladys said she heard voices, didn't she?"

Watkins got out his notebook. "It's definitely worth a try. I had him on my list for today anyway, to see if his story backed up Mrs. L.'s alibi. Okay. I'll put him down for this afternoon but let's get the two children out of the way first. We don't know how fond they were of each other, do we? Maybe they'll each be happy to incriminate the other to save themselves. And you know what else?"

He turned back to Evan as he pushed open the swing door to the cafeteria. "I wouldn't mind taking another look at that house. I know it was searched once and they didn't come up with a possible weapon, but I wouldn't mind looking again, especially through the wife's stuff. Perhaps she's got an incriminating letter or two?"

"Will the D.I. let you do that?"

"I'll ask him now, because I'd like to see how Mrs. L. reacts to her home being searched. Order a cup of tea and a bun for me, will you?"

EIGHTEEN

THE SMELL OF SUNDAY MORNING breakfast frying wafted through the open windows along Llanfair's high street as Evan parked his car outside the police station. He sighed deeply. A few weeks ago that would have been him enjoying bacon, egg, sausages, and even fried bread sometimes. Now there was no point in popping home to Mrs. Williams. She'd be feeding the Reverend Powell-Jones his presermon prunes and muesli.

Evan wondered if the two ministers would be holding their normal services this morning, since they were both competing at the *eisteddfod* later in the day. Perhaps they'd both want to save their voices for their bardic efforts.

Watkins's car drew up in the parking space beside him.

"That smells bloody good, doesn't it?" he asked as he got out. "Reminds me of the days before the wife went on a health kick. They don't seem to mind about cholesterol up here do they?"

"A lot of people up here work on the farms. I don't think it matters so much if you're out in the fields at five every day, come rain or shine," Evan said. He glanced up into the sky, which was heavy with cloud. The peaks were hidden and cloud fingers came down deep into the valley. The air was moist—what some of the older villagers called "a soft morning." If he wasn't wrong there would be rain later.

"I'm feeling a bit peckish myself," Watkins said. "There's no cafe up here, is there?"

Evan shook his head. "They serve food up at the Everest Inn, but not at prices you or I would want to pay."

"Pity. Oh well, let's have a quick look around the house and then I'll stop off at that roadhouse beside the roundabout in Bangor. They do a good fry-up."

"I might come down and join you," Evan said.

"You're alright. You've got a tame landlady."

"Not since our local minister moved in. It's all low-fat and natural now." His face lit up. "Now that's the one good thing about this murder. The Llewellyns will move out and the Powell-Joneses can move back to their own house . . . and I can go back to my old room and my old breakfasts."

"Now I come to think of it, you look a mere shadow of your former self." Watkins chuckled.

Evan chose not to reply.

"Looks as if the press have finally given up," Watkins commented as they stepped over the police tape and walked up the driveway to the Powell-Joneses' house.

"They're camping outside the Everest Inn now," Evan said. "Let's hope they aren't watching this place or they'll all come swarming back. What a life for that poor woman. You could understand it if she cracked, couldn't you?"

Watkins nodded. He put the key in the door. The house smelled cold and damp, with a lingering overtone of the chemicals used to collect the blood samples.

"Dreary place," Watkins muttered. "I can see why they turned the heat on. It feels like a bloody tomb in here."

He looked around. "Let's start upstairs in the bedrooms, just in case the lawyer arrives."

"We've got a search warrant, haven't we?"

"Yes, but you know what lawyers can be like. Talk the hind leg off a donkey. Alright, you take the rooms on the left, I'll take the right."

There were four bedrooms on the main floor upstairs. Two were untouched. One had clearly been the domain of Ifor Llewellyn. It was decorated liberally with framed photos of Ifor in various operatic roles as well as with heads of state, film stars, and other public figures. Tapes and CDs were littered over the tables and dressers. Evan scanned the titles: Ifor Llewellyn sings Wagner . . . or Verdi . . . Llewellyn and Pavarotti, The Paris Concert. There were also piles of personal tapes with bold scrawled headings: "Rehearsal, May 28th, including good version of Aria-Rigoletto. May 30th, rehearsal before Pagliacci." He certainly liked listening to himself, Evan decided.

The desk in the room was a jumble of papers. Evan started to go through them methodically: fan letters, theater programs, bills from tailors and a shirtmaker, letters from an accountant—all unincriminating. Ifor didn't seem to owe anyone a large sum of money. There were no letters from women; in fact the only feminine touch was a framed child's drawing of a house, family, and rainbow with the words "I love you, Daddy" printed on it in black crayon.

Then Evan noticed the envelope with an Italian stamp. He opened it and a smile spread slowly across his face. "In here, Sarge," he called. "I think we've got something."

Watkins appeared at his side and Evan handed him the letter. Watkins nodded as he read it.

It was from a law firm in Rome.

Esteemed sir, It has come to the attention of our client, La Signorina Carla Di Martini, that you in-

tend to write your memoirs. La Signorina wishes
me to convey to you in the strongest terms that
her name is not to be mentioned in this proposed
work. I am sure you understand that any reference
to my client would be potentially damaging to her
career and her international reputation. It is hoped
that you will behave as a gentleman should and
not attempt to embarrass the lady in question.

Should you decide to proceed with the mention
of our client in these memoirs, please be assured
that we will take all legal steps to block publica-
tion and seek damages against you for defaming
her good name. I need not remind you that such a
legal process would be both detrimental to your
career and financially devastating to you.

This is to advise you that our partner, Signor
Angelo Rossi, will be coming in person to obtain
your personal assurance that you will respect our
client's wishes.

"You think this could explain the Mafia type who
threatened him?" Watkins asked.

Evan nodded. "It makes sense, doesn't it? That was
obviously the representative they sent over."

Watkins folded the letter and put it back into its envelope. "I can't wait to show this to the D.I. He's got
half the police in Europe running around trying to locate
a possible Mafia hit man and all the time the explanation
was lying under his nose."

"It doesn't seem that this has anything to do with Ifor's
death," Evan said. "They could get what they wanted out
of Ifor legally—and make money doing it."

"Unless the signorina got desperate when he sent her
bloke packing," Watkins said thoughtfully. "You said
yourself that Ifor wasn't scared of any threats. Maybe
she decided to take stronger measures and the next mes-
senger she sent was a hit man."

"It's possible," Evan said, "but a hit man wouldn't kill so messily, would he?"

"Unless something went wrong. Ifor was a big bloke."

Evan paused then shook his head. "No, I still think the answer lies with the family. They're covering up for each other somehow. Did you find anything in Mrs. Llewellyn's room?"

"Not a thing," Watkins said. "Come and look. It's like a hotel room—nothing personal about it. No photos, no letters, nothing."

"Maybe she took the important stuff up to the Everest Inn with her," Evan suggested. "She went upstairs alone to phone her children, didn't she? And then she packed a bag."

"So anything incriminating might be in her room at the Everest Inn?" Watkins asked. He gave Evan a meaningful glance. "You know the manager there pretty well, don't you? Major something or other?"

"You want me to ask him to let us into Mrs. L.'s hotel room?" Evan asked dubiously.

"We have a search warrant for her personal possessions, don't we?" Watkins demanded.

"For this house," Evan said.

"Hotel staff come in and out of rooms all the time," Watkins said. "I agree that we probably can't use what we find in a court of law, but it would be nice to know if our hunches are going in the right direction, wouldn't it? After all, something made her come forward and confess."

"I don't think we're going to find a letter saying, 'I'm about to kill Daddy,'" Evan said dryly, "and we both agree that she's a clever woman. If she had incriminating evidence, she'd have destroyed it before she turned herself in."

Watkins nodded. "Probably true. All the same, it's amazing what women keep—old love letters from her boyfriend, letters from her kids. We might just turn up something."

"Alright. We can give it a try," Evan said, "but let's finish off here first."

Mrs. Llewellyn's room was neat and colorless, with no hint of the person who was currently inhabiting it. The artwork on the walls was definitely Powell-Jones's choice—a large stag standing over a Scottish glen, a framed picture of the slate quarry workers dated 1921, and a cloying portrayal of Jesus, surrounded by adorable children. Evan glanced around the room.

"I can tell you one thing," he said. "That shoe in the front hall never belonged to her. She has nothing with heels that high."

"Then why admit to it?" Watkins asked.

"Because she suspected that it might have belonged to someone else?"

"The daughter, you mean?"

"The lab techs did find a black hair, didn't they? And the little girl in the family picture has black hair."

"But the daughter adored her father. Her mother said so over and over again."

"She made a point of doing so," Evan agreed. "Oh well, no use speculating, is it? Let's give the rest of the house a quick search while we've got time."

Another half hour turned up nothing extraordinary, and nothing that looked like a possible murder weapon. They came out of the house into a blustery day. The early mist had now turned to a sharp driving rain.

Watkins turned up his coat collar. "I love summer, don't you?" he said.

"It's a pity it will spoil the last day of the *eisteddfod*," Evan said.

"You're not going to be singing today, are you?"

"No, thank God. Although I didn't think we sounded too bad without Ifor. Austin Mostyn had quite a nice voice. Not very big, but not bad at all. We might have been back for the finals today if he hadn't stopped sing-ing."

"Understandable enough," Watkins said. "He'd just lost his friend, hadn't he?" Suddenly he froze. "What on earth is that?" he demanded.

Evan was also listening to the great burst of sound. Then he realized that it was Sunday morning and the windows of Chapel Bethel across the street were wide open, in spite of the rain. A smile spread across his face. "Oh, that must be the Reverend Parry Davies, giving his sermon. He's obviously getting his voice ready for the *eisteddfod* this evening. He's entering the bard's com-petition, you know."

"And so I say unto you—you cannot love the Lord until you know the Lord. Which of you here can truth-fully say that he knows the Lord?"

Without warning another voice rang out. "And it says in the Bible the wages of sin is death! I am like John the Baptist—a voice crying in the wilderness saying Repent! Repent!"

This voice was booming from Chapel Beulah, which also, unaccountably, had all its windows open today in spite of the rain. The Reverend Powell-Jones was also getting his voice ready for the bard's competition. The whole street echoed. The voices drowned out the patter of falling rain, the hiss and sigh of the wind. The sound bounced back from unseen hillsides above and made star-tled sheep look up from their grazing.

"Bloody 'ell," Watkins said, turning up his coat collar even more. "Do you have to go through this every Sun-day up here?"

"Only when both pastors want to win the same com-petition," Evan said. Even as he spoke windows were slammed shut on both sides of the street. The first round of the current battle was declared a draw.

• • •

"I wonder what the son's doing while his mother's being held for questioning?" Watkins asked as they approached the looming shape of the Everest Inn. "He made a big fuss about our bullying her yesterday but he didn't show up to protect her at the station, did he?"

"No, he didn't," Evan said. "There was no sign of him this morning."

"He's an arrogant bastard, isn't he?"

"Or just young and scared," Evan said thoughtfully. "He's obviously got something to hide. We know he wasn't quite honest with us before. I saw him here a month ago. I'd swear it was him and yet he denied ever being here before."

"Now all we need is someone who saw him here a couple of days ago," Watkins said. "I'd like to have a little talk with Justin Llewellyn, while we're in the neighborhood . . . but I think the D.I. and the mother's solicitor would probably both want to be there."

"If we had a good reason, we could drop in for a friendly chat," Evan said.

"So come up with a good reason," Watkins said.

"Don't look at me. I'm already in big trouble if the D.I. finds I helped search Mrs. L.'s room!"

"Pity. I'd just love to hear how Master Justin explains away his last visit here."

"Me, too," Evan agreed.

A doorman opened the heavy oak-and-glass doors of the inn. Again the vast foyer was almost deserted. Everest Inn guests didn't hang around much during the day.

"We can try just asking for the key," Watkins said. "If the girl at the desk won't give it to us, then you go and find your friendly major."

As they approached the reservation desk the girl looked up and recognized them.

"Excuse me," she began before they could say anything. "Could I have a word with you?"

She beckoned them closer to the desk, even though the

foyer was deserted. "Aren't you the policeman from the village?" She gave Evan a shy half smile. "I thought so. I recognized you when you came to get Mrs. Llewellyn this morning."

"This is Detective Sergeant Watkins," Evan said. "We'd like to get some things from Mrs. Llewellyn's room."

The girl glanced around again. "If you don't mind, I'd like to tell you something first. I said I'd do it for Olwen. She's the room maid up on the third floor. She told me about it the other day and then when she heard that Mr. Llewellyn had been killed—well, she said that proved it, didn't it? And somebody better do something about it, as long as it wasn't her."

"I'm not quite sure what you're trying to say, love," Evan said.

She leaned closer. "It's about the man in number three twenty-one. He's been there all week and Olwen says he never leaves his room—just looks out of his window all day. Olwen says he's really creepy, and she thinks he's got a telescopic rifle—you know, one of those things that can shoot awful long distances. Olwen was wondering whether we should tell the major, but we didn't want to get in trouble."

Watkins glanced at Evan, then turned back to the girl. "What name is he registered under?"

She glanced down. "Forester. Robert Forester."

"Three twenty-one, did you say?"

The girl nodded. Watkins and Evan ran to the lift, then turned impatiently and took the stairs two at a time. Watkins knocked briskly on the room door and was answered with a curt, "If that's the girl come to clean the room, go away, I'm busy."

"North Wales Police, sir," Watkins called through the door. "Open up right away."

The door was opened by a serious-looking young man with round owlish glasses and prominent teeth.

"Yes? What do you want?" he demanded in a flat Midlands accent.

"Detective Sergeant Watkins and Constable Evans, sir. We've received a complaint about this room," Watkins said.

"You mean because I won't let the maid come in and clean when I'm working?"

"Exactly what kind of work are you doing, sir?" Watkins asked. Several aluminum boxes were piled on and around the table by the window. A tripod was set up at the window itself and on it was something with a long barrel.

"That's pretty obvious," the man said scornfully. "I'm a photographer. This is one of my cameras."

"Your window doesn't face the mountains," Evan said. "Exactly what sort of pictures are you taking from here?"

The man was about to tell them to mind their own business, Evan could tell. "You've probably heard," he cut in, "there has been a murder in the village. Anyone with a camera trained on the house in question would naturally be a suspect."

The young man's face flushed. "If you must know, I work for a French magazine. They sent me over here to keep an eye on Llewellyn's house and see if anything interesting was going on—you know, Welsh love nest for famous tenor and his latest flame!" He reached into his pocket and handed them a card. "Robert C. Forester. *Paris Match*."

"So you've been watching the house for a few days now, Mr. Forester?" Watkins could hardly control the excitement in his voice. "And have you seen anything worth reporting?"

"Not a thing. Dull as ditchwater." The young man sighed. "I thought things might liven up when the wife went away on Tuesday, but nary a sexy chick in sight. I would have packed up and left if this new story hadn't developed."

"So you saw everyone who went in and out this week?" Evan asked.

"I don't watch twenty-four hours of the day. I pop down to get a bite to eat or out to get some cigarettes from time to time. But most of the time I'm here, especially evenings."

"What about Friday evening? Did you see anyone then?"

"I saw a little red Mini arriving—you were in it, weren't you?" Forester turned to Evan.

"That's right. About eight-fifteen, that would have been."

James Forester nodded. "And then a whole lot of policemen. That's when I got on the phone and got a full crew out here."

"But before I arrived," Evan said, "say around seven o'clock, seven-thirty?"

The photographer shook his head. "Nobody. Not a soul at that time. I popped out for a pack of ciggies around six . . ."

"No, that would have been too early. Mr. Llewellyn was still alive well after six."

"I was back and watching by six forty-five at the latest," James Forester said. "It was all quiet on the western front after that."

"What about earlier this week?" Watkins asked. "Did you see anyone unusual going in or out?"

"I've got all the pictures, if you want to look," Forester said. "I develop them right here in the bathroom. The maid doesn't like it because I won't let her in to clean."

He opened a drawer and brought out several pages of contact sheets. "Here's everyone who has visited the house since I started shooting last weekend."

Watkins carried the sheets over to the window. Evan joined him. "There's Gladys," Evan said. "And that's Evans-the-Post, and Evans-the-Milk, and there's Evans-the-Meat."

"They led a bloody exciting life, didn't they?" Watkins commented. "Who's that?"

"That's Mostyn Phillips." Evan peered closely at the picture of the little man, stalking up the front path with a worried, but determined, expression on his face. "He went to talk to Ifor a couple of times last week."

"That's right," Forester said. "I got him here and again here. Poncey little bloke, wasn't he? Always wore a bow tie!"

"Was there anyone unusual at all—anyone who didn't go right up to the front door with groceries or milk?"

"There was one young chap, but it was back on Wednesday, I think, and quite early in the day, too. Yes, that's the right sheet. That one there. See the one in the dark trousers?"

"I certainly do," Evan said. "That's Justin Llewellyn!"

NINETEEN

"I THINK THIS CONSTITUTES A good reason to bust in on Justin Llewellyn, don't you, Sarge?" Evan asked excitedly.

"It bloody well does," Watkins agreed. "Let's hear how young Justin wriggles his way out of this one."

He turned to James Forester. "I'm going to need these photos for a while, if you don't mind. Maybe we should take the whole lot along, just in case."

"Be my guest," Forester said. "They're worth bugger all to me, unless I happen to have snapped the murderer. Just give me an advance tip if you're going to arrest somebody, will you? I have to earn my keep somehow."

He escorted them to the door.

"Pick up the house phone and find which is Justin Llewellyn's room," Watkins said impatiently. "I'm going to enjoy this, lying supercilious little snot."

"Take it easy, Sarge. We don't want him to think that we suspect him. Just let him tell his version and then we'll point out to him where he strayed from the truth."

Watkins nodded.

Justin Llewellyn looked as if he had just woken up.

His hair was still tousled and he was wearing silk pajama bottoms with a matching silk robe over them.

"What now?" he asked, rolling his eyes with exaggerated boredom.

"May we come in for a moment, sir?" Watkins asked. "We have a few questions we want to ask you."

"If it will finally satisfy you that I had nothing to do with my father's death, then I suppose so." He opened the door wide for them.

"Have you seen your mother this morning, Mr. Llewellyn?" Evan asked as Justin indicated the two chairs, then flopped onto the bed.

"As you can see, Officer, I've just woken up. I was planning to join her for breakfast . . ." He faltered as he picked up something in Evan's expression. "What? Nothing's happened to her, has it?"

"She called headquarters very early this morning and said that she wanted to make a full confession before her lawyer could get here and stop her," Watkins said, clearly enjoying Justin's look of horror.

"The bloody fool," Justin muttered. "What on earth made her do that?"

"We thought you might have some idea about that, sir." Watkins's tone was still pleasant.

Justin sat up impatiently. "Oh come on, Officer. You must know as well as I that she didn't kill my father."

"Why should we know that, sir?"

"For one thing she hated the sight of blood. If she was going to kill him she'd have done it neatly, not bashed his head in. And for another, she loved him. However much grief he gave her, she still loved the bastard."

"But you didn't?" Evan asked.

"I loathed him. I couldn't stand to be in the same room with him. The feeling was mutual, of course. I was the world's biggest disappointment as a son—totally unmusical, rotten businessman, shy, hated publicity—I wasn't any of the things my father wanted me to be. So I kept well away."

"Except you did pay a couple of visits to the house," Evan said.

"What are you talking about?"

"You were seen here, on two occasions."

"Absolute rubbish! People will say anything and they always get it wrong. Who claims to have seen me?"

"Me, for one," Evan said. He paused to let this sink in. "But you were also photographed going into this house earlier this week." He handed Justin the contact sheet. "This is you, isn't it, Mr. Llewellyn? The photograph is quite clear."

"Bloody paparazzi," Justin muttered. "They always manage to get you, don't they?" He looked up with a genial smile. "Alright. I can explain the visit very easily. I needed some money: I had some debts that needed to be paid right away. I knew my mother would give me the money if I saw her in person. She's always a soft touch where I'm concerned. So I waited until the old man went out for a walk, then I sneaked into the house. But she wasn't there! I looked at her appointment book and found that she'd gone up to London. So I got out again, pretty darned quick and went up to London to try and catch her."

"And did you?"

"Oh yes. I met her and we dined together at Simpsons."

"And then?"

"And then I flew back to Milan on Wednesday afternoon, only to be summoned back here yesterday morning. My frequent-flyer account is growing by leaps and bounds!"

"Have you come up with anyone who can verify your being in Italy on Friday, sir?" Watkins asked.

"The servants were there in the morning," Justin said. "I spent the afternoon alone, reading and relaxing. I ate some bread, cheese, and fruit around seven. I was there when my mother called, absolutely distraught, at nine o'clock. I suppose you could check whether the phone call went through or not. I caught the first train in the morning down to Milan and took the first flight out."

He was relaxed and confident, as if he sensed that this was the best they could throw at him and there was nothing they could make stick.

Watkins looked at Evan. "Now about your other visit to the house, sir," Evan said. "I saw you on two occasions, just before your parents arrived here. You were quarreling with a young girl and I heard her yell, 'bugger off, Justin.' " He watched Justin's Adam's apple go up and down, although the young man's expression didn't change. "And I saw you again later that day, beside a lake, just before a car went into the water."

The reaction was instant this time. "A car went into the water? What car?"

"I'm sure you know that, sir," Evan said. "You were standing right behind it one minute and the next minute it was in the lake."

"I have no idea what you are talking about," Justin said. His voice was now high and strained. "She was fine when I left her. I got out of the car because I couldn't make her see sense. I left her and walked back through the woods. The car was fine when I left it. She's alright, isn't she?"

"Luckily," Evan said. "I pulled her out before the car went into deep water. I couldn't get her to say what had happened. It was possible she was shielding somebody—shielding you, sir. Because attempted murder is almost as serious as murder successfully carried out. And you've got one count of each hanging over you right now."

Justin sighed. "Okay. I suppose I'd better get this over with and stop all this nonsense. I haven't been quite truthful with you up to now."

"No sir?" Watkins's tone was still pleasant.

A spasm of pain passed across Justin's face. "Alright, Sergeant. It was me." He held his wrists out. "Clap on the handcuffs. Book me, read me my rights, or whatever it is that you do. I confess. I killed him."

An hour later Justin was shown into the same green-walled room that his mother had occupied earlier. He had showered and dressed before Watkins and Evan had driven him to headquarters in Caernarfon. His hair was still wet and slicked back. He was wearing a black turtleneck and tight black jeans, looking very much like a tragic young poet or a ghost from the Beat Generation.

D.I. Hughes held out his hand. "Please take a seat, Mr. Llewellyn. Let's try and make this as painless as possible."

"Oh, not the electric cattle prods, please!" Justin said, with more than a touch of sarcasm.

"This isn't a game, sir. Life in prison isn't much fun, I can assure you."

The Adam's apple danced nervously again. "Look, I've confessed. What more do you want?"

"We'd like to hear your version of how you did it, sir. And before we begin—do you wish your mother's solicitor to be present? He's in the building."

"Good Lord, no. That bumbling old fogey would probably manage to get me hanged, even though there's no death penalty anymore."

"Very well." D.I. Hughes switched on the tape recorder and began the official interview. "Mr. Llewellyn, maybe you'd like to tell us the story in your own words. Take your time."

Justin reached into his pocket. "Do you mind if I smoke?" he asked.

"Go right ahead." The D.I. pushed an ashtray across the table to him.

Justin lit up a Gauloise and the pungent acrid smell wafted across the room. Evan stifled a cough.

"It's all very simple," Justin said. "I hated my father. I couldn't stand the way he treated my mother. I hated watching her suffer with such dignity while he chased anything in skirts that didn't play bagpipes. Then he cut off my allowance because I wouldn't take any of the jobs he found for me.

"Recently I got myself in a tight spot financially. I came here earlier this week, to ask him for money. He turned me down. So I waited until my mother was away, so that she wouldn't be involved. Then I came back to Llanfair and killed him."

"How?" D.I. Hughes asked.

"What?"

"How did you kill him, sir?"

"I—I hit him over the head with a blunt instrument when he wasn't looking."

"What kind of blunt instrument, sir?" D.I. Hughes asked.

"A golf club. His golf clubs were on the hallstand. I took one out, hit him over the head with it, then I wiped it clean and put it back in the bag."

"Whereabouts on his head did you hit him, sir?" Watkins asked.

A spasm of annoyance crossed Justin's face. "I didn't exactly stay around to look. I swung my blunt instrument. I made contact. He fell. I got out of there in a hurry."

"Excuse me, sir," Evan interrupted, "but that's just not possible."

All three men looked across at him.

Evan turned to the D.I. "Could I have a word with you, sir?"

"If you insist." He leaned forward and switched off the machine. Then he followed Evan out into the hall. "Alright Constable, what is it?"

"Justin Llewellyn couldn't have killed his father, sir."

"Oh? And why not?"

"I didn't realize until now, watching him sitting at the

table," Evan said. "I watched him light his cigarette. He's left-handed. If a left-handed person had struck Ifor Llewellyn, the blow would have been behind the other ear. There's no way he could have swung a golf club and hit his father where the wound was."

"By Jove you're right, Evans." D.I. Hughes looked almost approving, for once. "That's why it makes so much sense to have an observer at these sessions. You were able to notice that from where you were standing. I was too close to him and too involved with the tape recorder, or I would have seen it, too."

Evan stayed wisely silent.

"So now the question is what made him confess?" D.I. Hughes asked, almost rhetorically.

"He thinks he knows who did it and he's covering up for whoever it was."

"That much is obvious, but the question is who? The mother?"

"But we know she didn't do it."

"I wonder." Again the D.I. seemed to be speaking more to himself than to Evan. "Is it possible that this is a well-thought-out conspiracy between them? What if they both planned his death together and they agreed to take it in turns to confess and then be proved to be lying? All they needed to do was to tell stories that didn't jibe with the facts. And until we turn up the weapon, we can't prove otherwise."

"We will test those golf clubs, won't we, sir?" Evan asked.

"I'm sure that's already been done, but I'll get the lab to go over them again." He stared out past Evan. "We may have to start playing games, Constable. Maybe if we let the mother think that we believe the son and we're arresting him . . . or the other way around?

"So you got nothing more out of the mother this morning then, sir?" Evan asked.

D.I. Hughes frowned. "Not after the bloody solicitor

got here. He wouldn't let her say a word without interrupting."

"I suppose it is his mother that Justin is covering up
for?" Evan said thoughtfully.

"Who else do you have in mind?"

"Well, it's just possible that—" He broke off at the
sound of voices on the other side of the swing doors. "If
my mother and brother are here, then I want to see them
right now." A young autocratic voice with the same arrogance as Justin's. "I've been dragged here from Milan
because you had to see me and I'm not going to sit in a
bloody waiting room and drink tea!"

The swing doors were pushed violently open and a
young girl swept through them. She stopped short as she
saw Evan and D.I. Hughes blocking the hall in front of
her.

"Can I help you, miss?" the D.I. asked.

"I bloody well hope so," the girl said in an annoyed
voice. "I've just arrived here and I understand my mother
and my brother are both in jail. I'm Jasmine Llewellyn."

Evan stared at her, taking in the chin-length black hair,
the very white face, the mouth like a red gash, and the
black-lined eyes. He realized he was looking at a
stranger, a person he had never seen before in his life.

───── TWENTY ─────

"YOU'RE IFOR LLEWELLYN'S DAUGHTER?" Evan blurted out.

"I just said I was, didn't I?" The same confident arrogance of her brother. A definite look of her father in the toss of her head.

"Ah, Miss Llewellyn." The D.I. extended his hand to her. "So good of you to come. My condolences on your father. Detective Inspector Hughes. I am an opera buff and I can tell you that the world has lost one of its greatest—"

"If you're so sorry about it, can you please tell me why you've thrown my entire family in jail?" Jasmine demanded.

"I can assure you that they're not in jail, Miss Llewellyn," D.I. Hughes said, flushing at her belligerence. "They are here, in this building, helping us with our enquiries."

"That's what the police always say when they're about to get a confession out of some poor bastard," Jasmine Llewellyn said. "He was helping police with their enquiries, and now he's inexplicably dead."

"We don't use strong-arm tactics here, Miss Llewellyn. You've been living in Italy too long!" D.I. Hughes gave her a patronizing smile. "Your mother was reading the Sunday papers in the cafeteria when I last saw her. But we've been having an interesting conversation with your brother. He just confessed to killing your father."

Jasmine threw back her head and laughed. "Justin? He couldn't kill a fly without throwing up. He probably thinks that Mummy did it and he's being noble on her behalf. The Sydney Carton of Lake Como! He worships her, you know."

"Before we go back to your brother, Miss Llewellyn, maybe we could ask you a couple of questions."

"Of course. Fire away."

"You live in Milan—is that correct? And you were in Milan all this week?"

"No, I wasn't, actually."

"Oh, where were you?" Evan noticed the D.I. tense up.

"I work in the fashion industry, Inspector. I coordinate shoots. I was up in the Alps for a fur coat shoot on Tuesday. I was in Tunisia for bathing suits on Thursday. We got back Friday afternoon. Late Friday afternoon."

"That pretty much rules her out, doesn't it, sir," Evan ventured after they had escorted Jasmine to the cafeteria and left her with her mother and the solicitor. "She wouldn't have had time to catch a flight over here and get to Wales to kill her father."

"If she really was in Tunisia. That will be easy enough to verify. I'll get someone onto calling Milan right away. I've established personal contact with the chief of police there, so it should go smoothly. He's only too willing to help us in any way he can."

Evan remembered the lawyer's letter that must still be in Sergeant Watkins's pocket. He decided to say nothing for now. Better let him find out the truth about his Mafia hit man from Watkins! Evan had already one-upped him on the left-handedness and the D.I. didn't take kindly to that. This was confirmed when the D.I. said, as they reached the interrogation room, "Well, I shouldn't keep you from your duties in the village any longer, Constable. I expect you've got a whole slew of lost tourists and missing car keys waiting for you up there."

"It's Sunday, sir. My day off," Evan said innocently. "I'll be happy to assist in any way I can . . . and you might need me to drive some of the Llewellyns home—whichever of them ends up not confessing to the murder, that is."

The D.I. managed a tight little smile. "Ha ha. Very droll. Quite. Very well. I suppose you could hang around for a while, just in case we need a driver. Go and get yourself a cup of tea."

"Thanks a lot," Evan muttered, not loud enough to be heard as D.I. Hughes headed purposefully back in the direction of the interrogation room. Evan watched him go, then sighed, and walked in the other direction, toward the cafeteria.

Mrs. Llewellyn, Jasmine, and a bald-headed man, presumably the solicitor, were sitting at a table by the window. They looked up when he came in.

"Well?" Mrs. Llewellyn asked. "What's happening with Justin? When will we be allowed to see him?"

"I've no idea, madam," Evan said. "I'm just an ordinary P.C. I don't make any decisions."

"Yes, but any idiot could see that Justin didn't do it," Jasmine said. "He's not the head-bashing type."

"I can't understand why he doesn't want me in there with him. It's most dangerous to be in these situations without a solicitor present," the elderly man said. "I hope he doesn't say anything he regrets later. He always was impetuous, Margaret."

"I'm sure the inspector will come to the right conclusion fairly quickly now," Evan said. "You'll probably be able to go home soon."

"Home," Mrs. Llewellyn said with a sigh. "Doesn't that sound wonderful. Lake Como, sun, fresh peaches. Soon this will all seem like a terrible nightmare."

"Except that Daddy's gone," Jasmine pointed out.

"Yes, except that Daddy's gone," Mrs. Llewellyn repeated.

Evan bought a cup of tea and a cheese sandwich, only realizing as he ate it that he had missed breakfast and it was now close to lunchtime. As he ate he tried not to look too obviously at the Llewellyns. Jasmine was relaxed and laughing now. Even Mrs. Llewellyn's face had lost the pinched, strained look of earlier that day. Was it possible that the D.I. had been right for once? Had it been a family conspiracy, cleverly thought out to confuse the police and make them all seem innocent?

A disturbing picture was still nagging at the back of Evan's mind—the figure on the shore, the car in the lake and the defiant young girl, so like Jasmine that she could almost be her double.

Double . . . he spun the word around inside his head. Was it possible that Jasmine Llewellyn had needed a double for some reason? He had to find the truth.

He had just finished eating when Sergeant Watkins came in. He motioned Evan to the door.

"Justin's changed his tune now," he muttered to Evan. "Now he's not saying another thing until the lawyer's in there with him. It was when the D.I. started probing into why he'd lied that he became very defensive. He's covering up for someone, sure enough."

"It can't be the sister. She's got a pretty watertight alibi."

"Then who?"

"Listen, Sarge," Evan said. "Is there any way you could arrange to let me have a private talk with Justin? It's about this car-in-the-lake business. It has to tie in somewhere. I have to find out who the other girl really is and what she was doing here. If I could just sort it out, it might solve a lot of things. But I can't ask the D.I."

"I'm not really sure what you're getting at," Watkins said, "but I'll see what I can do."

"Thanks," Evan said.

"It shouldn't be too hard. I can't imagine the D.I. would want to keep Justin Llewellyn around much longer, especially now he's not willing to talk. What we have to do is arrange that the others leave without him and you can give him a ride."

"Brilliant." Evan nodded. "This might be the missing link we need."

"And now I'm going to check up on our other missing link," Watkins said.

"Mrs. Llewellyn's boyfriend?" Evan asked.

Watkins nodded. "We still can't rule him out, can we? It could be him that she's been covering for all along."

Evan nodded. "Or he could be part of the family conspiracy."

Watkins sucked air through his teeth. "I get the feeling that this whole confession nonsense is all a series of misunderstandings. Mother thinks lover or son did it and confesses to save whoever it was. Son thinks mother did it and confesses to save her. Bloody heroic either way."

"Or clever," Evan pointed out. "By the end of today we might even know the truth."

"Or we might be back to step one and looking into Mafia hit men again." Watkins sighed. "I wish we could come up with the weapon with a nice set of prints on it, or a friendly shopper who saw Gladys pushed under a car. The photos have gone down to the computer center in Colwyn Bay, by the way, just in case we've missed something. Oh well, on with the next round."

He went into the cafeteria and Evan watched him talk to the elderly solicitor, who then followed him out again.

"They are going to release Justin soon, aren't they?" Mrs. Llewellyn asked Evan.

"I expect so, ma'am," Evan said. "At least for the time being."

"I just wish this was all over." Mrs. Llewellyn ran her fingers through her hair. "Any idea when we can go back to the house and get our things packed up? I'd like the children there when I have to go through Ifor's effects."

"I'm afraid I can't tell you anything, ma'am," Evan said. "As soon as the case is solved, you'll be free to arrange the funeral and get on with your lives."

"Unless you decide that one of us did it," Jasmine said with biting sarcasm.

"Jasmine, that isn't funny," Mrs. L. snapped.

"Oh lighten up, Mummy. Where's your sense of humor?" Jasmine sounded ridiculously like her father. Evan suspected that raising her had been no piece of cake for Mrs. Llewellyn.

They looked up as the solicitor came back into the room. "They've decided no more questions for the present," he said. "Justin is free to go."

"Thank God." The relief was obvious on Mrs. Llewellyn's face. "Do you really mean he's not a suspect?"

"For the moment. It was tactfully suggested that he not try to leave the area while they check with the servants at Como."

Jasmine got to her feet. "Now we can go and find some edible food. I'll die if I have to drink another cup of this filthy tea. Do you think there's a halfway decent restaurant in this godforsaken place?"

The solicitor put a restraining hand on her arm. "The inspector would like to see you, Jasmine."

"Me? What on earth for?"

"He needs names and numbers to corroborate your movements last week."

"Bloody cheek!" Jasmine's face flushed scarlet. "Oh

well, I suppose I'll have to give them to him to shut him up."

"Don't worry, darling, we'll wait for you," Mrs. Llewellyn said. "Even if it means drinking more disgusting tea."

Evan had been studying Jasmine Llewellyn's legs. She had very nice legs, for one thing, but he had seen something else that interested him. "By the way, Mrs. Llewellyn," he said, "they never found the other shoe when they searched your house. That was strange, wasn't it?"

"What shoe, Mummy?" Jasmine asked.

"A black shoe with a thick sole and a high heel," Evan said. "I suppose that type must be fashionable right now. Looks sort of dangerous to me."

Jasmine laughed. "My mother doesn't wear shoes like that, Constable. *Que stupido.*"

"No, but you do, Miss Llewellyn," Evan said, glancing again at Jasmine's feet.

"Then it was lucky that Jasmine was far away in Italy, wasn't it?" Mrs. Llewellyn said smoothly.

There was definitely something going on here that he didn't understand, Evan decided as he went looking for Justin Llewellyn. He found him standing in the waiting area with Sergeant Watkins.

"We have reached an impasse, Constable," Justin said in an amused voice. "I keep trying to tell the inspector I did it and he keeps insisting I didn't. Strange but true. Anyway, the shackles are off for the time being and I am going to faint clean away if I don't get something to eat soon."

"I'm going back to Llanfair," Evan said. "I'd be happy to drive you back to the inn if you like."

"What about my mother and sister?" Justin looked around.

"The inspector has a few details he needs to get from your sister first. I understand that their solicitor is going to be driving them."

"That settles it," Justin said. "I'll ride up with you. I couldn't stand being in a car with that pompous old snot."

"You asked for him a few minutes ago," Evan pointed out.

"Only because I was tired of answering questions," Justin said with a grin. "I knew once he was there nothing would be accomplished. And I was right. The inspector soon gave up, didn't he? The old fool bores everybody into submission."

Evan held open the door for Justin and buttoned his jacket as they faced the blustery day outside.

"Bloody Wales," Justin muttered as he climbed into Evan's car and slammed the door shut on the rain. "Thank God mother had the sense to move out of that cold, damp house. At least the Everest Inn has efficient central heating."

"But they had the central heating on at the house when I was there," Evan said.

"My father? With central heating? You've got to be joking. Mother always called him the Welsh mountain goat because living with him was like being on a bloody hillside—all the windows open and a howling gale blowing through the place."

"But I thought—" Evan began, then shut up.

"Anyway, I'll be back in sunny Italy soon."

"I hope so, sir," Evan said evenly.

Justin shot him an alarmed look. "What do you mean by that?"

"Only that this case is far from being solved and no-body goes anywhere until it is. Now if you could help us in any way . . ."

"I've tried to help you, haven't I?" Justin said petulantly. "I've confessed to the bloody crime. What more do you want?"

"The truth would be nice."

"I don't know why they won't believe me. Do I look too fragile to be a killer?"

"Oh no, sir," Evan said. "Many of the worst killers are inoffensive people. They kill because it makes them feel powerful. It's just that you're left-handed. A right-handed person had to have hit your father. A left-handed blow would have been on the other side of his head."

"Ah. Very clever." Justin nodded. "I should have thought of that."

"So why don't you tell us why you confessed—it can't be because you actually wanted a lifetime in jail. You must have done it because you thought you knew who the real murderer was and you wanted to spare . . . her."

"Her?"

"Your mother or your sister, I would assume."

"Policemen do too much assuming."

They passed the housing estate, dripping drearily in the rain, and Caernarfon gave way to green fields, gently rising to the mountains. Evan dropped down a gear as the road began to climb.

"I'm still interested in this car-in-the-lake business," Evan said, staring past the windscreen wipers. "Who was the girl, Justin?"

"None of your business."

"Oh, but it is my business," Evan said. "I was there. I saw you behind the car. I rescued her from the lake. To me that looks suspiciously like attempted murder and being left-handed won't get you out of that."

"Don't be absurd," Justin said. "I told you before, I had no idea that her car went into the lake. We had another argument, she was being unreasonable, and I left. The car was sitting there on the lakeshore when I last saw it."

"Then can you explain how it got into the lake?"

"She knocked the brake off by accident? The brake was faulty? How should I know?"

"And if the brake wasn't faulty?" Evan asked. "What

were you quarreling about? She said she wasn't your girl-friend."

"That's right. She wasn't." He said it so firmly that Evan glanced at him.

"So what connection does she have to your family? Why did she come to the house trying to find you that day before your family moved in?"

"She wasn't trying to find me, you idiot. I was the last person she wanted to see," Justin snapped. "She was looking for my father."

"Your father?" Evan was caught completely off guard.

"It's rather obvious, isn't it? She was one of his acquisitions. He liked having young girls around him. They kept him eternally youthful—at least that's what he said."

Evan's thoughts immediately went to Betsy. He saw Ifor holding her hand, inviting her to the opera in Cardiff . . . suggesting that black hair would suit her better.

"I thought maybe she was your sister," Evan confessed. "She looks very like her."

"They all do. That's how father liked his women—skinny, dark, and waiflike. It didn't matter how they started out, they all ended up looking like Jasmine."

"So she came here looking for your father and was upset to find you instead—why?"

"Because it was rather uncomfortable for both of us. She used to be my girlfriend, before my father acquired her. Foolishly I brought her home. It only took him one evening." Justin laughed bitterly. "He promised her a backstage tour of La Scala. His backstage tours always ended up in his bed. She was, as they say, swept off her feet. What she didn't realize was that he never kept them long. He was like a little child with new toys. He soon tired of them and went on to something else." He paused. The rain drummed on the car roof. Spray flew from the windscreen wipers as they clicked back and forth. Evan's heart went out to him.

"Unfortunately she fell for my father in a big way.

They usually did. He was a very overpowering man. You either loved him or hated him. She wouldn't admit that it was over. She kept pestering him, begging him to come back to her—totally ridiculous actually. He never cared for them at all. He didn't care what happened to them after he'd dumped them."

"So she came here, hoping to find your father and get back together with him," Evan said. "Instead she saw you."

"And I tried to get her to see sense and go away before she got hurt again," Justin said. "My father didn't handle upsets very easily. He could be pretty bloody if he wanted to be. Christine and I drove up to the lake to talk. She was still convinced that he loved her and everything would be fine if he saw her again. I tried to make her see sense. I gave her a good reality check. She said some pretty crushing things about me—compared me unfavorably to him in some unmentionable ways. I was so angry I got out and walked."

"And then the car went into the lake," Evan said. "Why?"

"I presume she wanted to do something to make my father sit up and take notice. She's unstable and unbalanced and she overreacted. As usual."

───TWENTY-ONE───

THERE WAS SILENCE AS THEY both considered the implications of this statement.

"She tended to . . . overreact, did she, Mr. Llewellyn?" Evan asked quietly.

"She's highly strung. Very emotional."

"And you think she might have killed him?"

Justin didn't answer.

"Do you suspect that she killed your father?" Evan insisted. "Do you have proof that she killed your father?"

Justin looked out of the window.

"Mr. Llewellyn, if she's as unstable as you say, she may take her own life, too. Is that what you want?"

Justin sighed. "No."

"You must still love her, or you wouldn't have risked your own life for her."

"Of course I still love her, dammit." He dropped his voice. "Okay, I was in the house last week. I told you about coming to see my mother. She wasn't there. I was in the house alone when the phone rang. I didn't answer it. I didn't want anyone to know I was there. The answering machine picked it up and it was Christine. She told my father she had to see him again. She was staying at a local hotel. She knew his wife had gone out of town for a few days. She left a number. She said . . . she said she couldn't live without him and she was going to make him see that he couldn't live without her."

He looked at Evan with the scared, hopeless eyes of a young man who was carrying a terrible burden.

"So what did you do then?" Evan asked.

"I went downstairs and erased the message." He stared ahead into the rain. "Don't you see—I might have been the one who drove her over the edge into despair."

"You did what you thought was best for everyone," Evan said. "You don't happen to know what hotel she was staying at?"

Justin shook his head. "All these Welsh names sound the same to me."

Evan swung off the road as a petrol station loomed ahead. "I'll call HQ. They must have taken a list of all incoming calls to the house last week."

He ran to the phone booth and dialed. Not too long after he was back in the car. "The Plas Coed at Betws-y-Coed. Do you mind driving over there with me? We might be able to find out when she left and where she went."

Nestled in its narrow valley on the other side of the mountain, Betws-y-Coed was in the full swing of its tourist season, although strictly in a genteel way. There was nothing here for the funfair crowd. There wasn't even much for families. There were refined tea shops, as well as shops selling local wools and crafts, the Swallow Falls just beyond the village, and bucolic pastures along the river. Well-bred tourists were strolling along the river as Evan drove through the village. They wore tweeds and brogue shoes and many of them looked like the Queen at Balmoral, with scarves around their heads and dowdy raincoats.

Evan found the Plas Coed on the other side of the river, crossing by the narrow stone bridge with the waterfall roaring underneath. The hotel looked more like a country house—a refined black-and-white half-timbered building, set back from the road among tall larch trees. Old-fashioned and somber, with high gables and little tables on a manicured lawn, it was the sort of hotel that retired colonels and spinster schoolteachers might go for bracing fresh air and good long walks, but was probably lacking in modern amenities, like bathrooms.

Justin and Evan leaped out of the car as soon as it stopped. Evan had driven over the mountains with a sense of urgency that Justin had now also acquired.

"Christine Danvers?" The young redhead at the desk looked at them with interest, fluttering her eyelashes hopefully. "Hang on a sec." She flicked through the registration book. "Room twenty-one. I think she's still up there. Her key's not on the hook."

There was no lift and their feet echoed from the uncarpeted narrow stairs.

"Yes?" A cautious voice responded to their knock. The door was opened.

"Oh." She stepped back, for a moment speechless. Then she recovered herself. "What do you want?"

Evan answered. "Remember me, miss? I'm the police officer who pulled you out of the water."

"Oh, but I thought everything was settled with the car." She was clearly flustered, looking past Evan like a trapped animal, estimating whether she could make a run for it. "They said it was an accident . . ."

"It's not the car we've come about. It's Mr. Ifor Llewellyn."

"He's dead," she said, then repeated with utter hopelessness. "He's dead, isn't he?"

"We'd like to talk to you, please." Evan didn't wait for an invitation. Justin followed him into the room.

"It was the message on the answering machine, wasn't

it?" she blurted out. She walked across to the window and stared out across the valley. "I realized what I'd done right away. It was so bloody stupid of me to leave that message. I knew they'd find me, so I just sat here and waited to be found."

"Why should they want to find you, miss?" Evan asked. "Do you know something about Mr. Llewellyn's death?"

"Oh yes," Christine said. "Of course I do. Why else are you here?" She paused and then added, "I expect you found my fingerprints, didn't you?"

If the lab boys had found unidentified prints, they hadn't mentioned it. Evan smiled in anticipation of pointing this omission out to them.

"My fingers had blood on them," she added. "I must have touched something."

"Are you trying to tell us that you killed Mr. Llewellyn?" Evan asked.

She turned around, looking directly at him with surprised, innocent eyes. "Oh no. He was dead when I got there."

"Would you like to tell me exactly what happened?" Evan asked.

She looked around the room. "There's nowhere to sit, I'm afraid." This was true. Just a narrow bed and one hard upright chair with Christine's washing things on it. A room that belonged in a convent, not a three-star hotel.

"Don't worry. We can stand," Evan said. "Go on."

"Alright." She paused, biting her lip. "You put me on a train down to London, didn't you? But I couldn't stay there. I had to see Ifor again. See, I knew it was all a mistake. I knew he wanted us to be together when he got to Wales. Why did he tell me the address where he was going to be staying if he didn't want to see me?" She glared at Justin. "So I came back. I called but nobody was home. I left that bloody stupid message, but he didn't call me back. I waited and waited and then by Friday I

couldn't wait any longer. I called him on Friday afternoon. He answered the phone. He said he never checked
answering machines and he was glad to hear my voice.
He told me to come on over. He said his wife wouldn't
be back until quite late." Her face had become alive
again, as if she was reliving the thought of seeing him.
"I'd rented another car so I drove over to Llanfair. Ifor
told me to park up at the Everest Inn above the village,
so that nobody would notice a suspicious car. He said
people talked in villages. I went down the little path to
his house . . ."

"What time was this, miss?"

She wrinkled her button of a nose. "It must have been
after six. Probably closer to six-thirty."

"Are you sure it wasn't later than that?" Evan asked.
"Closer to seven?"

She frowned again. "I don't think so, but I'm not sure.
It could have been, I suppose. It might have taken longer
to walk down that path than I thought . . ."

"It doesn't matter. Go on."

"The door wasn't properly shut. I pushed it open and
I called. Nobody answered. I went in. I called again. I
went into the living room and then I saw him. He was
lying there, sprawled on the floor. I thought he was ill or
something—maybe he'd had a heart attack. I went over
and I touched him and I said, 'Ifor, are you okay . . . ?' "
The horror was clear on her face. "That's when I saw the
blood. I got it on my hand where I'd touched him. It was
all warm and sticky. It was horrible . . ." She paused to
compose herself. "I didn't know what to do next. Then
I heard this sound and I thought *oh-my-god,* the murderer
is still here, in the house! I was so scared, I just ran. I
tripped over in the back garden and I lost my shoe, but
I kept on running."

"Wait a minute," Evan said. "You lost your shoe in
the back garden?"

She nodded. "The heel got caught between paving

stones. I didn't want to wait around. I just kept on going in case the murderer was still coming after me."

"Interesting," Evan said. "And did you see anyone?"

"No. Nobody. Maybe I imagined the sound. I don't know. I was so freaked out. When I got back to my car I tried to get a grip on myself. I knew I should call the police, but then I thought what if they suspect me and I remembered the message on the answering machine and I knew that I must have touched something with my bloody fingers. I've been so scared. I didn't think anyone would believe me."

"I believe you, Christine," Justin said.

She looked up at him fiercely. "You shouldn't be so willing to believe things about me, Justin. I'm not a nice person, I'm really not." She covered her face in her hands and burst into noisy sobs. "Oh God, I wish I were dead."

Justin went over and put his arm around her. "It's going to be alright, Chrissy," he said. "I promise you it's going to be alright."

Evan was just coming out of police headquarters, where he had delivered Christine and Justin, when Sergeant Watkins drove up.

"I think we're onto something," he yelled to Evan. "Finally we've got some evidence." He waved a large manila envelope as he got out of the car. "I've just got the photos from the computer center and you'll never guess what's shown up."

He stepped into the shelter of the porch and pulled a stack of photos out of the envelope. "Take a look at this," he said, handing one to Evan. It was a poorly lit shot of the village street with Mrs. Llewellyn walking toward the Powell-Joneses' driveway.

"Yes? What about it?" Evan asked. "Isn't this when she arrived home to find us there?"

"Right," Watkins said. "And she said she took a taxi, remember?"

"And?"

"No taxi in the picture, but right down here, in the corner, you can just see the front bumper of a car?"

Evan nodded.

"With computer enhancement we can read the license plate. It's a green Jaguar belonging to James Norton— Mrs. Llewellyn's boyfriend."

Evan whistled. "So he was in the village after all, at least around eight-thirty."

"And there's more," Watkins went on excitedly. "I've taken a look at the statements from people who were in Pool Street when Gladys had her accident. Several of them mention seeing a green Jaguar."

"Very interesting," Evan said. "Did you go and interview him this afternoon?"

"Yes I did and I can tell you, the gentleman was very nervous. Sweating buckets. And he had no alibi from the moment they checked out of the hotel at four o'clock until he arrived home after ten." He grinned at Evan. "He tried to deny the whole thing to start with. He claimed he just happened to bump into Mrs. L. at the hotel, where he was staying on business. Surprised and delighted to see an old friend, ha ha. It will be interesting to see what he says this time."

"Are you going back there now?" Evan asked.

"I'm going to show this lot to the D.I. and then I imagine he'll want James Norton brought in. What's the betting they planned it between them—him and Mrs. Llewellyn? And I think we've got a good chance of getting the truth out of him. He'll be easier to crack than she was." He pushed open the door. "Come on. Where are you off to?"

"Home," Evan said. "I've been patted on the back and sent back to Llanfair."

"Oh come on," Watkins said. "Can't you find an excuse to hang around and be in at the kill?"

"I'd like to but the D.I. made it pretty clear. He

thanked me for my invaluable help as chauffeur today and said he wouldn't be needing my services any longer."

"The man's a fool," Watkins said. "He knows as well as I do that—"

"Let it be, Sarge," Evan said. "He's right. It is none of my business. And it's my day off. I'm going to try and enjoy some of it."

"I'll call you and let you know how it went," Watkins said.

"Be careful, won't you," Evan called after him. "If he's already killed once, he won't hesitate to do it again."

"Don't worry, I'm not stupid. I'm not going back alone," Watkins said. He gave Evan a friendly wave as he went into the building.

As Evan drove home, he tried not to feel annoyed that he had been dismissed, just when things were beginning to get interesting. He had to face the fact that he was only the village bobby and it was none of his business. But he would have liked to be in that interview room when James Norton broke down and told the truth. And he would have liked to see Mrs. Llewellyn's face when they confronted her with it.

They had to have been in on it together. She was probably the one who planned it—she was certainly cool and calculating enough . . . except that it didn't seem like a planned killing. Hitting someone over the head was a risky way of dispatching them. What if they had missed, or the first blow wasn't hard enough, or it turned into a fight? A giant of a man like Ifor was very likely to win. No, anyone planning to kill Ifor would have used a more guaranteed method, like a bullet.

Which had to mean that it wasn't planned at all. Evan considered a new scenario. What if they had intended to talk to Ifor civilly, begging him not to make a fuss and give Mrs. Llewellyn the divorce she wanted? What if Ifor had then lost his temper and become violent? Might one of them have struck him in self-defense? But then why not admit it?

Oh well, there was no more point in speculating tonight. He'd know more when Watkins called and in the meantime it was his day off.

The rain had stopped as he drove back up the pass. A watery sun was making hedgerows steam and dotting sheep's wool with diamonds. Streamlets danced down both sides of the road. The fresh smell of green things after rain came in powerfully through the car windows.

He'd go and see Bronwen, he decided. He hadn't even had a chance to tell her about Maggie Pole. Bronwen deserved to know the truth. He wanted to tell Bronwen the truth. It had been like a gnawing wound he had kept to himself for a couple of years now.

He tapped on Bronwen's door. No answer. As he turned away he saw two little boys hanging from the climbing frame in the school playground. "Teacher's not here, Mr. Efans!" one of them called. "She's gone down to the *eisteddfod* again. She took some of the girls to see the finals of the dancing."

The other made vomiting noises, to show what he thought about girls and dancing.

"Thanks, Aled," Evan said. "Maybe I'll go on down there myself."

He went home and changed out of his uniform, then he drove down to Harlech.

The main car park was full and he had to park in the nearby housing estate and walk. Progress was slow and difficult in the main *eisteddfod* field as the mass of spectators had to pick their way around puddles and through mud. Some of the outer booths, not fully enclosed from the weather, were now a sorry sight, with torn and dripping signs and sagging tarpaulins. He found that he was wandering past the beer tent, maybe with the subconscious hope of finding Maggie there. He didn't want her to think that he had stood her up last night. Funny that he still didn't want her to think badly of him, after the way she had behaved!

As he was passing the tent, he decided that a pint might not be such a bad idea for someone who had had to subsist on tea and buns all day. He went inside and was greeted by Evans-the-Meat.

"Well, look who's here! Finished your crime solving for the day, have you, Evan *bach?*"

"What are you lads doing here?" Evan asked, as he joined a circle of Llanfair men. "Come down for a dose of culture?"

"We thought we ought to come and cheer for Mr. Parry Davies and Mr. Powell-Jones," Roberts-the-Pump said.

"I didn't know the bard's competition took place in the beer tent." Evan raised an eyebrow.

"Ah well, the chairing of the bard is the last event tonight, so we thought we had time for a quick pint first," Evans-the-Milk explained. "What are you having, Evans-the-Law?"

"I wouldn't say no to a pint of Brains, thanks." He held up his glass to them. *"Iachyd da,"* he said raising his glass to them before taking a long drink.

"Poor old Austin Mostyn is here, too. He's putting himself through agony, listening to the winning choirs give their command performances," Evans-the-Meat said.

"He came so close this time," Roberts-the-Pump said. "He'll never get that chance again."

"If only we'd had time to think, we should have used a tape of Ifor and got one of us to lip-synch, like the pop stars do," Barry-the-Bucket joked.

"We could have done that, man," Evans-the-Milk exclaimed, giving him a hearty slap. "He had loads of tapes of himself, didn't he? And he always recorded all his rehearsals, too."

"Drink up, man," Evans-the-Meat nudged Evan. "I've never seen you so slow with a pint before.

Evan put down the glass. "Look, I've got to go," he said. "I'll see you all later. Something just came up."

Then he ran out into the twilight. He found a phone in the first aid tent and made a call to HQ.

"Look, I know there's only you on duty, Dai," he said impatiently to the young constable at the desk, "but this is an emergency. I need to have a detailed list of everything in that drawing room right away. Tell the sergeant it's very important that I get it now."

It seemed to take forever. If he didn't get it soon it would be too late and he didn't want to have to act without it, just on his suspicions.

"Sorry about that," the young constable said at last. "Sarge didn't want to give me the file because you're not officially on the case—so I just sneaked it out when he wasn't looking. Don't tell him, will you?"

"Thanks. I appreciate it."

"Now what was it you wanted?"

"A list of everything found in the room where the murder took place."

The young constable started reading. Evan interrupted him halfway. "On the windowsill, you say? Great. Perfect. Thanks, Dai. You've just helped catch your first murderer. Tell the duty sergeant I may just be calling him for help soon. I'll see how things go here. I'm at the *eisteddfod.*"

He hung up the phone and stood for a moment, collecting his racing thoughts in the brisk night air. Finally he saw how it had been done. It hadn't seemed possible before but now he saw that it had been cleverly orchestrated.

TWENTY-TWO

EVAN MADE HIS WAY ACROSS the muddy field to one of the three big pavilions. The rich sound of a Côr Meibion was overpowering the lesser sounds of piano and poetry in the other tents. Evan stood at the back of the tent, letting his eyes adjust to the darkness. The Ffestiniog choir was on stage, giving a rousing version of "Sauspan Fach."

Then Evan spotted him, sitting alone in one of the back rows, staring intently at the stage, his glasses glinting in the reflected stage lights. Evan slid into a seat beside him.

" 'Ello, Mostyn. They said you'd be here, listening to the other choirs."

Mostyn nodded. "They're not as good as we could have been," he said. "We could have won."

Evan put his arm on Mostyn's sleeve. "You and I have to talk, Mostyn. Let's go outside."

"Not now. I'm listening to this."

Evan tightened his grip. "Yes now, Mostyn. It's important."

"Oh, very well." Mostyn gave a sigh of annoyance, picked up his shabby briefcase, and got to his feet. It was now almost dark. Lights reflected from puddles. The crowd had thinned out. The sound of clapping and cheering came from the pavilion next door.

"Now what is it, Mr. Evans?" Mostyn asked. "I really want to get back there to hear the choir from Rhondda Vale. They're truly excellent."

"So why did you do it, Mostyn?"

"Do what?"

"Kill the goose that laid the golden egg?" Evan said gently. "Kill Ifor before he had a chance to win you the first prize."

"What are you talking about, man?" Mostyn demanded. "Have you lost your mind? How could I have killed Ifor? I was down here, waiting for the rest of you when he was still alive. Everyone heard him, didn't they?"

"They heard a tape of him, Mostyn. One of those tapes of himself he had lying everywhere around the house. I checked with HQ a few minutes ago. There had been a tape recorder on the windowsill behind the curtains, but no tape in it. There was no tape anywhere in the room. That's why you went straight over to the window, didn't you? It wasn't to see if the radiator was on, it was to take the tape out of the machine while I was examining the body."

Mostyn said nothing so Evan went on. "And you turned the radiators on, too, didn't you—so that the body would take longer to stiffen up and we'd put the time of death later than it really was? Then you fed me that nonsense about Ifor feeling the cold. He hated stuffy rooms. He always had the windows open, even in winter . . . didn't you remember that about him from the days when you roomed together? Funny how criminals always slip up on the little things."

"I am not a criminal!" Mostyn blurted out. "And you've no proof at all. I wiped everything clean."

"Did you now. Thanks very much for telling me. What

I can't understand is why. Why then? Why not wait until you'd won your first prize?"

"Because he made me, that's why," Mostyn said flatly. "I never meant to kill him, but he goaded me. You know how he was, Constable Evans. He kept on and on until something snapped."

Evan did know how it was. He remembered Mrs. Powell-Jones saying the same thing. She had been pushed until something snapped. If it was possible for a stable, unemotional person like Mrs. Powell-Jones, how much more possible for someone like Mostyn Phillips.

"I went to the house that evening," Mostyn said slowly. "I was going to drive him myself to make sure he was on time for once. He said he wasn't riding in my little tin can of a car. That upset me to start with. It's a good little car, isn't it? Plenty of power still."

Evan nodded.

"I told him what I thought of him and the way he treated his wife. She used to be my girl once, you know." He looked up at Evan with despair in his eyes. "She came to visit me at college. Ifor and I were sharing a room. He took one look at her and . . . and he took her away from me. The only girl I ever loved, Mr. Evans. He took everything away from me. Whatever I did, he did it better. I would have won the outstanding student prize if Ifor hadn't been there. I worked harder. I deserved it more. But he won it. He had the damned trophy sitting there on the sideboard—Polymnia, the muse of harmony, carved on a base of Italian marble.

"He laughed at me. Meeting him was the best thing that ever happened to Margaret, he said. He told me what she thought about me—that she laughed about me and how . . . inadequate I was. I couldn't stand it any longer. He turned away to pour himself a drink, still talking and laughing, telling me what a miserable failure I had been. I grabbed the trophy, the one that should have been mine, and I hit him over the head with it. I don't know what I meant to do—not kill him—just make him stop."

Mostyn shut his eyes and a shudder went through his body. "I did make him stop. He fell to the ground. I saw the blood. I tried to pull myself together. I thought I'd go and tell the police exactly what had happened. They'd understand. Then I thought, what if they didn't—what if they locked me up for life?

"That's when it came to me that I could make it look like an accident. I moved him across to the fireplace so that it would look as if he hit his head on that fender. It was hard work because he was so heavy. But I did it. There were blood spatters on the carpet. I moved the desk to cover them. Then I splashed whiskey around to make it look as if he'd been drinking and had fallen over blind drunk.

"Then I realized I had to give myself an alibi. For the first time in my life I was making full use of my brain— the fine brain I had been given and never had a proper chance to use.

"I knew he always recorded himself, every time he sang, vain bastard. I found a warm-up tape. I hid a tape recorder out of sight on the window ledge and I turned it on at full volume. That would give me half an hour to get safely away. That's when I saw the radiator. I remembered reading that bodies didn't stiffen up as quickly in a hot room. I went and switched on the central heating and turned the radiators in the room on full.

"Then I went into the kitchen to wash my hands. I'd been very careful but I'd got some blood on them when I moved him. I was just coming down the hall again about to leave when I heard someone knocking on the front door. And then it opened. I hid in the hall closet. It was a girl. She found Ifor and she ran out. I can tell you, Mr. Evans, that my heart nearly stopped beating with fright. I was sure she'd gone to get the police and I'd be trapped. I slipped out and then I found that she'd dropped her shoe. I picked it up with my handkerchief, so I wouldn't leave fingerprints and tossed it back into the house, outside the living room door. That would give the police something else to think about.

"My car was parked over at the pub. Nobody was around when I got in and drove away . . . and anyway, if someone had seen me, they'd swear that Ifor was still alive. It was a perfect alibi . . . if you hadn't stuck your nose in and ruined it for me."

"What did you do with the murder weapon, Mostyn?" Evan asked.

"It's on my mantlepiece, where it belongs," he said. "I gave it a good going-over. You won't find a trace of blood on it. You won't find anything to incriminate me. I was meticulous. I wiped away every trace."

"And Gladys?" Evan asked. "Did you have anything to do with Gladys?"

Mostyn sighed. "How was I to know she was still in the house, silly woman? I knew it was only a matter of time before she recognized the voice was mine."

"So you pushed her under a car."

"It wasn't hard. I followed her and waited for the right moment. It's funny how easy it is to kill someone." He looked up at Evan and smiled. "But all this is just between you and me, Constable. I think you might have a hard time proving it."

"Do you think you're the only one who uses tape recorders, Mostyn?" Evan said.

"You mean you've recorded this conversation?" Mostyn asked indignantly. "That's very underhanded of you, Constable Evans."

"I'm afraid the police have to be underhanded sometimes, Mostyn," Evan said. "Now we ought to take a ride to headquarters, don't you think? It's good to get the truth out, isn't it? It would only have preyed on your mind and haunted you."

"Do you think it hasn't already?" Mostyn asked in a broken voice. "Sitting in there, listening to those other choirs . . . do you think I haven't regretted my reckless act over and over. I would do anything in the world to undo it, Constable. I might have hated him, but I would never have wished him dead. He was . . . the greatest living tenor. I deprived the world of that talent. I can't tell you how sorry I am."

Evan put a hand on his shoulder. "Come along, let's go now."

Mostyn came with him willingly enough. As they passed the next pavilion Mostyn hesitated.

"Just a minute, Mr. Evans," he said. "I just need to get something out of my briefcase."

Evan waited patiently. Mostyn rummaged around, then he said, "You really are very naive, aren't you? Did you think I'd come without a fight?"

His hand emerged from the briefcase and Evan saw that he was holding a gun. It wasn't just a little pistol, either. It was a sleek new semiautomatic, the sort of gun Evan had seen in the hands of drug dealers but the last thing in the world he would have expected to see in the hands of Mostyn Phillips.

"Where on earth did you get a thing like that?" he blurted out.

Mostyn gave a satisfied smile. "You can buy them quite easily these days. I got it on my last trip to Ireland. Everyone is armed there. Nobody asks questions. I always sensed I'd have to protect myself someday."

"Come on, Mostyn, don't be—" he was about to say "a fool" and stopped himself. Being labeled as a fool and a failure had already made him kill once. He had to make sure that Mostyn didn't do anything stupid with so many people milling around them. "Don't make it harder on yourself," he finished. "I'm sure the judge and jury will understand that there were extenuating circumstances. We can testify that Ifor goaded you to the limits of your endurance. You'll probably get off with manslaughter— maybe only a couple of years."

"A couple of years?" Mostyn's voice was high and dangerous. "Do you know what prison would be like for a man like me? You saw how Ifor picked on me. That's what it would be like every moment, only worse." He shook his head. "I'm not going to jail, Mr. Evans. I'm going out in a blaze of glory. I'm going to make bigger headlines than Ifor, for once!"

Suddenly he dodged into the tent behind him, ran up the center aisle, and leaped up onto the stage. "Nobody move," he instructed. "And nobody gets hurt."

There were screams and the sound of chairs being knocked over as people dived for cover.

"I said nobody move!" Mostyn's voice was almost a scream now. "And stay in your seats!"

But some people had already left. Spectators standing near the entrance had managed to slip away. It was only a matter of time before the police got here in full force, and then what would happen? Evan was sure Mostyn was serious about going out in a blaze of glory. He'd probably be quite prepared to shoot it out with the police, and how many other people would wind up dead?

Evan ducked out of the back of the tent and ran around to the stage entrance. He slipped inside and for the first time he was able to assess the true horror of the situation. Mostyn was standing in the middle of a group of young folk dancers. There were white dresses and flower garlands all around him. They were standing rooted to the spot with expressions of bewildered horror on their young faces. The audience also sat as if mesmerized as Mostyn's gun swept over them, first left and then to the right. Then Evan's heart missed a beat. Bronwen was sitting in the middle of the front row, her arms around two little girls. Nothing was going to be allowed to happen to Bronwen!

It was now or never. *Go on,* he commanded himself silently. *Get on with it, before it's too late!* But his legs didn't want to move. He was fairly sure that Mostyn wouldn't shoot him in cold blood, but Mostyn was not himself tonight. He was already a man driven over the edge. Who knew what he would do?

Evan took a deep breath and stepped up onto the stage. Mostyn turned at the noise and pointed the gun at him. He heard gasps from the spectators.

"Come on, Mostyn *bach*. You don't want to do this," Evan said, fighting to keep his voice calm and genial. "We don't want one of these little children to get hurt by mistake, do we?"

"Stay away from me, Evan," Mostyn said, waving the gun dangerously. "I'm warning you!"

"Just think what you're doing, Mostyn. Any jury would understand how you killed Ifor. But if a little child gets killed tonight, they won't forgive you so easily. They'll put you away for life."

A spasm of pain crossed Mostyn's face. "I don't care," he said. "Why should I care about anything? Who's ever cared about me? Now get back. I don't want to hurt you."

Evan took a step closer. "I know you don't. You don't want to hurt anyone, Mostyn. You're not a violent person. And you like children, too. You've devoted your whole life to children. Why undo all that good in one stupid moment?"

He took another step closer. "Give me the gun, please, before someone gets hurt by mistake."

"Don't come any closer!" Mostyn was crying now, the tears mingling with beads of sweat that ran down his face. "I'm not going to let them take me alive. I'm going out in a blaze of glory."

"You call this glory?" Evan demanded. "Little kiddies getting hit by stray bullets is glory? Look at those little faces, Mostyn. Look what you're putting them through. Don't do this to them. Come on. Give me the gun."

He took the final step. He saw the muscles in Mostyn's forearm tighten, his fingers curl around the trigger. Mostyn let out an almost primal "No!" as Evan grabbed the gun and wrenched it out of his hand. Mostyn sank to the floor with a great sob as security men leaped onto the stage and yanked him to his feet.

"Go easy with him," Evan commanded. "He's sick. He doesn't know what he's doing."

Mothers scrambled onto the stage, sweeping up and enveloping now-crying children. Evan stood on the stage, unnoticed for the moment, too stunned to move. He was just coming down the steps when flashbulbs went off in Evan's face.

"How does it feel to be a hero? Were you scared? What made you do it?" He was being buried under an avalanche of questions.

"I'm a policeman. It's part of my job," he said, squinting in the glare of the lights. "If you want to know any more, you'll have to talk to my boss in Caernarfon."

"Wait. Let me get to him," a female voice yelled and someone pushed through the circle of media. "Evan, darling, you were wonderful! So brave! You saved us all! I was so proud of you!" Maggie flung herself into his arms as the flashbulbs popped around them.

"I realize now what a fool I was and how badly I treated you," she went on. "Please come home and let's start over."

Evan removed her arms from his neck. "You don't understand, Maggie. I am home," he said. "I've no desire to go anywhere else, or to go back to any part of my old life. Now, if you'll all excuse me . . ."

He walked calmly past the microphones and cameras. As he came down the steps from the stage he heard the wail of an approaching siren. It hadn't taken the police long to get here. He had only just been in time.

Bronwen was standing now, her arms still around the little girls who were crying.

"It's alright," Evan said, bending down to them. "It's all over." He looked up at Bronwen. "Are you okay?" he asked simply, because that was the first thing that came into his head.

"More to the point, are you okay?" she said fiercely. "I never want to go through that again, as long as I live. Must you always be the Boy Scout and do the good deeds?"

"I was pretty sure he wouldn't really have shot me," Evan said, recoiling at her anger.

"Pretty sure?"

"I had to do it, Bron," he said simply. "If I hadn't got the thing away from him before the police got here he would have been happy to die in a Rambo-style shoot-out."

Bronwen let go of the little girls and came up to him. "You were incredibly brave," she said. She slipped her arms around his neck. "Just don't ever do it again!"

"I can't promise that," Evan said, wrapping his own hands around her waist. "As I said to those media types, I'm a policeman. It's all part of the job."

"Miss Price, I'm scared. Can we go home now?" One of the little girls tugged at her skirt.

"I have to get them home," Bronwen said regretfully.

"Of course you do. And I suppose I'd better make my way to HQ and file my report when they bring Mostyn in," Evan said. "Come on, let's get out of here." He ushered them through the confusion in the center aisle, pushing aside persistent cameras that were still following him.

"Don't you want to say good-bye to your girlfriend?" Bronwen asked as they reached the exit.

Evan glanced back. He could no longer see Maggie amid the chaos on stage. "That was all over and forgotten long ago," he said. "She let me down rather badly once. When we've got time, I'll tell you all about her."

"Is that why you're so reluctant to get involved again?" Bronwen asked.

Evan nodded. "Once bitten, twice shy, don't they say?"

"Oh, she did that, too, did she?" Bronwen asked. There was a challenging sparkle in her eyes.

"Did what?"

"Bite?"

Evan took one of the little girls by the hand and put his arm around Bronwen's shoulder. "Come on, let's get these little ones home. I said I'd tell you all the details later."

Outside the activities were winding down. The outer booths were lit by kerosene lamps and the sky was glowing pink on the western horizon.

"We never did manage to go around the *eisteddfod* together, did we?"

"There's always next year," Bronwen said.

"Right. I'll mark it in my calendar. No crime allowed that weekend."

They stood smiling at each other.

"I really have to get going," Evan said. "They'll be waiting for me at HQ."

Bronwen nodded. "Why don't you stop by on your way home, if it's not too late," she said. "I'll make you some cocoa."

"People might talk."

"Let them. And anyway, they'll be too busy gossiping about poor old Mostyn to notice us."

Evan smiled. "Alright. I'll see you later then."

He watched Bronwen disappear into the twilight, a little girl at either hand. Then he headed back in the direction of his car.

A burst of applause made him pause at the grand pavilion. On the stage were tiers of figures in white robes, their heads draped in what looked like tablecloths. In one case Evan knew that the headdress was a tablecloth. Although he knew that this was the traditional Druid dress, he still thought it looked bloody silly. His eyes scanned the rows until he picked out the Reverend Powell-Jones, sitting at one end and the Reverend Parry Davies at the other.

In the center was an empty chair, decorated with vines, surrounded by several men in splendid green robes with crowns of leaves on their heads. Those were the past bards and the Arch Druids. Little girls in green dresses, their heads wreathed with garlands of flowers, sat at their feet.

"And now we come to the most solemn moment of the *eisteddfod,*" one of these green-clad figures announced. "Now we pay homage to this year's bard, by crowning him and seating him in the chair of honor. We have heard all the candidates for the title of bard. We have been truly impressed with the quality of their eloquence and the richness of their poetry this year. The choice has not been an easy one, but one contestant stood out from all the rest. He spoke with fire, he spoke with eloquence, he spoke with passion.

"I am delighted to say that this man is one of our own, from here in North Wales. I call forth to be chaired the bard of the Harlech *eisteddfod,* from the little town of Llan . . ."

Mr. Powell-Jones had already risen to his feet. So had Mr. Parry Davies.

". . . from the little town of Llanrwst in the beautiful Vale of Conwy, Mr. Rex Beynon!"

An inoffensive-looking little man with a toothbrush moustache rose to his feet, his head bobbing to the applause as he walked toward the bardic chair. Powell-Jones and Parry Davies remained standing, staring in disbelief.

Then, almost as if they had orchestrated it, they marched down the steps at either side and off the stage.

They kept on walking until they met at the back exit of the pavilion.

"Rex Beynon!" Mr. Powell-Jones exclaimed in disgust. "He had no fire, no spirit, no rhythm to his verse. No voice at all."

"He sounded like a mouse squeaking in a cathedral."

"He'd never preached a rousing sermon in his life, I'll be bound."

"Never made people weep to hear him, eh, Edward?"

"Never had a conversion on the spot, eh, Tomos *bach*?"

They stood there, looking slightly ridiculous in their white sheets and tablecloths.

"You should have won it, man," Powell-Jones said huskily. "You had the voice and the fire and the passion."

"So did you, Edward. So did you. Either one of us should have won it. It would have been hard to decide between us."

Edward Powell-Jones's face lit up. "That's it!" he exclaimed. "That's why they did it! They couldn't decide between us and they didn't want to hurt either of our feelings, so they chose that little squeaking windbag Rex Beynon."

"You may just be right there, Edward. There was nothing to choose between us, was there? We were both streets ahead of the rest of the competition."

"Next year you should enter alone. I'll bow out and give you your chance for glory," Edward Powell-Jones said.

"That's very good of you, Edward, but maybe I'll step down next year and let you have your chance."

"Oh no, I insist. You've been working for it longer than I. It's only fair."

"Let's not think about next year yet. Let's go and get a drink and toast the true winners, eh, Edward *bach*?"

"I don't usually imbibe, Tomos *bach,* but seeing the solemnity of the occasion . . ."

The two men set off together, white sheets flying in the breeze.

Who would have thought it, Evan mused. It was definitely a night of minor miracles.

————TWENTY-THREE————

THE NEXT MORNING EVAN WAS back at work at the Llanfair subpolice station when Mrs. Llewellyn came in.

"I suppose we'll be free to go now, won't we, Constable?" she asked.

"I expect so, Mrs. Llewellyn."

"And Ifor's body will be released to us?"

"I see no reason why not. They've got a full confession from Mostyn Phillips and he's in custody. This time I think the confession was genuine."

Margaret Llewellyn smiled, then the smile faded. "Poor Mostyn. I feel so sorry for him. He could never understand why I chose Ifor . . . but it was no contest, was it? How could anyone want Mostyn when they could have an Ifor Llewellyn?" She smiled sadly. "In spite of everything he put me through he was the only man I ever loved. I truly loved him, Mr. Evans. Mostyn could never understand that."

Evan could think of nothing to say.

"I'm taking the body back to Italy for the funeral," she went on. "They want to give him a state funeral with all the trappings—black-plumed horses, the lot. Ifor would appreciate that. Going out in style."

Evan smiled. "Pity. Mrs. Williams was rather hoping for a good funeral here."

Back at Mrs. Williams's house Mrs. Powell-Jones was busy packing up her husband's clothes.

"It will be so nice to be back in our own place, won't it, Edward," she said. "It's not easy living out of a suit-case."

"It has been disagreeable," Mr. Powell-Jones said. "The whole thing has been very uncomfortable and in-convenient. I think that's why I lost the competition—I couldn't put my mind fully to the task in hand, because I wasn't in my own house and you weren't there to look after me."

Mrs. Powell-Jones put her arm awkwardly around his shoulder. "I'm sorry, Edward. I won't go running off again. And next time anyone offers us a large sum of money for our house, I'll resist the temptation and turn it down."

"They won't want a refund, will they?" Edward Powell-Jones asked. "Just because they're going home early?"

"I hope not!" Mrs. Powell-Jones said. "I've already got a deposit on a new three-piece suite!"

Over in the Red Dragon Betsy was doing the morning dusting.

"You can wave bye-bye to that date with Constable Evans, Betsy my girl," Harry-the-Pub commented as he came in with a tray of clean glasses. "Rumor has it that he was seen going into Bronwen Price's house very late last night."

"I heard that, too," Betsy said. She looked at herself in the mirror decorated with the words WHAT WE WANT IS WATNEYS. "I don't understand it, Harry. What's she got that I haven't, I'd like to know. I keep myself looking nice, don't I? I wear trendier clothes than her. I've got a better figure . . ." She paused and examined her hair. "Maybe it's my hair. Maybe Mr. Llewellyn was right and I should dye it. How do you think I'd look with black hair, eh, Harry?"

"Bloody daft," Harry said. "Now stop gawping at yourself and put away those glasses."